A PLACE IN

SOCIETY

DENISTHORN HALL
BOOK ONE

Yellow Teapot Books Australia

ISBN: 978-0-6486502-8-7

Yellow Teapot Books Australia

Cover picture *Equestrian portrait of Mlle Croizette*
By Carolus Duran, 1876
Author picture by Mark Flowers
Designed and typeset in Constantia by
Ding! Author Services

Also by Rosanne Dingli

Death in Malta
Camera Obscura
According to Luke
The Hidden Auditorium
The Frozen Sea
The White Lady of Marsaxlokk
How to Disappear

For more about this author visit
rosannedingli.com

For Maggie

A Place in Society

DENISTHORN HALL
BOOK ONE

CHAPTER ONE

*In which Lady Croukerne makes a decision
and plans a dinner*

The sound of the bedroom curtains being drawn open. A dull shaft of morning light illuminating the end of her bed, the silk carpet, and the head and shoulders of Prudhomme. Her head ached and she was still full of foreboding. Struggling to summon what it was that filled her so with anxiety, she remembered the previous night's conversation.

A telegram had arrived, delivered to the drawing room, where they sat after dinner. The girls had already gone up. The yellowish envelope was presented by the footman on a salver with a matching paper knife, and her husband slit it and extracted the message, placing the knife back without a look.

'What is it, Ninian? At this time of night?'

'Oh dear.'

She waited.

'Well, my darling, Mater announces she will be ...' He read aloud. '... *abbreviating the grand tour and making my way home*. Stop.'

Silence descended on the drawing room. The storm outside could be heard raging against their heavily curtained windows. Lord Croukerne lowered his head, raised it again and his eyes met his wife's. 'So.'

'Your mother is returning! Ninian! So soon?'

'It will take her some time, Edwina.' He consulted the top of the sheet. 'I knew it was not advisable for her to go on a grand tour so soon after Pater's passing. What a to-do! She must still be overtaken by grief.'

'Grief!'

'Edwina, please. She's now in ... let's see ... Istanbul. So, it will take her a week at least. Perhaps a fortnight. Or three weeks.'

'She's cutting short a tour that might have taken a good year, Ninian.'

'Let us not sound too disappointed, my dear. The children need to be filled with respect for their grandmother's position, and her venerable age.'

'I hardly think sixty-nine is venerable.'

He laughed. 'She makes it feel venerable.'

'I'm going to get a headache.' Edwina raised the back of a hand to her forehead. 'Perhaps I should retire early.'

'Good. I'll leave you in peace then, and sleep in my dressing room.'

'Perfect, darling, thank you.'

But she slept fitfully, even though she slept alone. The thought of her mother-in-law coming back early to upset the entire household's peace and order of its days, was not a palatable consideration. Her mother-in-law, grandmother to her children, mother of Ninian Crownrigg, Lord Croukerne, fifth earl of Denisthorn, Baron of Brockworth, was a formidable woman. She had turned suddenly taciturn and unfriendly when her husband died; she emerged after a lifetime of living in his shadow a stern and demanding woman.

It was almost bearable when the old baron was still alive. Now, most vitally, they were never allowed to forget she was dowager marchioness, *widow* of the fourth earl of Denisthorn, a woman who had years before inherited the title of Marchioness of Harpensted from her father, a title that put all of them in the shade from which she strode out, forceful and energetic. This most important *marchioness* played a living, scene-making role in all their lives.

Little had changed for Edwina's family; they had lived at Denisthorn since the baron had taken ill years before. It was a drawn-out illness, which had thankfully ended peacefully and without much anguish.

The morning came and she did not feel the least bit rested. It was Prudhomme's black dress that told Lady Edwina Croukerne it was Saturday. The lady's maid wore a narrow dress at the end of the week, with a white jabot; and a pin-tucked blouse and black serge skirt from Monday to Friday.

'Good morning, my lady.'

'Prudhomme, it can't be morning. I feel I haven't slept a wink.'

The maid reached for the curtains and started to draw them back. 'I'll let you rest, then. I'll bring your breakfast up later.' The bed tray stood on a side table.

On it, the countess could see her special teapot and cup, a lidded muffin dish, and a specimen vase with a yellow rose from the garden. 'No. No, Prudhomme, thank you. There's no point. And look – it seems the storm has cleared. There might be an opportunity for a walk before luncheon. I do need to clear my head. Has Lord Croukerne been down for his breakfast?'

Prudhomme arranged pillows and helped her ladyship sit up in bed, then placed the footed tray gently in front of her. 'And the young ladies – yes, my lady. They're all in the small dining room now.'

They rarely came down to breakfast at the same time, but when they did, Lord Croukerne and his two daughters launched on some disagreement that took them through the long hours to luncheon in a surly mood. The displeasure would lift suddenly when Lady Croukerne emerged from her day sitting room. She always had to strive to instil calm, and the very thought tired her.

At this moment, strong tea was just what she needed. And Prudhomme had cleverly laid out her lavender day dress, so in under half an hour, with her voluminous hair trapped in a matching net snood, she felt strong, refreshed, and ready for anything. Even her fear of a headache had dissipated. She went down and took a brief constitutional back and forth on the raised terrace outside the garden entrance, and faced the day.

'What is it today, Athena, my dear?' Edwina Crownrigg's light-hearted question at the luncheon table was nearly always the same, sent across the small dining room like a benign paper dart, to land on her daughter's shoulder; a dove of peace. The small dining room was bathed in sunlight that morning, watery sunshine that gleamed from behind a small bank of dispersing cloud, so she had sat in a shaft of brilliant light after her walk, ignoring the peril of what sunlight could do to her complexion, and did nothing but stare out at the west garden, which that early spring was starting to green and show promise of blossom and bloom.

Without a further thought of the early return of the dowager marchioness, she filled with expectation of a good season, one in which her daughters would finally display the level of maturity she had hoped for, the accomplishment she had made them work at, and the beauty they inherited from Lord Croukerne's side. Since the time they began to come downstairs to have their meals as a family, there were small but regular signs of success.

For some years now, the day nursery was occupied solely by Frederic, who was no longer a baby. They would start preparing him to go off to boarding school before too long. The second nursery girl had long since been promoted to housemaid. Some said – downstairs where conversations were lively about staff engagements, promotions, and dismissals – that it was not a real promotion at all.

The last thing on Athena's mind that day was what happened downstairs. 'Papa said something at breakfast about my London ball.' Her voice was not shrill, it would never be, but there was a note of distress in it, which her mother had labelled in her mind as a dull whine. 'Something about my gown, and it ...'

'I hardly think Papa would have mentioned anything at all about your wardrobe, my darling. It's for me to ...'

Athena looked down at her plate of ham, piccalilli and boiled potato and sighed, avoiding her sister's eyes. Geraldine sat further down the table from her mother, silent but bursting with mirth.

'What are you smirking at, Geraldine?'

'Leave your sister alone, Athena. Let's discuss your problem. I do declare it's become a daily thing for you to have a *problem*.'

'Well, I'm coming out this season. I'll be nineteen in Christmas. So I'm coming out late as it is. And I think I might be allowed to discuss – at least *discuss*, Mama – what I should be wearing to be presented at court.'

'We have two rather large books of samples and illustrations, and patterns. And a mountain of swatches. We shall sit in my day sitting room for as long as you like, Athena.'

'And we shall come out having decided on a whole wardrobe *of your choosing*.' Athena shot a petulant glance at her mother, then a sharp meaningful grimace at Geraldine.

'Have you seen the latest issue of *Harper's Bazaar*?'

Athena restrained herself from stamping a foot and leaving the room, but her fists were clenched. 'That magazine reaches us from America almost a full year after it is published. Your friends kindly send it, but we receive it far too late, and when we do see it, Mama, it's frightfully outdated. Besides, the fashions we see in it are mere copies of the *previous* year's French ones.'

'When it's my turn to come out ...'

'That won't be for another two long years, Geraldine. There is absolutely no point in discussing it now.'

'It's less than that, really. And you cannot despise me for having a June birthday, because I had nothing to do with that.' The younger sister looked at her mother for permission to rise from the table, making sure she was seen to put aside her starched napkin.

It was, however, the moment chosen by the butler to enter with a salver covered in envelopes.

'The post is a touch late, Herring.' The sentence was raised from being a reprimand into a bright observation. Lady Croukerne's voice rose on the butler's name, making him beam a little, rather than produce an outright smile.

'My lady, it is. There is a new postman, and I'm afraid he takes his time.'

'Which is not anything we can control from here, is it, Herring?'

He gave a small bow before leaving the small dining room. 'No, indeed, my lady. The Royal Mail is quite out of our bailiwick.'

Geraldine was already standing by the time Herring had left the room. The countess gave a half glance in her direction and the girl sank into her seat again, looking with some dismay at the small pile of correspondence in her mother's hands.

Lady Croukerne sorted through the top letters and gave her third sigh that day. Then she looked up and gazed into her daughters' faces in turn. 'Go. I expect you will be in the library until it's time to change, Athena.'

The older daughter nodded without a word.

'And you, Geraldine?'

A dusky blush rose to the younger daughter's cheeks. 'I think I'm already ...'

'All you need to complete that riding habit, Geraldine, are hat, veil, and gloves.'

'And whip.'

'And whip. So I think you're quite ready to accompany Papa on some jaunt. Why he has not taken luncheon with us I cannot imagine. And why you must ride every day is really quite beyond me.'

The girl raised her chin an inch. 'What is quite

beyond *me* is why I continue to ride side-saddle while the whole world is sitting astride.'

'Really! The whole world.'

'Mama, we are reaching the end of a century. It is eighteen *ninety-four*. Things cannot stay the same forever.'

'Things that matter will, my darling girl. And you will not ride a horse like a man. What would you do, wear *breeches*? We should be the talk of the entire county if you did. Clothing is what distinguishes us, one from the other. Ladies will *never* wear trousers.' She raised a hand, to draw a line under the argument. 'I shall see you on your return. Where are you bound today?'

'Papa hasn't said.' All that mattered to Geraldine was the ride, not the destination. 'I think he had luncheon with Swinnart. I think he has a *problem*, too.'

'Don't be arch with me, darling. We all have problems, not just your sister. Papa's problem today is probably his luncheon with Lewis Swinnart. Having a very voluble agent means he must listen and listen and listen, and then listen some more, and try to pick out what the problem is out of all those *words*.'

'Papa is patient.'

'I think he needs to be, with Swinnart, and with this estate to run, and all its farms and tenants, and all the people working the land. It takes my breath away. And then he must travel to London to sit in the House.'

'I've never really understood why.'

'What – why he sits in the House of Lords? Well, he's a peer of the realm ...'

A maid put her head around the door and retreated quickly.

'Let's allow Alice in to clear. I'll tell you why Papa sits in the House of Lords while you walk me to my sitting room. Do you have time?'

'Not really. Papa will already be mounting by the time I run to the stables.' She turned, poised to leave.

'Don't run, Geraldine. It doesn't become you.'

But Geraldine had already flitted across the gallery towards the ante hall and the garden entrance. Lady Croukerne knew her riding things would have been put on a chair there by the girls' maid, and Geraldine – despite all instruction to the contrary – would pull on gloves and hat as she bustled along to the stables.

Her mother gazed absentmindedly at the fast-retreating figure of her second daughter, turned, and made her way back to her sitting room, knowing that the instant she sat, she would be joined by Mrs Beste.

There was the infinitesimal suggestion of a knock and the diminutive housekeeper entered.

'I am not yet used to the new way you wear your hair, Mrs Beste.' A bright smile with slightly lowered eyes made the remark a positive one.

The housekeeper glowed. She took the neutral words as a compliment, partly seeing her mistress was very adept at making the servants feel good about themselves and their work, and partly inclined to see there was a touch of sarcasm in her mistress's tongue. Not that she would ever think it aloud. 'I am hardly used to it myself, my lady. But it is infinitely more practical, especially early in the morning.' The slight refinement she gave to her broad Lancashire speech tempered also her tone, which she modulated to suit that of the countess.

'You're a very adaptable person, Mrs Beste, which is why I am sure you will not mind when I say we shall be nine to dinner on Tuesday.'

'Nine, your ladyship.'

'How well you contain your surprise, Mrs Beste, and how well you take the odd number. And please note I did not say *dismay*.' There was a twinkle in the countess's eye.

The housekeeper smiled. 'Perhaps the dismay will be reserved for Mrs Jones. Any alteration to her menu sends her into paroxysms of panic. But it's only display.'

'Display of importance?'

'Of over-inflated heroism. The responsibility is after all on Mr Herring's shoulders. And mine.'

Lady Croukerne laughed. 'Naturally, in a way. I think Cook considers her department a universe unto itself. I need not ask her up for a chat, need I?'

'Indeed not, my lady. She and I will adapt and adjust – it is only quantities after all, and my store will cover another four persons comfortably. I take it little Baron Brockworth will dine early, in the nursery.'

'We are in a quandary about my son, aren't we? He is at that awkward stage of childhood where no one knows what to call him, and no one knows where he is to sit. It was all so much easier in the olden days. So much easier when the old baron was still alive. And it will be a blessing when Frederic goes off to school. Then we'll have to wonder what on earth his governess Miss Purl will do. And dear little Frederic will miss us all so.'

'The little baron will eventually return to us a man, my lady. And the awkward stage will be over.' She took a silent breath. 'About Tuesday – I shall see that the store will accommodate the numbers, despite Mrs Jones's panic.'

'You still do not allow her access. Cook must be so curious to know what's in your store.'

'There is no need for anyone except myself and Mr Herring to enter my store, or to know its contents. I hold inventory, and it is all correct.' She patted the bunch of keys hanging from her belt.

Her mistress made a tiny grimace of acceptance. 'So thank you, Mrs Beste. I take it you are in control.'

'Very much so, my lady.'

'I shall make out a full list of names and so forth for Herring.'

'Glover will come and collect it this afternoon, if that is quite all right, my lady.'

When she left, thought of doubling numbers around

the dinner table gave Lady Croukerne a shiver. She counted on dainty fingers laden with beautiful rings. Lord Croukerne and herself, their two daughters, her sister Lady Marguerite, who they all called Margery, with her second husband, Sir Herbert Fanshaw. She now regretted asking the Baroness Brindlebarb and her commoner husband, Mister Barton-Amery, but there was no going back. Their stodginess and immense commercial wealth would be nicely – and humorously – balanced by the presence of their closest neighbour, the widower Lord Ullingsbroke. He was touring the countryside to entertain his cousin, who none of them had yet met. With a commission in Australia, the man was rarely in England. A colonel, perhaps, or a brigadier. She could not remember.

'A dinner will brighten up the week, I suppose,' she said to no one at all.

'I should have to wear my pastel organdie again.'

Lady Croukerne twisted round in surprise, to see Athena standing by the door Mrs Beste had just shut.

'Well, we'll meet someone new and ... whatever's wrong, Athena? You have been wearing a long face for hours.'

'Two things. Two things I've heard, without being told directly. It seems I must hear things from the servants, or as I pass an open door, or try to decipher something Papa says when he is completely unconscious of the fact I'm listening.'

Would she never be able to stop sighing? Lady Croukerne patted the seat of the small settle she sat in, and Lady Athena sank next to her.

'Now give me your hand and take a deep breath.'

'Mama, my age forbids the first of your requests, and my corset the second.' She kept her hands tightly clasped.

'Oh, what nonsense. I take your Grand-mama's hand all the time, and she is very nearly seventy.'

Athena gave her mother a cool dry hand.

'There. Start with the first thing.'

'I heard Papa say something rather strange about Grand-mama's return from her tour.'

'Yes, she is cutting it short. She is a bit unhappy.'

'More than that. As if it weren't enough. Is she really unwell?'

Lady Croukerne put her free hand to her lips. 'Oh, no! I was not aware, and the thought never came to mind. My dear girl. It must worry you.'

'Not least because she will be unbearable. She has changed. Ever since Grand-papa died it's been dreadful.'

'Dreadful! Hardly that. I know we wore mourning for some weeks, but...'

'It's hard enough to have her here when she is well. I hate to be unkind, but it is a trial. If she is sick ...'

'Don't use that word, dear.'

'If she is ill, I doubt I should be able to stand being here.'

'You can keep ...'

'I *cannot*. You will not bear for me to keep out of her way. How impolite and unfeeling you would all think me.'

They looked at each other for a long silent pause.

'Your Aunt Margery is coming to dinner on Tuesday.'

'Is that a good thing or bad?'

Lady Croukerne shook her head. Sarcasm did not suit her older daughter, but she was not about to scold her again and make things worse. 'We can suggest a sojourn.'

Athena's eyes lit up. 'At Gallantrae House? Up in the hills? Just me?' Her face took on a downcast aspect again. 'Please let it be just me. I could not bear to go away with Geraldine – not all the way to Gallantrae.'

Her mother relented. 'Just you. After all, Geraldine is still officially a child. We'll see what my sister says. I have no doubt she will put you up splendidly at Gallantrae. She has had it decorated in a splendid way and has a wonderful staff. It's only a matter of whether my sister has anything on the calendar that might prevent it. Perhaps a note is in order.'

'And I should travel with a maid?'

'Yes, of course. Milly will think it's a promotion. But it won't be. I'll speak to Mrs Beste. Geraldine will do with one of the housemaids until your return.' She rose and moved to an elegant *bonheur du jour*, the desk where she spent some of the calmest moments of each day, writing lists and instructions for the servants, and several notes which were delivered here and there by footmen and coachmen and even postmen, for which it was necessary to use a stamp.

'We are very nearly out of paper.'

'Herring is very good with paper. Only yesterday he let me have almost half a box.'

Her mother turned. 'Why do you require so much paper?'

Athena diverted her eyes for an instant, then seemed to make a quick decision. 'I write a bit. And draw. I wish I had ...' A rapid shake of her head, and she bit her lip. 'Not since Geraldine and I had a governess, have I ...'

'My darling girl, we must get you some bound journals. There are some lovely ones in the new catalogue. With marbled end papers, and some with feint lines.'

'Feint lines?'

'Straight printed lines. What a very modern thing! For writing on. And I suppose a nice set of pens will not be turned down?' Lady Croukerne looked at her daughter and tilted her head, a kind interrogative stance to which Athena had to respond.

'You are so perceptive, Mama.'

'Now look at this. Stand here.' She held her daughter and positioned her a few feet from her little desk. 'This is my *bonheur du jour*. You do know what that means.'

'We had that French governess here for two years, Mama. We did learn something. Mademoiselle Clerque was not perfect, and her clothes were strange, but yes, I do know it means *the day's happiness*.'

'A lady is happiest when sitting quietly at her desk, reading and writing. Organizing her household, setting things to rights, corresponding with family and dear friends, writing in her personal journal, and generally putting things on paper to be recorded.' She pointed at a glazed bookcase. 'All my journals are in that case. A few – or sometimes a great many – words each day, to record incidents and accidents!' She laughed. 'More happens than one might think, even in a single day, on a great estate such as Denisthorn.'

'Every day since you married?'

'Every day since I met your Papa. I wrote every day from the year I was seventeen, so it's about time you started, perhaps, my dear Athena.'

'What, put everything in writing?' She looked horrified.

'Oh don't worry, Athena. No one will see or read it – except by explicit and personal invitation. Or upon your ... um ... demise.'

'At a desk like yours?'

'Would you like one?'

'Oh, yes please.'

'We shall order a nice one for you. My catalogues are here somewhere. And we can place it by the window in the small library. Would you like that?'

'And will it really be entirely mine?'

Lady Croukerne saw where her daughter's anxiety lay. 'You do mean, don't you, whether you will be required to share it with Geraldine? Would you rather it were placed in front of the window in your room?'

Athena nodded. There was a note of sadness in her eyes which her mother still wondered about.

'It will be entirely yours, my very dear girl. You can write or draw every day after you dress in the morning, or before bed at night.'

Chapter Two

In which Lady Geraldine drinks coffee and
little Baron Brockworth comes down to breakfast

Lord Croukerne paced solemnly and steadily down the grand staircase, with the two house-trained lurchers, Cosmo and Damian, at his heels. They were inseparable dogs, part of one of several litters to dear old Connie, short for Constantinople; the scent hound who always followed his late father around. She had died so soon before the baron's demise one could be forgiven for thinking his grief was such that he departed after her. Connie's grave was on the Denisthorn grounds, with a small granite statue of the dog on top. It was like a shrine to both hound and master.

The present master of Denisthorn had left his wife to her breakfast in bed, and prepared himself mentally for breakfast with his daughters, which was never free of some heated discussion or other. With Geraldine wanting to assert her decision to ride astride in the saddle, it was proving to be a difficult week. The gallery was well lit that morning, with slants of dust-mote laden sun entering diagonally from the long rectangular glass light two storeys above his head.

'Good morning, Herring.'

'My lord.'

'I should like to see little Baron Brockworth after breakfast, if you could let Nanny know.'

'Of course, my lord. In the small library?'

'The big one, please. I shall be at my desk there for the better part of the day.' He patted Cosmo the lurcher on the rump. The placid hound did not look round, but proceeded towards the small dining room for the unbroken breakfast routine. A footman would let the dogs out to the care of a stableboy for their breakfast at the stables, through one of the French windows in that room. In the early morning, just after dawn, the fire in the small dining room was laid by a skivvy or lower housemaid. The curtains were drawn open, and the table set for breakfast by a footman.

Dishes of scrambled egg, braised kidney, fried bacon, grilled tomato and hand-toasted bread were placed on the warmer just before Lord Croukerne came down the main staircase for the day.

He always rose early, and was dressed for the day's work in a three-piece tweed suit with parallel vents and a gusseted belt, by his valet, Thorn. Their conversation nearly always went the same way.

'Has it stopped raining, Thorn?'

'Not yet, my lord. I trust it will be bright and sunny before luncheon.'

'You're nearly always wrong, Thorn.'

'About the weather I am, my lord. We live in hope.'

It was two days before the dinner Lady Edwina had planned, and there had been another telegram from the dowager marchioness, his mother, so the day promised to be a mixture of things already.

'Good morning my darlings.' The girls were already at their places. Breakfast was the kind of unstructured repast where everyone helped themselves and did not stand on the ceremony of waiting for elders before they could sit. But what they had before Lord Croukerne arrived and served himself was just a sip of tea. They would eat together and wait to be served with coffee in due course.

'I have longed for years to be served coffee.' Geraldine started with a minor bone of contention. 'How much longer am I to wait?'

'Good morning to you too, my darling girl.'

'Oh, Papa. Is today the day we are all insistent on the proper salutation, in the right order, to the right person?'

'It is the day you will be served coffee at breakfast for

the very first time.'

Her eyes widened.

'You might ask what happened, for you to deserve the privilege.' Her older sister interjected before Geraldine could open her mouth. 'Offered a small biscuit when cake is not forthcoming.'

The earl turned to Athena and stared her in the eye. 'What a magnificent metaphor, Athena.' But he saw his older daughter had guessed Geraldine would be once more denied the dubious satisfaction of riding a horse like a man. 'I have a yen for doing things early. We might dispense with formality and convention with a few things at Denisthorn.'

'Such as what?' The girls spoke at once, glanced at each other across the table, and returned gazes to their father.

'Such as having Frederic at table with us for breakfast.'

'*Frederic*?'

'And before you utter it together, in harmony, using exactly the same words, no – your brother is *not* still a baby.'

'But ...'

'Athena, he will be twelve rather soon, and it probably means, seeing he is such a tall fellow, that he will be fine at the breakfast table and will not embarrass himself. Surely he can handle a fork and spoon by now, without the help of Nanny.'

'Grand-papa might have ...'

'Mama will be shocked.'

'Grand-papa is no longer with us. And Mama does not come down to breakfast.' It seemed an obvious thing to Lord Croukerne. Married women had breakfast in bed and were rarely seen before eleven.

'So little Brockworth will turn into a little man and join us.' Athena's quiet voice seemed loud in the silence.

'I think it's a jolly turn for the better.' Geraldine saw this as a twist to convention of which she might take advantage in the future. She lowered her head and said not a word more before finishing. She placed a tentative finger on the tablecloth above her right hand, and a footman presently placed a coffee cup and saucer there. She gave an incredulous smile. 'Thank you, Formby.'

'Lady Geraldine.' He poured a stream of dark coffee from the silver pot.

Geraldine looked at it, glanced at her father, and promptly proceeded to pour cream and stir sugar into her cup.

'You would do well to take as little sugar as you can stand.' Athena saw opportunity to give advice.

'And why is that?'

'Mama says it can make you short of breath.'

Lord Croukerne thought the remark very humorous, and then thought of his wife's generous form. 'Ha ha! Sugar can make your dresses and stays feel tighter, and that is a certainty.'

The girls looked at him like he had said something most unsuitable at table, but not a word left their lips.

'Is it delicious, Geraldine?'

'It's more bitter than tea, Papa.'

'And that is the whole point. Do not dredge it with so much sugar that it tastes much like any other brew.'

'Ah.' Geraldine saw sense in his words. 'So from tomorrow we shall have Frederic at table. Is he to have coffee too?'

They all laughed together at the droll suggestion.

'I think one privilege at a time is the seemly way.'

Later, in the library, Lord Croukerne's only son stood and fidgeted, breathing through reddish lips. 'Am I really to come down for breakfast?'

'You are indeed.'

'But Papa, who'll have breakfast with Nanny? She can't go down to the servants' hall.'

'Of course not. What a thought. A girl will take up a tray to her and she can eat in the day nursery as usual.'

'Without me.'

'Without you.'

'That will be very strange at first. What about lessons?'

'You will have those as usual. Miss Purl will expect you at the usual time.'

'Oh.' Frederic looked at his boots.

'What is it, son? You seem distracted and quite out of sorts.' Lord Croukerne looked closely at his boy.

'Nanny says there's to be a fair at Brockworth, starting this afternoon, until Sunday, and ...'

'And you'd like to go ... or would you like to be excused?'

The boy's eyes brightened. 'To go, rather. To go, please Papa.'

'Well, your mother and the girls are helping to judge the produce competition, and the flowers and plants. I've heard them discuss it at length. I shall be there early with Swinnart, to look at the livestock and all that. It won't be much different from last year's affair.'

'I don't remember last year's.'

Lord Croukerne remembered Frederic had a tooth out last year and stayed behind. And the previous year they had all stayed in because they were still in mourning. 'In any case, we'll all go and make a good day of it.'

'And may I have the rides?'

'Of course, Formby will be there. All the servants will be going and some will no doubt spend the whole evening enjoying the rides and such. We can get Formby and one of the other fellows to see you have some fun, eh?' He gave his son a mock punch in the chest.

'Thank you, Papa.'

'Your Mama will insist you are home by dusk, so will you not tarry or dawdle, please? She will surely be home earlier than that and will fret and send someone out to find you.' He beamed and laughed. 'You know how Mama can be. Now off with you, and let me work.'

At his ample and deceptively elegant Regency desk, which was made from seven kinds of inlaid wood for the first earl of Denisthorn, Lord Croukerne pulled open a huge ledger and consulted a row of costs and disbursements. He drew a finger around his stiff starched collar and prepared for a day of difficult mental wrestling with facts and figures totally incompatible with his requirements and wishes for Denisthorn.

It was becoming increasingly hard to reconcile expenditure with income. The place would start to lose money if he were not exceedingly careful, and he knew Swinnart would agree with every word of the concept of frugality, but not find the wherewithal to come up with any useful expedients. The most frightful expense, unlike in the past, was wages and salaries. Why was it so rapidly getting out of hand? Paying for the household, garden and stable staff was becoming ridiculously expensive, and he could not for the life of him figure out why.

Worry and confusion with figures, statistics and complicated calculations kept him preoccupied well into the evening. He hardly remembered being dressed for dinner, recalled nothing of his pre-dinner whisky taken alone in the drawing room, and did not take in any of the conversation at the table.

'I find you rather absent this evening, Ninian.' The countess, in her glittering evening dress, seemed relaxed and calm.

'I wrangled facts and figures all day, Edwina. All day.'

'Wrangled? Is that a new word?'

'No. No. I have always used it. It cannot be new. I used it at school. It's a school word.'

She rocked her head and raised napkin to lips. 'The things one learns in school!'

'Well, it wasn't exactly Rugby, but we made a jolly good job of it, I think. Pollenhurst School, in hindsight ...'

'Made a man out of you.'

Lord Croukerne turned to his tittering daughters. 'You might laugh, but schools in my day were not the same as they are now.'

'We should never know, should we, Papa? We had French and embroidery and the classics and piano lessons right here at Denisthorn Hall.'

'And we memorized innumerable historic events and figures, military ranks and how to recognize uniforms!'

'Mademoiselle Clerque was good. And Miss Point. Was that her name? I remember Miss Point.'

There was silence from the girls, and two straight faces.

'You might not agree,' their mother said quickly, 'but some day you will come to bless deportment and elocution.'

'That was Mrs Cobbleham.'

'We could say your education is complete, my dear daughters.'

Lady Croukerne gave her husband a sharp look. 'There is still a lot to learn. Why – you are both still quite young.'

The earl put down his spoon. 'Only by today's modern standards. My dear, you were seventeen when we became engaged, and very nearly nineteen when we married.'

Both daughters regarded their mother. They knew that in her day, peeresses married younger. What they could not guess was that her three children resulted from a number of failed pregnancies and still births that had weakened her, as well as broadened her frame, both physically and in spirit for a number of years.

'School might have been enjoyable. Why is it that girls are so ... I might have liked school, but it's only the heir to all this, little Baron Brockworth, who gets to have fun.'

'Being sarcastic about your brother's title does not persuade us of deep intellectual worth or value, Athena.' Lord Croukerne threw down his napkin in a benign kind of huff and rose when his wife and the girls moved away from the table. His face did not indicate he relished returning to his desk the following day, but not a word about his work left his lips.

Geraldine, perceptive and understanding of what her father wrestled with, tried to save the evening. 'She was rather sweet, I remember Mrs Cobbleham well.'

'Oh so do I, but she was a *widow*.'

'What that has to do with anything I really do not know.' Lord Croukerne's face was still a mask of concern and his mind full of something unmentioned at table. 'I'll smoke a cigar and have one glass of port and join you in the drawing room for coffee in a little while.'

*

He was still preoccupied a day before the planned dinner, and descended the grand staircase with the dogs as usual, but a bit dazed and absentminded.

'Good heavens, what are *you* doing down here at this hour?'

Little Baron Brockworth stood at the door to the small dining room in a new tweed suit. His voice was bright and full of early morning spirits. 'I think it was you who invited me down, Papa. Yesterday.'

'Yes, yes of course. Silly of me.'

'Silly of you to invite him, or silly of you to have forgotten, Papa?' Athena's deceptively soft voice teased and provoked her father.

He led the way. 'You will gain little and make few friends if you continue along this path to becoming a sarcastic scold, Athena.' His tone was just as quiet, and just as piercing, as hers. Accompanied by a bland smile, the remark was cutting.

Disappointed, the older daughter lifted the lid on one of the warming dishes, lowered it, and lifted another. 'Could we not have pancakes for breakfast more often? Or muffins?'

Her father helped Frederic to eggs, ham, kidneys and tomatoes. 'Do you not find tomatoes exciting enough?'

'I think they come from our own gardener's glasshouse, and that's not very exciting.' Geraldine helped herself to some anyway.

'I wonder what kind of breakfast they will have at Gallantrae.'

'Gallantrae? Why on earth would you think of breakfast at Aunt Margery's?'

Athena's face fell. So her mother had not yet discussed with Papa her sojourn in the hills. Was she to hope for nothing?

'Athena? Are you tongue-tied?'

'I just wonder, that's all.' It was probably wise not to say more.

CHAPTER THREE

In which little Baron Brockworth takes a piggyback
and
a footman is promoted

Mrs Jones tied around her lean waist a gathered apron, whose hem reached just above that of her dark green uniform dress. It was brilliant white, correctly laundered and pressed. She made sure her bonnet was firmly fixed on her small birdlike head with two great brass hatpins, and pushed steel-rimmed spectacles up her nose.

The recipe she read was not complicated, but it required time. Behind her, two kitchen maids carried baking trays to the scullery to be washed.

'Will you need a lot more sugar, Cook?' A modulated voice came from in the doorway to the passage.

'If we are doubling quantities for the unexpected numbers at dinner, Mrs Beste,' she said without looking up from the sheet of paper, 'then yes. We'd need a lot more sugar.' She mumbled and counted on her fingers. 'I need seven ounces more, to be exact, for this alone. If you add an extra ounce, it will leave me a margin of error.'

'Eight ounces of sugar! Do you know how much that is?'

The cook finally lowered the recipe, took a deep breath, and slowly inserted the sheet of paper between the pages of a big cook book. 'I do. I do know that eight ounces is eight ounces.' The twinkle in her eye went unnoticed. 'We shall probably need to refill the kitchen canister.'

'Oh! Really! And butter?'

'When the dairy boy comes round presently, we'll have plenty of time to tell him to double the order. He hangs about the yard and smokes with that new stable boy.'

'New! He's been here since little Baron Brockworth's last birthday, and he's about to have another.'

Mrs Jones undid her apron and knotted it back in place more firmly. 'Indeed he is. Didn't the year go fast?'

'He comes down for breakfast now, the little baron.' Mrs Beste saw no reaction in the cook's demeanour. 'Hm? Breakfast with the family, as you must indeed know, in the small dining room. He'll be donning a white bowtie next ...'

'And dining with his mother? I don't think there is much chance of that before he's sent up to school.'

'Formby says he's coming to the village fair. He's to keep an eye on the little baron.' She turned, but did not move from the doorway. 'Ah, it's you, Formby. You're in charge of the young master at the fair.'

'And shall aim to show him a good time, Mrs Beste.'

'The family will all be there, mind. The young ladies are judging the flowers again this year.'

'And I suppose, Mrs Beste, you'll be in the company of Mr Herring?'

She moved slightly to let Formby past. 'Hm. I ... no, Mrs Jones. Mr Herring is staying behind to reconcile the wine ledger and count the silver before her ladyship's Tuesday dinner.' She fidgeted with the keys at her waist. 'Well, I'd better get busy.'

Mrs Jones pushed her glasses up her nose. 'You'll be walking out with that fellow from the village then. The shopkeeper.'

'Oh!'

'You can't keep anything a secret at Denisthorn.'

Formby stooped his tall frame, seeing the opportunity to have a tease. 'Nothing at all.' He walked away quickly, tugging at his livery jacket and straightening his gloves. 'Nothing is secret here.'

If Mrs Beste called after him to keep it to himself, it would be an admission. Mr Pillow was a shopkeeper, and he was from the village, and she did walk out with him every now and then. It was also true that keeping anything hidden was impossible in both the village at Brockworth and at Denisthorn Hall.

*

The fairground was fenced off diagonally from the top field at the north end of the fallow ground Lord Croukerne liked to think would be developed one day. A small stand of birches sheltered part of the ground from the worst of the wind. Within the temporary boundary, pitches were roped off. Some did a roaring trade in cider, pickles and preserves, others had games of chance, designed to take as many pennies from a willing crowd as possible. Noise, laughter and organ music was loud and raucous, and it was obvious from the expressions on faces everywhere that the break afforded by the diversion was well needed. Smiles were broad, and foreheads were freed of frequent frowning caused by the anxieties of serving at and running households and farms.

'The housemaids need the occasional interval – they rise before the dawn, work very hard all day, and drop onto their beds exhausted when the sun goes down.'

'The footmen too, Mrs Jones. Footmen too.' Mr Glover, the under-butler, looking so very different in a pork pie hat and brown sack jacket, pulled at a cuff and swept a finger underneath a bristly moustache.

'Did Mr Herring say nothing about your new face fuzz?'

'I don't think he can treat me like a footman any more. I've been under-butler now for over a month, and I don't think he can complain. Breakfasts are now running without a hitch. Every morning, Mrs Jones. Every morning.'

'You were a footman a long time, Mr Glover.'

'I was – and when suddenly, out of the blue, Mr Herring brought in the first footman from the London house, I thought my days were numbered. But no ... it was the surprise of my life.'

'You went from footman to under-butler, just like that. You never even served as first footman.'

'Not for one day. And it wasn't *just like that*, Mrs Jones. Not just like that.' He snapped fingers in the air. 'I was a footman, and a good one, for nigh on seven years.'

'I remember you got the job because you are so tall, and hale and hearty.'

'Well – you have to be, haven't you, Mrs Jones? Moving furniture for the maids to clean behind is no job for a weakling. Godwin and I – as regular as clockwork – moved the chiffonier in the small dining room like it was a feather.' He puffed his chest and swept a finger under his moustache again. 'Hey, wait a minute – who's that with little Baron Brockworth?'

Mrs Jones could not see through the crowd. 'What do you mean? What do you see?'

'There's a strange fellow giving our young master a piggy-back. Look! Look there I say, Mrs Jones.'

But the cook was too small to see past the throng gathered in front of the coconut shy. Gaggles of young men and groups of servant girls in their Sunday best walked back and forth; some arm in arm, some carrying baskets of produce and purchases, and most laughing and shouting at the tops of their voices to make themselves heard. An organ grinder went past, working his crank and leading an exhausted collared monkey by a worn rope.

'Where is he, Glover?'

But Glover was gone, weaving through the crowd and craning his neck to see where Lord Croukerne's son had moved off to, and who the man was who held him on his shoulders.

'Hold fast, Master Frederic!'

'Address Baron Brockworth properly, please. And put him down forthwith.'

The robust man who held the heir of Denisthorn on his shoulders turned. He swung round suddenly, which made the boy teeter; a child too old to be carried, being not much shorter in stature than the man who bore him, but slim and pale.

'Put him down. I say – put him down, mister.'

'Don't mister me, Jack Glover. Don't you know me?' He allowed the boy to slither down his back, laughing, and pulled off his cloth cap to fully expose his face.

It was only then Glover recognized who it was. 'Well I never – Alfie Tanner. Are you still at Ewlyn House?'

'I reckon I'll be there till I die, polishing shoes and running hot water up those back stairs until I cark it.'

'We at Denisthorn had plumbed bathrooms put in, we did – on two floors. There was a-coming and a-going, let me tell you. And enough dust for an 'undred maids for an 'undred days.'

'You're a posh lot at that house in the valley – the only house in England where footmen are hailed by their last names. You'd just be Jack anywhere else. Plain, plain Jack.'

'Every house has its ways, Alfie Tanner. And I'm under butler now.'

'Huh – Denisthorn ways are peculiar ways, if you ask me.'

'No one asked you.' But Glover watched his young master out of the corner of his eye, standing by patiently. 'I beg your pardon, Baron, to stop your fun. But I thought you were with Formby.'

'I was, Glover. With Formby and with my sister Lady Geraldine.' She was quite his favourite sister. Unlike Lady Athena, she understood fun. 'Here comes Formby now.' He indicated the footman with a nod of his head.

Alfie Tanner leaned forward as far as his rotundness allowed, and addressed the boy, peering close into his face. 'I hope you had a very good time, my young lord.'

'Hey – you don't have to touch noses with him!'

Alfie Tanner laughed, coughed, and pulled at his tight collar. 'You folk at Denisthorn are all the same. You can get so possessive.'

'It's just manners, Tanner. Manners, I say.'

'Well – take your manners and your young master back to the big manor in the valley ... and perhaps we'll meet at the public house in Brockworth one fine evening, eh?' Tanner flipped his cap back and took off into the crowd.

Formby looked apologetic. 'I thought it was fine. We know everyone at Ewlyn House. Tanner is a fine fellow.'

Young Frederic hopped leg to leg, awkward and hesitant. 'We could not be in trouble, could we? I'm sorry.'

'No need to worry at all, my young sir.'

'Tanner is a fine fellow,' repeated Formby, anxious now.

'He'd have been a fine fellow with a fine bloody nose if I hadn't remembered who he was. I think you'd better take the young master back to the house now. It won't be long before it's dark. Look – those men are lighting lanterns already.'

CHAPTER FOUR

In which there is trouble in the nursery

Lady Croukerne liked the way Prudhomme styled her hair the evening of the dinner. It was important for her to appear well-groomed when her sister came visiting, because Margery was obsessed with fashion. 'Will I do, do you think, Prudhomme? Thank you for this style.'

The lady's maid nodded through the mirror, gave one last brush stroke and an adjusting pat to the successful coif, which included a most fashionable Newport knot, and inserted a spangled comb, whose gems matched the colour of her ladyship's gown. 'Your hair is still freshly washed from last week, my lady. It is very manageable.'

The countess nodded. It was always an ordeal to have her hair washed, even now that they had hot and cold running water in a bathroom close to her rooms. Prudhomme knew a lot of tricks, and would have a pile of towels to hand, and a little jar of brilliantine. She would always add a few drops of eau de Cologne to the mixture of shaved Castile soap and water she shook vigorously in a bottle to make what she called *shampoo*.

'I read in *The Delineator*, my lady, that it does no harm to wash the hair even twice a month.'

'Oh! But that is an American periodical, I think.'

'It is, my lady. Glover, the under butler, has a brother who works in New York. He frequently sends useful periodicals laden with hints, tips, recipes and suggestions which keep servants up to date with current usage.'

'How admirable. I feel so well looked after.'

'And it would be even better if you were to order one of those new brushes with wide bristles set into a rubber back. I've heard a lot of good things about them.'

The countess admired her hair in the mirror; first one

side, and then the other. 'Are we not going to curl the side fringes, Prudhomme?'

'That is now an extinct fashion, my lady. And Lady Margery is sure to know it.'

'Oh, I do not in the least want to seem outdated to my sister.'

'This Spanish comb suits you admirably.'

The comb went well with the evening gown; a silk and tulle confection in emerald green with a neckline that dipped just enough to show the countess's clavicles and an emerald pendant.

'It does not do for married women to show too much skin. That is for the younger set. Which brings me to the realization ... oh Prudhomme, both my daughters will soon be attracting attention.'

'Lady Athena will have a proposal or two in the coming months, perhaps.'

'Only if she gets to see anyone at all, Prudhomme. I must devise some invitations to come her way, for house parties and balls. But having a house party at Denisthorn? No – even the thought makes me thoroughly exhausted.'

'When the dowager marchioness returns, my lady, there might be occasion to host a gathering, perhaps.'

'Ah – so you have heard downstairs of her imminent return.' The countess drew her mouth straight. 'Of course you have. I doubt we should be in the mood for a party.'

'There's always the hunt.'

'Lord Croukerne loves hosting a good hunt. I wonder whether it's the right occasion for Lady Athena to meet some young people, though. And it is such a lot of work. Do the servants really dread it?'

'November is a long way away, my lady. The little hunt is in August. That is very manageable. We have a lot of time to get ready, as we do every year. Cook is already putting up preserves and having hunt meetings with Mrs Beste. And no, I think everyone downstairs likes a bit of activity and special tasks. It is a lot of work, but it's worthwhile, even if only to have a bit of company in the servants' hall.'

'I hear not all gentlemen and ladies are travelling with servants, though. At Lord Marchton's hunt last year, two of the guests turned up without valets!'

The maid smiled through the mirror. 'Perhaps it is a delusion to expect the years to roll along without change.'

'How philosophical of you, Prudhomme ... what a startling observation that is.'

What Prudhomme observed about gradual change was a rise in the sons of gentlemen taking on such roles as banking, commerce, and medicine. It was not unheard of to entertain wealthy guests who had created some dynasty in trade. Knighthoods bestowed on successful businessmen, of course, made this kind of evolution a bit more acceptable than it otherwise might have been. Prudhomme could not imagine what it might be like to attend to a lady without a title. It was a thought of which she could not conceive. Fancy putting a comb through the hair of someone called plain *Mrs*. The thought accompanied her all the way down the back stairs.

*

The Tuesday dinner seemed to be going without a hitch. With each platter or dish presented to her left, Lady Croukerne noted the presentation and abundance devised by Mrs Jones and her kitchen staff, and was well satisfied. Perhaps Mrs Beste's tight retention of possession over the store was something subject to compromise and negotiation. She looked at a garnished platter of very nice portions of salmon and nodded when she saw appreciation on her guests' faces too. The pressed tongue was perfect, and she looked forward to the pudding, on which the eye should feast, as well as the other senses.

Conversation was lively if a bit predictable. At the head of the table, Ninian seemed to be chatting amiably with the Baroness Brindlebarb, who nodded sagely, without the flutter of eyelashes which, with her, signified boredom. A very attractive hairpiece caught the light when she moved her head.

Lady Margery was elegant in shimmering blue, and had the sides of her hair pulled tight. Prudhomme was right, the fashion for curled side fringes was gone.

When it was time to turn for conversation with diners on their other side, Ninian had to talk to Colonel Kirksduff, on his left, who seemed to have a lot to say. The younger man lived in Australia, on a commission that seemed rather onerous because of the heat and the conditions.

The countess waited for a few seconds. If Ninian shot her a blank glance, she would immediately know he was not enjoying the conversation. A few snatches of what the colonel said reach her at the end of the table.

'I must compliment you on your family.'

Did she hear correctly? Did the colonel have his eye on one of her daughters?

'... coming out this new season.' Her husband did not give many details, leaving the lion's share of the conversation to the colonel. To be absolutely polite, the countess turned to her left, where Sir Herbert was making short work of the sorbet before it melted in the warm room. She wondered how long one of the kitchen maids had to hand-crank the ice machine to make the delicacy, which was flavoured with rose water and gin. Her mind was wandering, so she glanced once more in her husband's direction. Good; he did not seem to need to converse.

Her gaze went once more past the etched crystal decanters, the silver salts lined with blue glass, and the heavy silver epergne and flower arrangements in the centre of the table, towards her guests, and Ninian. His satisfaction with the evening was plain, but she detected a lingering aspect about him, which signified he was tired or concerned about something. She tilted her head to watch him, past a bouquet of peonies. Running the estate was becoming difficult, with an agent as slow, wordy, and rigid as Swinnart. But this was no time to worry. She turned her thought to how her evening was progressing.

Herring directed the footmen with minute movement of eyebrow and chin, and an occasional index finger waving left and right. She saw that the baroness beamed when she put down her spoon after the sorbet. The footmen were waiting for her to finish, so they could clear the footed bowls away. Herring nodded, and the footmen moved, but the butler surprised her when he leaned over to say something in her ear. 'I am sorry to interrupt, my lady. You are needed in the nursery.'

'The *nursery*. Is little Baron Brockworth quite all right?'

'Nanny sent word. Apparently he is a bit unwell.'

Her son had to be more than just a little unwell for her to be summoned to the nursery in the middle of dinner. Nanny Arthur could deal with most childhood malaise. This must be something a touch more serious. Frederic lost a tooth some days ago, so his mouth must be a bit more sore than manageable. He was probably calling for her.

'When you can, my lady.'

'I'll come up when we rise after the pudding, Herring. I shall go up between dessert and when the ladies adjourn to the drawing room. You might pour the sweet wine with a bit of alacrity.'

He signified his understanding, and nodded past a half-open door. There, out of sight of the guests, stood a discreet housemaid, who had arrived with the message. Herring unobtrusively held up fingers of both hands to suggest the number of minutes that would elapse before Lady Croukerne appeared upstairs.

Drawing breath as far as a tight corset allowed, even

though she had not eaten much after the message came, Lady Croukerne made her way with some trepidation to the nursery fifteen minutes later, as her lady guests rustled and wafted to the drawing room in billowing evening dresses. It made her breathless to hurry up the staircase.

She opened the nursery door a crack, to find Nanny Arthur and Miss Purl there.

'Miss Purl! You are to be found in the nursery at such an hour.'

'Little Baron Brockworth called for me, my lady.'

A shot of alarm caught Lady Croukerne in the throat. 'He called for *you*. Oh. Let me see my dear boy.'

Frederic lay in the high metal-framed bed, with the covers up to his chest and both arms lying straight, on top. 'My darling boy – what is the matter?' She looked at Nanny Arthur. 'Has someone sent for Dr Gable?'

'Yes, my lady. Mrs Beste thought it would be better. He should be here within the half-hour.'

'My poor darling's forehead is very warm. He is looking rather feverish. Look at his eyes. Is there nothing we can do?'

Nanny looked confident. 'We have sponged his face and head with cold water. It seems to relieve him a little.'

'But he does not speak. Frederic? Will you not speak to your Mama?'

There was a soft groan.

'Where does it hurt?'

The boy lifted a hand to his throat and neck, and grimaced.

'Open your mouth, darling.'

He shook his head weakly, squeezed his eyes shut and open again.

'It looks as though swallowing is painful.'

He nodded.

The countess looked at his eyes and at Nanny.

'Yes, your ladyship. I know. His eyes are bright and

feverish, which is why I asked Mrs Beste to send for Dr Gable. One of the stable boys ran to the village and back.'

Miss Purl came up and stroked the boy's head. She moved away and brought a nursing chair. 'Please sit while you wait for the doctor, my lady.'

The brilliant green dress was creased and pulled out of shape, but she did not care, and watched with great concern as Nanny once again passed a cold cloth over the child's face.

'I feel it is going to be a long night.'

CHAPTER FIVE

In which disease comes to Denisthorn and
Mrs Beste acts as nurse

If anyone at all were standing out of doors, even at some distance, many lamps would be seen to be ablaze at the windows of Denisthorn Hall, burning far beyond midnight.

Lady Croukerne and Nanny stayed up. The doctor, who had been summoned by a breathless stableboy, watched them as he paced by the window. He consulted his pocket watch, rubbed his stout cheek and paced a bit more. If the boy's throat was so infected, as his examination starkly revealed, his fever would take some time to abate.

He had rarely seen such a constricted inflamed gullet before. Little Baron Brockworth's breathing had become more laboured and noisy as the night wore on. The rapid pace of regress startled even the old practitioner. The women were exhausted. One of the daughters had peeped in, huddled in a wrap, looking concerned, but she was sent away rather summarily by the nanny.

Every now and then, the exhausted mother rested her head back on the nursery chair and seemed to doze fitfully. She woke with a start after a few minutes, and took the cloth from Nanny's hand to apply it to the boy's face, throat and head with her own hands. 'Frederic, my poor dear Frederic.'

'It is tonsillitis, my lady. He might ... his throat will be back to normal in a week ... when his temperature goes down, when his fever abates, he will be himself again. We should hope for that before morning.' But Dr Gable's voice contained more than just a trace of uncertainty.

With hands shaking slightly, the worried mother pulled and pushed at the neckline of her dress, and at the comb in her hair. She shook her head. 'He trembles when awake. He cannot speak. His voice is gone. And the swelling around his throat is much worse. This is real malaise.'

'Yes – it truly is. I sense your concern, but this is a hale and robust little man. He is ... ahem ... fighting the fever well.'

Lady Croukerne did not agree with their doctor. She had never seen Frederic like this before. He had had his share of childhood illnesses, just like the girls. Goodness knew; when there was something in the village they were sure to get it.

'All children get tonsillitis at some point or other. We might make a case to have them taken out.'

'Taken *out*, Doctor! His tonsils! Surely they are there for a reason.'

Nanny came to stand near her mistress. 'I ... I've heard one should not ... um ... it's very ...'

The doctor shook his head. 'It is not as dangerous as it once was to perform a tonsillectomy, with the new instruments. It is a short, sharp operation.' He looked as though he regretted his description.

'Sharp!' Dismay was plain in the mother's face.

'But if his fever abates?' Nanny Arthur's question went unanswered.

'I shall re-examine his throat when some of the swelling goes down, my lady. I have administered some efficacious linctus.'

Such hope in her eyes, such exhaustion. The room was close and stuffy.

'Might we not open the curtains, perhaps? And let some fresh air in through a window?'

Both women were horrified at his words. Fresh air was not something one let into a sick room.

'Are you certain, Dr Gable? Surely the night air will not do my son any good.'

'His breathing is laboured and noisy. This room is airless.' His arms rose a fraction and fell by his sides. 'Yes – I suggest we open a window. In a few minutes I shall give the boy another spoon of linctus.'

The countess rang the bell.

'I also suggest we call Lord Croukerne.'

'Really, Doctor. It is bad enough he had to see our guests off on his own last night. I am quite certain the first thing my husband will do on rising in the morning will be to come up to the nursery. Disturbing him this early might suggest a sense of urgency that would fill him with unnecessary dread.'

Nanny's face was crushed with concern. She caught something in the physician's eye and raised both hands to her face. 'Oh no. Oh, no.'

Lady Croukerne turned, face aghast. 'What are you saying? What are you thinking?'

'I think it would be advisable for his lordship to visit his son now, or as soon as you deem possible.'

'Am I going to have to raise the household?' Lady Croukerne consulted the nursery clock. 'Well, I suppose there already must be people up and about in the servants' hall.'

For the twelfth time that night, the doctor compared his fob watch to the mantel clock. 'Five thirty is not as early as one would suppose, below stairs.'

A housemaid appeared at the door.

'Alice. Please get one of the footmen to raise Thorn. His Lordship needs to be woken to come and visit little Baron Brockworth.'

Alice bobbed and went away as silently as she had arrived.

Dr Gable stepped into the hallway and called her back. 'Alice!' He motioned urgently and she returned to the nursery door.

'Kindly open the curtains in there and open the window a crack, will you?'

'Open the *window*?' It seemed such a strange request.

'Please.'

She lowered her voice. 'Is it true the village fishmonger's daughter has died, Doctor?'

'Alice, do not spread gossip in the household. It's bad enough to have illness in the nursery. This is no time to be chattering.'

'But she has died, hasn't she?'

The doctor's head lowered in assent. 'Yes. Now open that window, please.'

Alice entered the room and fixed her eyes on Lady Croukerne. 'My lady, I ... the doctor ...'

'Do as Dr Gable says, Alice. It's all right.' She watched the maid part the curtains, lever open the solid shutters, and then push out the casement to a slight angle. The girl turned back into the room, cap fluttering slightly from the fresh breeze that wafted in and stirred the heavy curtains. Her eyes were wide in astonishment.

Lady Croukerne turned to see what caused Alice's surprised expression. Her husband stood shock still in the nursery doorway.

'Oh, Ninian. I hope you do not ...'

'Is he bad? My son!' He rushed to Frederic's bedside. 'Gracious me, Gable. This boy is burning up.'

'I have administered a tincture. His throat is very inflamed.'

The two men looked at each other. A communication, tacit and instantly understood, passed between them.

Lord Croukerne took the doctor by the upper arms. 'Oh no. Oh, *no*.'

'It's in the village, my lord.'

Lady Croukerne rose. 'Ninian? *Ninian!* What are you saying?' She turned to the doctor. 'What's in the village?'

There was a moan and sniffle from Nanny, who backed away from the bed. She looked faint. Alice took her arm and stood her by the window.

'Edwina, my dear.' Lord Croukerne's eyes were

reddened by distress.

'Do you and Dr Gable know something I don't?'

Her husband stroked her arm, and stumbled to his son's bedside, going down on one knee. 'Frederic, my boy. Frederic – can you hear me?' He put a hand on his forehead. 'Ah. It does not seem to be too bad.' His eyes searched those of the doctor, and then his wife's. 'Perhaps the fever will break by breakfast time.' He held out his hand and Dr Gable passed him a wrung cloth, which he tenderly placed on the boy's forehead. 'Open that window wider. Open it – we must cool this room. There are too many of us in here.'

'Alice, you may go.' The countess sat back on the nursing chair, exhausted. She looked at the nursery clock. The night was over, and soon it would be dawn.

Nanny withdrew, and came back with a fresh basin of cold water.

'This is no tonsillitis, is it, Doctor Gable?'

There was no immediate reply.

Lord Croukerne looked at his wife's querulous face. 'It's all my fault.'

'How could it be, Ninian? Is it tonsillitis? Can anything be done?'

'His tonsils, his whole throat, are very inflamed.' The doctor said no more, looking at the master of the house.

Lord Croukerne had his head in his hand, kneeling as he was by his son's side. 'There is diphtheria in the village, Edwina. Diphtheria. And I thought there would be no harm in allowing Frederic some fun there at the fair. It's my fault.' His voice was suffocated with guilt.

'Your lordship might not be to blame.'

'Of course I am, Gable! I should have forbidden anyone to leave the house. That abominable fair did more harm than good.'

'The germ must have infected little Baron Brockworth long before his visit to the fair, my lord. Diphtheria has an incubation period of more than a week.'

The tormented parents looked at each other and then at the doctor.

'How were we to know? A dozen souls have been stricken in the village. We did not know what it was at first.' Gable held his arms out.

'And was no warning given? I only heard two days ago. Swinnart was rather casual about it.'

'Frederic could have caught it from anyone then. People and tradesmen are coming and going from the village all the time.' Lady Croukerne sat back on the chair. She leaned forward again and took her son's hot hand.

'And all ...' Nanny stopped and raised a hand to her mouth. Tears ran down her cheeks. She took a corner of her white apron and mopped her face unceremoniously, leaving her skin chaffed and red.

The morning did not bring relief. The little boy struggled for breath, and did not respond to words or touch. His face reddened, and his throat inflamed more. The ladies Athena and Geraldine were instructed to stay away from the nursery, and everyone in there now wore squares of linen, dampened and tied behind their heads; they covered nose and mouth in an effort to keep the germ from being breathed.

'But is it not too late?' Lady Croukerne pulled at her makeshift mask, her eyes dull with fatigue and fear.

Her husband stilled her hand. 'Keep it on, Edwina. We must all do what Dr Gable tells us.'

'How could Frederic have caught it? From whom could he have caught this dreadful disease?'

'It's impossible to say, my lady.' Dr Gable was so tired he could hardly stand. He leaned against the mantel, wishing for a cigar.

The door opened and a trolley was wheeled in. On it, laid out with the utmost care and foresight, were coffee and a great platter of buttered toast. Mrs Beste herself stood behind it. Her face was grim.

'Thank you for such thoughtfulness, Mrs Beste. Please wheel it into the day nursery.'

'How is little Baron Brockworth, my lady?'

Edwina shook her head and looked at her hands lying in her lap. Her helplessness was discomforting to observe.

'Perhaps, my lady, you might be more comfortable in a more ...'

The mistress of the house looked down at the creased evening dress she still wore. How she longed for bed. But she would not move from that room.

The doctor drew Lord Croukerne to one side. 'Your son is getting worse, my lord. I am going to have to clear everyone from the room and ask Nanny to act as nurse.'

But Nanny had long disappeared to her room. 'I'm afraid she is exhausted.' The countess shook her head again.

Mrs Beste stepped forward. 'If you require nursing help, sir, I am very willing. I am not without such experience.'

'But you are ...'

'I am very willing, Doctor Gable.'

CHAPTER SIX

In which Lady Geraldine makes an early visit to the stables

It was still inky black outside. The chill that accompanied the setting of the moon came from a barely-visible mist that rose from the mirror lake outside Denisthorn Hall.

Lady Geraldine thought neither of the cold nor of the earliness of the hour. Already in her riding habit, she hurried from the garden entrance down the back stairs toward the ornamental rose bower and the gate to the walled vegetable garden, which she knew was always open early. The gardeners were up and about at dawn.

But it was not gardeners she sought. Past the gate she continued, the long way round to the stables. The soothing scents of grass, hay, and dry feeds were dampened by the morning mist, there but not there, and the strong aroma of horses, and their warmth, was also sensed immediately she treaded the cobbled stable yard. Although there was no one about, she knew the stables were hardly ever empty of staff. The head man lived in an abode above the tack rooms.

She entered the breezeway between two rows of stalls that faced each other, and sought her favourite mount. The stall's top shutter was still closed. Geraldine fumbled with the catch, fingers numb with the morning chill. 'Hello Buttercup. Hello, hello.' There was no cheer in her voice.

At last the catch gave, and a large brown head nosed toward her hand. 'Oh, Buttercup!' She reached up and patted the mare between the ears with a confident steady stroke, caught the horse's head between both arms and sank her face into the warm smooth neck. That was when tears threatened to come, but Geraldine breathed deeply of the horse's scent and calmed.

'They're all in the nursery, Buttercup. And they won't

let me in. They think I will catch whatever Frederic has. Oh, he is so, so ill with whatever it is. And you and I know I could never catch it. Could I, Buttercup?'

She started to sob, and the mare shifted nervously, horseshoes muffled by stable straw.

'I can't ride you so early, Buttercup. Don't get excited.'

She ignored the sounds of early morning work behind her. Someone was mucking out a stall. The resounding clatter of empty tin buckets came closer. A wheelbarrow rumbled on the cobbles.

'My poor little brother. My poor, poor Frederic.' She buried her face in the horse's neck, eyes closed and arms fast around the massive beast.

Someone cleared his throat behind her. 'I can get her ready for you, Lady Geraldine. Is that what you'd like?'

She did not turn.

'Or I can leave you for a while, my lady. I'm around if you should need me.'

Footsteps retreated after she gave a small nod. She wore neither hat nor veil, and her gloves were still in a pocket of the voluminous habit skirt. She cared little of what anyone thought. She felt disaster was around the corner. She knew something awful was taking place in the nursery, although exactly what she could not tell herself.

She could not believe she heard a female voice, but there it was. Not wanting to turn, Geraldine blinked against the horse's rough coat. 'Hm? Yes?'

'Are you quite all right, my lady?'

Geraldine turned. She had to turn. The voice was deep and yet soft and friendly.

'No, my brother is ...'

Before her stood a person in cap, jerkin, riding breeches and boots, with neck and chin swaddled in a thick scarf against the mist.

'Are you new?'

'No, my lady. Nothing like new. I've been helping out

here in the early mornings for quite a while. From First Farm, up beyond the copse there.'

'So ...'

'So I'm Mark, my lady. Mary Mark. Luke Mark's daughter.'

'Daughter! In breeches and cap, doing the mucking out.'

The young girl laughed. 'Daughter, in son's clothing, you might say.'

'It makes ...'

' ... practical sense, yes.'

'Oh.' For a moment, Geraldine forgot the nursery, and Frederic's plight, and the sadness that was in her heart. She looked the girl up and down, noting her clothes. But it all came flooding back in a few seconds and her eyes welled with tears.

'Oh, my lady.'

'Well, Mary Mark – I do wish I could wear my brother's breeches, but he is very ill and his clothes are very small, and he ... and he ...' She very nearly burst into real tears, real sobbing, but remembered where she was and held it all back.

'Oh my lady.' The girl rested a broom against the stall gate, rubbed both palms firmly down the front of those breeches, and held one hand out in a comforting gesture.

Geraldine took the rough warm hand and squeezed it.

'How old are you, Mark?'

The girl squeezed her hand and put the other on top of their clasp. 'Nineteen, my lady.'

'Do you ride?'

'I'd be quite useless around here if I didn't.'

They smiled together.

Geraldine knew in a second that if she had not been burdened with thoughts of Frederic lying there, they would have laughed. They would have laughed companionably.

The sensation of silent laughter in the stables buoyed

her spirits a little. 'If you ... by the time you saddle Buttercup, and another mount, it will be light outside. And we can go up to the copse and back across the west stretch and ...'

'If you think so, my lady.'

'I do think so, I do. Please saddle two mounts and I'll wait for you outside the breezeway. Please tell Attley I said so.'

'Very good, my lady.'

Geraldine watched Mark walk away, wondering at the breeches and how it might feel to walk so free of petticoats and stays and skirts and heeled boots.

Within fifteen minutes, they were cantering steadily, approaching the long bank of trees that hid the ridge from Denisthorn Hall.

Mary Mark led, on a young mount that had only last year been broken in by one of the more experienced men. He moved well, and Geraldine could see how nicely he avoided obstacles and took hill and dale, which was also due to his rider's handling. The stable girl was not a bad rider at all.

It was good to watch and also quite annoying to see a woman astride in breeches, comfortable and natural, riding with a measure of freedom and ability Geraldine wanted for herself. What it might feel to be free of stays and corset, of petticoats and skirts, stockings and heels.

'I want to ride like you,' she said when they dismounted for a short while near the chattering brook below the ridge on the west side. 'I want to wear a cap and scarf, shirt and jerkin. 'Women are so trammelled by what society thinks we should wear and how we should look, trussed up like fowl before the oven.' A sudden breeze wafted up, and Geraldine had to hold onto her hat and veil. 'Hats and veils and gloves and too many petticoats!'

'You do not ride badly, my lady.'

'I'm hampered by all this, Mark.' She shook her skirts,

a touch of anger making her sound strangled with frustration.

'Yes. I must say riding in breeches is free and fast.'

'Fast and free ... which is what I want to be.' But Geraldine knew it was time they turned back. She would be missed at the house and that would not do on a day when there was such a to-do in the nursery.

What she found on her return was nothing short of catastrophe.

CHAPTER SEVEN

In which disaster strikes

Coffee and toast in the day nursery was a meal Lady Croukerne would not easily forget. She had spent ten minutes in her room with Prudhomme, emerging in a grey day dress and a bit refreshed, if seen from a certain distance. Up close, her eyes were clouded, with hairline creases appearing on her lower lids. She had dispensed with any face powder, thinking it frivolous at such a time.

Sunlight streamed in past the parted curtains and fell on her skin; and on a partly-open cardboard box on the nursery floor, in which could be glimpsed the parts of a train set. The maid moved it aside and brought in extra chairs, and the trolley was placed at a convenient angle.

They took it in turns to administer to the boy, moving in and out of the sick room. Dr Gable only stayed away for a few minutes, downing a coffee and swallowing a morsel of toast. He was grateful for it, but would never let it be said he was not by the boy constantly. Constantly by the boy. Anxiety and dread ate at him.

He looked in his bag and of course did not find a throat tube of the new kind. He had only seen the tubes in a book. But he searched anyway, his fingers numb and tired. He doubted there was even one at the hospital. The things were so new – he had seen one in a catalogue of instruments that must still be on his desk.

His roll of scalpels brushed against the back of a hand. 'No.' He mumbled to himself and shook his head. 'No, no, no.'

Behind him, he could hear a footman arrive with the boiling water he had requested. He hardened his resolve and took up the rolled instruments, approaching the housekeeper with dread in his tone; dread he sought to disguise with kindness. 'You say you have experience. I do hope, Mrs Beste, that you are not squeamish. In any case, you can help me, but you can avert your eyes.'

'I shall do my best, Doctor.'

He had no doubt she would. 'Drop these instruments into the dish of boiling water now.'

Giving orders for Lord and Lady Croukerne to leave and get some rest was not easy, but they eventually left; his lordship to his dressing room where Thorn was waiting, and the countess to her bedroom to lie down.

'I am to perform a procedure that requires absolute silence and concentration, my lord.'

Without asking what that procedure might be, the earl had nodded.

The doctor took it as consent. He was in charge.

Performing a tracheotomy outside the sterile confines of a hospital, and on a patient so young, and of such noble standing, was not something Dr Gable had ever done. He had to force himself to take breath. It would be criminally negligent of him to become lightheaded and clumsy. He had to keep his wits about him, his hand steady, his eyes clear.

He held the instrument and watched it tremble. Inhaling again, his grip firmed. It was done quickly.

Afterwards, out of breath and shaking a little with distress, he stood, groaned, and dropped eyes to carpet.

He walked over to the washstand and scrubbed needlessly at a spot on the back of his hand, where a tiny spot of blood had rested for an instant. 'We shall have to wait and see, Mrs Beste.' He scrubbed again, imagining the speck of red still on the back of his hand.

The housekeeper was visibly shaken. Her face was ashen and drawn, and her hands trembled as she gathered up bloodstained towels. She had seen the boy's chest fill with air as soon as the doctor made the deep incision, and she quickly moved in, despite her fear and revulsion, to stem blood flow with damp towels.

In a very short time, the wound was dressed, and the boy's chest rose and fell. He had uttered not a sound when the doctor punctured his trachea to insert a small rubber tube. The room was quiet, except for the eerie sound of air through the incision in his throat.

'I fear ...'

The doctor turned to the sound of the housekeeper's distressed voice, a stern but alarm-filled look in his eyes. 'Do not go and faint on me now.'

'No, no.' Mrs Beste lowered her eyes. 'It's not that. I just fear what her ladyship will think when she sees little Baron Brockworth with a tube emerging from his throat.'

'She is a fine, perceptive lady. She will know it has saved her son's life.'

*

The sounds of staff moving about, birds outside the open window, and clip-clopping of horses in the distance seemed to put the room at odds with a normal day taking place outside that sick room.

Dr Gable heard a bell tolling somewhere out there, wondering whether it was Sunday, and thinking he had somehow lost a few days. Perhaps the sound was only in his head, a head filled with hope that by Sunday, this boy would be out of danger. He looked at his shaking hands, which he angrily scrubbed once more, savagely wielding a nail brush so it stung his skin. Anger gave way to guilt, to disappointment; to asking himself once more if he had done all he could.

'Doctor Gable.'

He turned.

The countess stood just inside the door.

'My lady – your son has had a ... a minor intervention, which I hope will allow him to breathe with ease.' He held out a hand. 'Perhaps we ought to have his lordship here before we approach the boy's side.'

Her face was enough to increase his fear and guilt tenfold. 'What? Why? Why?'

But Ninian Crownrigg was by her side. One glance towards the bed and his face creased into grey folds of dismay. He led his wife away, and nodded at the doctor. 'We shall be in my wife's day sitting room. I shall not be seeing Swinnart today. I'll ring for Herring from the sitting room. Thank you, Doctor.' He swallowed several times.

When they left, Dr Gable swallowed too, stood by the window and gulped in the fresh air. It had gone as he expected, and the rush of air through the narrow tube attested to that, but he did not feel either justified or relieved.

Outside, a flight of swallows swooped close to the house and away, gliding like so many black paper triangles over the mirror lake. He hardly noted the beauty of the scene in front of him. He did not take much notice of two figures on horseback returning to the stable by the eastern gravel road in the distance. Exhaustion and dread finally took their toll. He leaned against the shutter and shut his eyes. How long he stood there he had no idea. It seemed like moments, but could have been long exhausted, numb minutes.

'I can do nothing. Nothing.'

Behind him, someone stirred.

'Lady Geraldine. You have been ...'

'Out – riding.'

He looked at her clothes. 'You should not be in the sick room.'

'I must have a look at little Frederic.' She seemed breathless. 'Is what he has catching?'

'Yes, my lady. Please keep your distance.'

'I heard your words, doctor. You say you can do nothing.' Her face was a pale mask of distress.

'We cannot move him. He should be in the hospital. But we cannot move him.'

'My brother is so very ill, then.' She turned towards the bed.

Dr Gable saw her blanch when she saw the protruding tube. He was there to catch her as she collapsed; a light slight figure limp in his arms. She had seemed so assertive and confident in her riding habit only a split second before she fell.

He had no need to raise his voice. Nanny and Mrs Beste were there to take her.

'Lady Geraldine, my dear. Lady Geraldine!'

Between them they half carried her away, and in their place, at the threshold, the figure of a man he had not seen for weeks. 'Doctor Winthrop! How timely. I ...'

The young newcomer moved forward. 'You are all in, Doctor. Your gig is at the front door. Leave it all to me now. You must rest now.'

They shook hands and Dr Gable made his way to the grand staircase. He walked past magnificent paintings, the busts of Greek philosophers on plinths, and a coat of arms hanging over an archway. His surroundings were the last thing on his mind as he slowly wound his way down to the grand hall. He knew Doctor Winthrop was very capable, but there was nothing anyone could do. It would be a miracle if the boy survived another day.

CHAPTER EIGHT

In which Denisthorn Hall descends into mourning

They walked in the rain, following a white coffin borne by six village worthies. Composed of a cluster of enormous black umbrellas, the sad procession wobbled among uneven ranks of tombstones behind the ancient church.

A knot of household staff kept a discreet distance, under their own amorphous sectioned canopy of bleak black umbrellas; the stretched silk of gloom. Mr Herring and Mrs Beste huddled under his umbrella.

'We could not have foretold this a month ago, Mrs Beste.'

'Indeed not. Only the other week, we were gladly noting how the little baron came down for breakfast.' She mopped at raindrops and tears on her face with a large handkerchief.

'Two more souls in the village have gone.'

'It is a strange and discretionary scourge, wiping out nearly all of one family ... and leaving another unscathed, even next door.'

'Our young ladies seem well.'

'They were kept well away.'

'Nothing can keep Lady Geraldine away from anything, Mr Herring. She was up there every hour, day and night. She will be the worst affected by this. Do you not remember her teaching him to ride?'

There was a faint smile on the butler's face. 'Even though he had a perfectly good master of his own? The boy will be missed in the stables.'

It was infection that bore little Baron Brockworth away in the end; a long drawn-out end, which took another four days. The two doctors took it in turn to ensure everything possible was done for the boy. Nurses were sent in from the hospital at Cheltenham, but it was plain that outside the sterile confines of a hospital, it was difficult to keep the wound in the boy's throat from festering.

Fever from the diphtheria broke soon after the incision was made, but infection of the wound set in the following night, and despite everyone's efforts, the boy took his last breath without regaining full consciousness on Sunday afternoon.

'Her ladyship is inconsolable.'

'If you could look inside his lordship's heart, you would find the same. But he soldiers on, like the true nobleman that he is, never giving in to emotion. Look at him – he stands there in the rain bidding farewell to his only son, in place of his wife, who definitely and understandably could not come out in this, for this saddest of reasons, as well as himself. He must be truly devastated.'

'Who will inherit the title now, Mr Herring?'

He seemed only a slight bit shocked that she would bring up the topic. 'I should think that question is the furthest thing from his lordship's mind at this moment. Here they come. Let us take a step back and let them past when the padre has finished.'

The family party streamed by, a monochromatic clutch of black damp figures, with wobbling umbrellas and sodden hats. All the servants from the house looked at the ground, heads bowed and just as soggy.

'My shoulders are freezing.'

'We shall soon be back at Denisthorn, Mrs Beste. The cold and wet will not be as memorable as the bleakness of the reason we are here today.'

'In a few days all will be better.'

'Perhaps not the weather.' He looked at the louring sky. 'But at Denisthorn, all the aspects and outcomes of this sad, sad event will emerge to confound us all. Her ladyship most of all will require a great deal of care.'

'We never mention Lady Athena.'

'Ah. Lady Athena, look at her. She follows her father, despite what she considers to be opposition to his thoughts and wishes.'

'Would it not have been wonderful if ...'

' ... if she were a boy, Mrs Beste? If she were male? Perhaps. It is not for us to dispute or discuss how the lines of inheritance go. They are set in stone by the norms and customs of our country.'

'And by the laws.' The housekeeper's voice was muted by the conditions in which they walked, tramping on the muddy ground and finally finding the gravel pathways that led to Denisthorn.

'And by the laws.' He felt her release his arm, to which she had clung when the footing was uneven.

Now, the housekeeper walked on as steadily and calmly as the butler, and they wound around, following the other knot of servants, towards their entrance at the side of the hall.

Two of the footmen had hurried onward and there was tea in the day sitting room, as well as a blazing fire. When they descended from changing out of damp clothing, Lady Croukerne was there to meet them, dressed in deepest black. She had been advised by both doctors to stay inside and miss the burial, and everyone was glad she had heeded their call.

Her face was lined and wan, her lips a silent straight line. She took both her husband's hands when he offered them, and simply nodded.

Lord Croukerne took the stairs one at a time, which was unusual. There was no hurry, it seemed, to get out of his damp clothing. His hair was pasted to his forehead, his skin glistening from the rain. He looked upward and climbed, passing underneath three portraits of the previous earls that had governed over his estate. The last picture was his father's, but as those still down in the hall watched him ascend towards his rooms, he did not raise his eyes.

The noble line seemed doomed to be severed, and the interruption would soon weigh on his mind as the day of his young son's funeral and its memories ebbed into the flood of time ahead.

*

In the servants' hall, there was hustle and bustle for a while, and Mrs Beste endeavoured to calm the staff back into some semblance of a routine.

She questioned the housemaids about fires in all the sitting rooms and the small and big libraries. 'Alice, have you seen to replenishing the coal scuttles this morning, in the ...'

'It's all been done, Mrs Beste.'

'Because the footmen will soon be checking those fires and they had better be going well.'

'Blazing, Mrs Beste.'

'Good. On a day like today, it's more than just necessary. You and Dora must prepare for high tea. I have no doubt that even without consultation, her ladyship would appreciate a high tea.'

Alice was surprised. 'Not in the sitting room?'

'We might as well lay it out in the small dining room, where breakfast is usually served. Glover and Formby will tray it up. So let's get more water boiling ...'

'Already done, Mrs Beste. And there is plenty of fresh bread.'

'Good. Let's cut a good quantity of cucumber sandwiches and ... wait, there is not enough of the good fruit cake, is there?' She opened both doors of a larder cupboard and considered what lay before her on the marble shelves. 'Oh, there is an as yet uncut cake here. Good, good.' Although glad at her foresight and good planning, there was heaviness in her heart that would take weeks to dispel.

Sending up three laden trays in the capable hands of the footmen was the easy part. Settling the staff around the long refectory table and seeing they were all suitably fed was another thing. How she longed for her office, her sanctum, where the fire would rid her of the clammy sensation caused by damp stockings, and perhaps soothe some of her distress away.

Mr Herring rapped knuckles on the table. He stood at its head in his usual place and waited until silence fell. He shot her a meaningful glance, but she could not decipher its true import.

'Thank you all for your attendance today, your discretion, and your comportment. Kindly understand, every one of you, that I expect this demeanour to endure for the remainder of the week. We are to sustain decorum and provide succour to the family. We are a house in mourning until we are advised otherwise, do I make myself plain?'

'How long must we wear black arm bands?'

'As long as necessary, Formby.'

'I will never understand these people.'

'*Formby!*'

'They are utterly confusing. They do not complain or shed tears.'

'Yes they do!'

'And they all have several names. What is it? Crownrigg? Croukerne? Why can't they be plain mister and mistress?'

'Formby!'

A soft voice came from among the younger maids. 'Yes, why? I have only one name – Brown.'

'Hush, Nancy Brown. Croukerne is the noble title his lordship has inherited. Crownrigg is the family's name.'

'And why was the little master called Baron *Brockworth*?'

'That's another noble title, which relates to the land

we all stand on. The little baron would have inherited the Croukerne title too. He was the only male heir.' It was plainly obvious. The butler had a wide-eyed expression which down-stared the maid. 'And her elderly ladyship is a marchioness, because she inherited the title, and her fortune, from *her* father, the late Marquess of Harpensted.'

'What, no brothers?'

'No, and the title was expressly bequeathed to her in his will. Or so the story goes.'

The response was evidently too complicated for the girl to understand. 'Why was there no wake, Mr Herring?'

'Yes, why? I fully expected having to wait on at least a hundred souls.' Formby reasserted his place in the exchange. 'Were all the relatives and family friends turned away, Mr Herring?'

The butler cleared his throat and waited for silence once more. 'It was made very plain that Lord and Lady Croukerne are in no state to receive visitors. The carriages were all directed to follow Lady Margery's to the village.'

'The village!'

'There is a wake for family members and close friends only, those who came from some distance, at the chambers of Judge Harding, under the auspices of Lady Margery and her staff from Gallantrae.'

'All that way in the rain, from Gallantrae!'

'It's hardly an impossible distance, Alice. Lady Margery will host a very seemly wake, I am sure. That household is just as capable as this one of feeding a crowd of esteemed ladies and gentlemen.'

'And the padre!'

'*And the padre.*'

'At the judge's chambers.'

'Just so.' Mr Herring's expression allowed no more to be said on the subject.

CHAPTER NINE

In which Lady Athena gets her way

Lady Athena stamped a foot in frustration and dismay. She stood in the middle of her mother's day room carpet and crossed her arms.

'Do you dare throw a tantrum, at your age? And at this juncture, Athena? I pray, put down your arms.' Her mother was most displeased. Her voice remained calm and modulated, but it was composure and elegance, and a life-long adhesion to serene comportment and sensible behaviour – behaviour that could never let her down or be held against her – which kept her composed.

There had been a telegram that morning, in response to the sad one sent to the dowager marchioness, of what had transpired in the nursery the previous week. 'Your Grand-mama is now in Greece, and is taking a train to the lakes, from where she will traverse to France. It won't be long before she is home again. Devastated, her telegram said. *Devastated*.' She looked at her hands, glanced up at the ceiling to clear her eyes, and took a breath. 'What is it with you, my dear?'

'Well, you led me to believe, Mama, that I would spend some time with Aunt Margery at Gallantrae, and it is suddenly out of the question.'

'Suddenly! Do you say suddenly? We are in *mourning*, my dear. Need I make a fine point on it? The entire family is crushed.'

Contrition stained Athena's cheeks scarlet. How could she forget, even for a minute, that they had lost Frederic? Her little brother was gone, it had only been a few days, and all she could think about was herself. 'I am so very sorry,

Mama.'

'*Well should you be.*'

There was an awkward silence, in which Athena twitched and fidgeted and her mother raised her chin and fixed her eyes on the window behind her daughter's back. She truly wished her daughter was thinking how she could emulate her calmness, and resist reactive mischief.

'We have had a very busy time of it, and I've had little time to ...'

'Please don't make excuses, my girl. I should not make excuses if I were you. You have had little in the way of firm commitments. Two seamstresses were here, that is all, two seamstresses who were quick and clever and rather capable, with two maids to tack and hem. We need to be suitably outfitted with mourning clothes. We have certainly not been exceptionally busy. We are merely ...' Her voice broke. 'We are heartbroken and confused.' She put a hand on her heart. 'We are inconsolable and ...' Her enormous sigh made Athena look down at the carpet. 'Look, my darling girl, I suppose grief affects us all in different ways. Your way is to seek distraction.'

Athena said nothing. She did not even dare nod.

'A good way to help you onward in your particular kind of anguish could be to spend some time away. I do concede it might be a solution. I shall write to your Aunt Margery this afternoon.'

'Really?'

'Yes – *really*. I shudder to think that anything can reduce you to uttering single-worded expressions. I used to pride myself in your articulation, Athena.'

'I am much better at writing than speaking.'

Her mother scowled. 'Everything might fall back in place by the time your new desk arrives. And what are you thinking of writing, might I ask? What in the world are you thinking of setting to paper?'

Athena took a step forward. 'I'm not sure yet, Mama. I

just have words milling around in my head, and I feel a need to capture them in some way.'

'Well, darling ... I don't know. I don't know about *capturing* words. Words can only be thought, spoken and written.'

The girl nodded at last. 'And kept close, and shared, and heard, and *read*.'

'Ah – how interesting. So you are intent in having whatever you write read?'

'A secret diary is no use to me, Mama. I do want ... well, writing is communication, is it not?'

'Is it always?'

'One communicates with the reader. Even if it is a secret diary, one communicates with oneself ... or oneself at another time. Oneself as a reader in ... in the future. It could almost be another person, if one reads what one has written a long time afterwards, could it not? A person does change.'

'Young people change. One is only truly prone to change when one is youthful. When one gets to my age one feels stuck in a kind of permanence of spirit. And then one is shaken to the core by the passing of a child. By something like this. By tragedy.' She raised a hand to her forehead, and sought the lacy handkerchief in her lap with the other. 'Will we ever get over Frederic's passing? Ever?'

'Oh, Mama ...'

'I must find a distraction. I must get to my desk and write to Margery.'

Athena stirred. 'It's not a truly opportune time, perhaps.'

Her mother looked up.

'Should I do better by staying here at Denisthorn, by your side? You need consolation too, Mama. You probably need more solace and succour than anyone else in the household.'

'Your father is torn and grief-ridden, and quite disconsolate.'

'I mean ...'

'And Geraldine retreats to her own spaces and leaves us to wonder where she might be. The stables claim her, I suppose. She and her riding clothes. She and her horses.'

'I mean ...'

'I see very well what you mean, Athena. I shall write to your Aunt Margery. She will have the clarity of mind and the presence of spirit to direct us. She will offer you a splendid visit. When and how ... the details I shall leave to her. She is a most capable person, and not as numbed and disabled by this bereavement as are we.'

'And should I be required ...?'

'Athena, yes. Look at me ... yes. I can forestall your question because I know fully well what it is you are thinking. Yes – you are required to wear your new black clothes until the mourning period is over. Do you understand? No matter where you are. Even if you do stay at Gallantrae.'

The young woman's eyes once more grazed the carpet at her feet. She gave a slight contrite nod.

'You will demonstrate to your aunt's household your respect, decorum, and observance of custom. As is ...'

'... as is right and fitting, Mama.'

'Exactly so.' Lady Croukerne rose and walked purposefully to the window, whose long figured damask drapes gathered gracefully on either side. She looked out towards the walled garden over the stretch of lawn and the parterre which looked dewy in the morning light. 'Do you know, I almost expect to see Frederic striding past, in that way of his, every time I look out of one of the windows.'

'Oh, Mama.' Athena watched her mother press the handkerchief to her lips. 'You are so pale and distressed. That is so sad. I too think I hear him coming down the stairs sometimes. Do you remember the sound of his boots on the marble?'

The sound of soft sobbing filled the day room.

Both women bowed their heads.

Athena moved forward and touched her mother on the shoulder. 'Mama, oh Mama.'

The older woman turned and embraced her daughter, falling into her arms and weeping.

'We shall never get over this.'

'Yes we shall, Athena.' Lady Croukerne stood back. Her back was straight, but her eyes were clouded with emotion. 'Of course we shall. Ring for Prudhomme. She will help you decide how to have your hair. A short veil, an abbreviated veil will be sufficient for the evenings, and you may have my jet comb and necklace.'

'*Prudhomme!*'

'Yes, you may borrow my lady's maid. There is nothing wrong with that. Prudhomme will be happy to style your hair.'

'Thank you.'

'And she will instruct Fairley how to do it, for when you travel together soon.'

'Thank ...'

'You are reduced to monosyllables again.'

Athena was tongue-tied.

'But you will get your way, my dear. I am persuaded somehow that there is no sense in you and I and ... I see no sense in imprisoning ourselves behind a wall of grief.'

Athena stood back.

Lady Croukerne swished her voluminous black satin shirts and left the room, still holding the handkerchief to her cheek.

CHAPTER TEN

A house party at Gallantrae

The mistress of Gallantrae swept down the main staircase in that magnificent castle-like mansion and held out an arm. She fanned a dainty hand to indicate the landscapes, representations of wildlife, and prize-winning livestock and horses in beautiful frames hanging around the stairwell. 'We might not have portraits of earls on our walls here at Gallantrae, Athena, but we do have a fine estate, slightly larger than at Denisthorn, and it is very capably run by our managers.'

'Managers!'

'It's what we call agents here. We do run things on very modern lines.'

'Lines!'

Lady Margery looked at her niece, but said nothing about her monosyllabic way of conducting a conversation. She had always felt her sister, Edwina Crownrigg, *Lady Croukerne*, whose husband was an earl, had unconventional methods for raising daughters.

Oh, if only she had daughters. There had been such hope, when she was younger. And she did bear two live infants out of a dozen pregnancies. That they took their first and last breaths within just weeks was for some time a constant source of grief. Her sister surely knew she understood the grief of losing a child. They never spoke of her childlessness, nor of her grief, because she had managed to emerge from it all with a solid determination, a modern kind of fortitude. But if she had had daughters, she was sure they would have spoken in full sentences. Perhaps she could talk to Edwina about that.

But Athena found a longer sentence or two to say. 'I must thank you. Um ... I am very well accommodated, Aunt Margery. My room is lovely.'

'You're very fortunate to be among the first to arrive. I urged my old faithful and very capable housekeeper Mrs Otton to give you the yellow suite, even though it's usually reserved for Lady Marchbinder when we have a house party, and even though you have not yet come out and are still to all intents and purposes a child.'

'I am due to come out this summer. I wonder if ...'

'Your mother is a sensible woman. She will not hold you back, mourning or no mourning.'

'And Lady Marchbinder?'

'She will be delighted to be placed in the crimson room for a change. Now ... will you join us for all the planned events? There will be a rather vigorous walk over the downs tomorrow afternoon, to watch the launch of the dirigibles.'

It was plain from Athena's face that she had no concept of what dirigibles might be.

'I wonder if you might like such an adventure, but your mother would never forgive me if something were to happen to you, my dear. Especially at this juncture in your family. I see in your face a trace of mystery.'

'Dirigibles?'

'A dirigible is a balloon!'

'Oh.'

'A very large balloon that flies! Up above the earth, filled with hot air warmed by a flame of some sort.'

'Oh.'

The older woman ignored the brief utterance and went on. 'From Grayson's Field, tomorrow afternoon, two Montgolfier balloons, with suspended baskets, will – if the winds permit – take a few passengers for a flight, and return to the field. We are not the first to host such an adventure, and definitely should not be the last. My husband does think it is the future of travel.'

'*Travel* – up in the sky, Aunt Margery?'

'It seems unbelievable, but some very long flights in a basket suspended from a balloon have been made. Some people think it will – before very long – be the ideal way to get across the English Channel, on regular excursions, much faster than any ferry!'

'Will you be riding in such a balloon, Aunt Margery?'

'I think we should sensibly leave it to the gentlemen. Uncle Herbert will lead the men.'

'Oh.'

Lady Margery restrained herself once more from commenting on her niece's monosyllabic way of responding, but doubted the whole visit would go by without her losing her patience and remarking on it. 'Your uncle and two or three of the gentlemen will have the opportunity to view the estate at a perspective from which no one has before. I find it rather exciting.' The older woman turned to see what reaction her niece might have. 'Do you have no thoughts on it, my dear? Will you not be eager to hear what your uncle and his companions will have to say?'

'Yes.'

'Well, let's have it then. What is your opinion of human flight?'

'I wonder whether it is flight, exactly. Does the word flight not suggest wings ... or ...'

'Oh, how delightfully imaginative of you, Athena! Would it not be wonderfully astonishing if someone invented a basket with attached wings? White wings, with enormous feathers fashioned out of silk, perhaps, or satin.'

'Or a million doves' feathers glued together with wishful thinking. Like Icarus. I find the thought rather dangerous.' The girl shuddered.

'It's positively enchanting to hear your thoughts. I do love listening to you speak.' Perhaps encouragement was better than rebuke. 'Now let us make our way to lunch. I do believe the gong will sound ...'

The sound of a melodious gong reached them from the second hall.

'My word, how timely. Come along, now. I do believe Mrs Otton has arranged to have a fresh ham upon the stand.'

And sure enough, when they entered the small dining room, which at Gallantrae had a dual perspective, with windows on adjacent walls providing an excellent view of the foothills, the sideboard was laden with a large ham on a blue and white ceramic stand, and various dishes of accompaniments, including piccalilli, rice and raisins, and a large tureen of something Athena had never seen before.

She stood in front of the sideboard and paused for a second, which caused a footman to rapidly reach her side. 'May I help you to luncheon, Lady Athena?' He took a plate and expertly laid two carved slices of ham onto it. 'Would you like some potato salad?'

'Is that what this is?'

Lady Margery gave a soft chuckle. 'I don't suppose you frequently have many German recipes coming up from Mrs Jones's kitchen at Denisthorn.'

'No.'

'The little potatoes have red skins, and they are prepared with mayonnaise and various other ingredients. You will find it delicious.' She nodded at the footman, who ladled a small helping onto Athena's plate.

Lunch went well, until the peace of the small dining room, which was an intimate space, was interrupted by the entrance of Sir Herbert.

Athena was surprised to have him join them after they had started. It was something that would not have happened at Denisthorn. The family ate together or they did not, but no one would enter once a meal was under way.

Lady Margery saw her face. 'We are rather modern

and informal for luncheon at Gallantrae, my dear niece. It is a frightfully busy estate, and needs fine management, which does not always adhere to the timing of the household gong!'

Athena's eyes stayed wide.

'We run several hundred head of cattle,' Margery's husband continued. 'And a sizeable flock of sheep. And I deal with two managers. Sometimes three.' He fluttered his napkin and placed it on a knee, quite out of breath, as if he had run the last few yards to the house, which perhaps he had. He gave a brief smile across the table and started on his ham immediately. His wine glass remained untouched. A footman came forward and filled a fine etched tumbler from a silver water jug.

'Thank you, Rogers. We shall continue from here.'

The footman left the room, and everyone served themselves. The conversation turned to the house party.

'You are first to arrive, I see, Athena.'

'Yes, Uncle.'

He waited for her to say more. After a slightly awkward pause, he went on. 'We have an adventure planned for tomorrow, which your aunt has no doubt intimated. I pray you hold that news to yourself, for us to announce to the other guests after they get here this afternoon. I think we should all get ready to meet and greet them at about five. I shall consult with our butler, Cotterell, and let everyone know.'

He waited for a remark from Athena. Then continued. 'We are expecting ... my dear – how many should we be in all?' He gazed across to Lady Margery.

'A dozen or so souls, I should say. There is a list on my desk, and Mrs Otton has her copies. Cotterell has everything under control.'

'There would be no control at all without your capable intervention and planning, my dear.'

Lady Margery smiled. 'Thank you, darling.'

Athena's eyes swung round to her aunt. It was surprising for a lady to use an intimate term of endearment at table. Her mother never addressed Papa with anything but formality when anyone else was in the room. She was not exactly an outsider, being a relative, but it still surprised her.

'I suppose you are prepared for a number of events, my dear?'

'Yes, Aunt Margery. My clothes however ...'

'... are all black? It's right and fitting. By the end of the fortnight or three weeks you are with us, my dear, after our house guests have departed, you might find yourself surreptitiously borrowing my grey stole.'

'It was a terrible business with your young brother. Has your father spoken at all about the estate ... or the title, Athena?' Sir Herbert looked curious and concerned, all at once.

It was an unexpected question. 'The title, Uncle?'

Sir Herbert saw it was an inopportune inquiry, even though he was getting used to her brief way of responding to questions. He put down his fork and waved a mild hand. 'Never mind me, my dear. I'm ever the inquisitive snoop. I might be what your father never fails to stress a *gentleman farmer*, but I have the mind of a village idiot.'

'Herbert!'

'My dear.' He nodded at his wife. 'I'm incorrigible, awkward, aren't I? Always the inveterate curious cat. Never mind me. I'm sorry, I apologize.'

His comment, however, did make Athena wonder. Indeed, what was going to happen now that her father no longer had a male heir?

CHAPTER ELEVEN

In which there is discord downstairs at Denisthorn

The fire in the servants' hall blazed, but the chairs around it stood vacant. The table was crumbed and cluttered with what remained of the first sitting's breakfast, but no one moved to clear it. A small clutch of kitchen maids stood by the door, staring at what was happening in the passage at the bottom of the stairs. It was a place they were instructed to keep clear. One of the first things Mr Herring or Mrs Beste did with new staff was to show them the spot at the bottom of the stairs, and to repeat strings of warnings.

'This place must be always clear. Never stand or dawdle here, do you understand? The footmen come rushing down and go up again bearing trays of hot food. It is a busy crossing, which no one must obstruct. The footmen are always in a hurry, and they are always carrying things.'

Mrs Beste liked to add that chambermaids carried buckets and jugs of hot water, and the ladies' maids often swept down bearing beautiful gowns and delicate fabrics that required spotting or laundering. Early in the morning, housemaids clattered up and down laden with cleaning materials and coal scuttles. 'Stay away from the bottom of the stairs!'

It had been a while since anyone ran up those steps bearing a long copper can of hot water, drawn from the eternally boiling cauldron on one of the kitchen ranges. There were now plumbed bathrooms, with drains that magically took waste water away, which dispensed with the use of slop pails. The new coal gallery at the end of the gentlemen's passage upstairs had a boiler, from which footmen carried hot water to dressing rooms for shaving, and to new bathrooms in each passage.

It had been a while since anyone slopped water onto the floor at the bottom of the stairs. The argument taking place in that very spot between Glover, the under butler, and Formby, one of the footmen, was neither loud nor aggressive, but it pulsed with something that threatened to take over the entire household.

'You cannot be serious ...'

'If you're going to argue, Formby, tell me things about *yourself*, not about me. All you utter is *you, you, you*.'

Formby stopped. 'Orright, Glover. Orright – I'll tell you how I *feel* if you listen for a second. Don't cut off the end of everything I say. Orr–?'

'The dowager marchioness is coming back to England. To this house, for four whole days. We're all at sixes and sevens. Surely we can leave this for another time.' Glover growled the words and started to turn away.

A high booming voice was heard to emerge from a doorway down the passage. 'You had both better remove yourselves from the bottom of the stairs!' Mr Herring appeared just outside his office. He held each lapel in a loose hand, but his chin was raised in an authoritative stance. 'Move. Move away now and settle your differences out in the courtyard. Now. Now, Glover.'

Glover turned on his heel and disappeared. Formby hung his head, looking at a loss.

'There's a table needs clearing, Formby. The second sitting will soon be down for breakfast. And they're not to find the crumbs, cold empty teapot, and used cups you others left behind.'

'Yes Mr Herring.'

There was another muted grunt.

'It's true what Glover said, Mr Herring.' Mrs Beste also emerged from her room.

The butler lowered his voice. 'Yes, of course. He's right that there is a tension in the household. The dowager marchioness is coming to stay for a few days, and that is always a nerve-racking prospect.'

'Always?'

'Since his lordship died, that is. The old earl's presence meant the dowager marchioness was calm and cool, and as close to being happy as one of her temperament could be. The death of Lord Croukerne's father has changed everything. Denisthorn is changed for good. It's a long time ago now, but the change still affects us all.'

'It's no excuse to break house rules, however.'

'Everything will be perfect.'

'Everything *must* be perfect.'

They both moved inside the butler's office.

'Why does she not return to her house on the other side of the village, then? Cheltenham House is at such convenient proximity.'

For the first time that morning, the butler smiled. 'And at such convenient distance, Mrs Beste.'

She smiled in response.

'She will be here with her lady's maid Burgess, for four days, to comfort the family after the tragic loss. Everyone is numb and muted after the little baron passed away. We are all still blanched by his death.'

'Scalded. But I should have thought ...'

'It's a blessing. Think of it as a blessing, Mrs Beste, for we have no alternative but to think of it as anything other.'

'A blessing!'

The butler waved her towards a seat.

'Yes. Think of it like this. We are all going to be so on edge and careful to do everything just right. We will all tiptoe around her ladyship and Burgess, who will, I suppose, be accommodated with ...'

'She will share with Prudhomme.'

'Then Prudhomme will have a difficult four days too.'

'Well, it's an unfortunate fact that the only suitable vacant bed in the servants' sleeping quarters at the moment happens to be in that room. Prudhomme is her ladyship's personal maid. Can you imagine the fuss if we accommodated Burgess with Alice and Maisie?'

They laughed together, but it was a strained laugh. Their experience and patience would prepare them well for anything, but some of the younger and newer staff would be well ruffled by the dowager marchioness's stay.

'It will serve us all well.'

'How, Mr Herring? How?'

'It will be a distraction. For four days, it will feel more discomforting and demanding than the little baron's passing. And when the four days are up, we will all hurt less. Especially the family. Think of the family, Mrs Beste, and what they must be going through. And what they will endure for the four days.'

'Goodness. I should not like to be at that dining table. Nor in that drawing room.'

'Indeed. Enough said on the matter.'

'Enough said then.'

'May I ask what the differences are that Glover and Formby are arguing about?'

'If we were to stand at the courtyard door in ten minutes, Mr Herring, after Formby clears the hall table of breakfast, we should be able to hear every word. Their voices are that loud and gruff.'

'What is it *about*?'

'Since Glover was promoted, Formby has been a lump of resentment. He has slowed, he is reluctant to help, gets in the way of the girls, and spends a lot of time out smoking with the stableboys and the delivery boy from the dairy. Glover thinks it's his responsibility to hurry him along.' Mrs Beste held a finger to her lips. She took a deep breath and placed a hand on her heart. 'Oh. I should not have said all that! Even I am on edge, and the dowager marchioness is not even yet within hailing distance of Calais and Dover.'

Herring lowered his eyes, and there was a moment's

silence.

Mrs Beste took up again. 'I apologize. The men are under your rule and guidance, Mr Herring.'

'I did ask, Mrs Beste. I'm thinking of asking Formby to take a few of his days of leave early.'

She shook her head from side to side.

'Yes – I know what you're thinking. It would not do to be one footman short when the venerable houseguest and her maid are here. There will certainly be more to do.'

'A lot of coming and going. I already have the girls airing and preparing Marlowe.'

'Marlowe? But the dowager marchioness has shown a preference for ... he consulted a leather-bound volume on his desk. 'Let me see. Wordsworth. She likes Wordsworth.'

'I keep notes too. And in my book, I have recorded that on her last visit, when Lady Geraldine sprained her ankle ...'

'Oh, I remember that. About two years ago.'

'Exactly. When that happened, she remarked there was a distinct cold draught in Wordsworth. Across the room, from behind one shutter to the gap under the door. And she won't stay in Keats, because that is where ...'

'Hm.' Herring gave her a warning glare. 'Hm. We shall not discuss um ... we shall not discuss what happened in Keats.' He looked up. 'Marlowe has an ante-room.'

'That's why I thought it would be ideal, despite it being the room closest to the gentlemen's passage.'

Herring smiled again. 'And since we have no gentlemen staying at the moment ... I see. Well planned, Mrs Beste.'

She needed no congratulating. 'The dowager marchioness also disapproves of the fact her ladyship has given literary names to the various guestrooms. She distinctly dislikes the one called Byron, even though the furnishings are deep blue.' Rising from her chair, she wagged a finger at the butler. 'We know enough about this household ...'

'... and about one another, Mrs Beste ...'

'... to be able to avoid second-guessing each other, don't you think?'

'Our departments are separate, but they are but one entity. We ...'

It was like a handshake, a tacit understanding that their departments might overlap, but they had discrete powers over distinct domains at Denisthorn. They both looked like they wondered how long it would last.

'When do we expect the arrival?'

'Wilson is taking the carriage to the station at Brockworth, to meet the five o'clock train, a week from Sunday.'

'We have eight days, Mrs Beste. Eight days to prepare and forestall.'

'Eight days of relative peace.'

CHAPTER TWELVE

In which Lady Athena shows reluctance to return to Denisthorn
and there are changes at the estate cottages

The girl pushed a barrow of stable muck to the end of the breezeway between the main stalls at the Denisthorn stables. Halfway along, she stopped, arched her back, stretched her arms, and sighed. It was hard work. Taking two steps to one side, she patted the head of a horse that nosed out of the top of the stable door. It was Buttercup.

'No ride today, eh, Buttercup?'

'Oh, yes – I shall take her out, Mark.' Lady Geraldine's voice came from the opposite end of the cobbled space.

'Good morning, my lady.'

Geraldine regarded the stable girl. She was sheathed in a long leather apron, underneath which it was plain she wore breeches and stout hide boots. Her neck and shoulders were as usual wound in a long reddish scarf, and a cloth cap hid her blonde curls.

'Mark, I'm going to ride into the village and back.'

'The village, my lady. I'll have Buttercup ready for you in a minute.' A hint of disappointment could be felt in her tone. Although they rode together often, Mary Mark knew it would not seem proper for her to be seen wearing breeches, riding astride, alongside her mistress in the village.

Lady Geraldine spoke even after the girl turned away to her tasks. 'It's horrible up at the house. Everyone is either weeping or consoling.'

'It must be a hard time, Lady Geraldine.'

'Did I interrupt you at your task?' She looked at the abandoned barrow in the middle of the breezeway.

'Tom!' Mary Mark called loudly and a young boy

appeared. He could not have been much older than Frederic when he died. 'Tom, push the barrow to one side, will you? Or wheel it down to the pile, please – that would be better.'

The boy tipped his hat to Geraldine and pushed the barrow away. She watched him retreat out of sight into the cold and wet, then turned to watch Mark saddle Buttercup.

'My sister's the lucky one. She's away at Gallantrae.'

'That's Lady Margery's house a bit of a ways over the two ridges, isn't it?'

'Oh, it's miles past ..... I do suppose ...'

'I have never been further than Brockworth village, my lady.'

'What – not even as far as Cheltenham?'

'My work is here.'

Geraldine looked at the girl in amazement, wondering what it might be like to go without a London season, whether one had come out or not. What it would be like not to know what lay behind the forest outside Cheltenham. Although she envied Athena's coming out that year, and her ability to entertain invitations to balls and dances, dinners and parties, and to be presented at court, it was a lot of fun just to live at the London house for part of the year. They all moved *en masse* to the great busy city, with two carriages and two box carts, and spent the better part of two months in that smaller but more elegant and formal Belgrave house. They received visitors every afternoon except Thursdays, when they did their visiting, and had an open house after dinner every Friday night, when they received gentlemen and ladies with some connection to the House of Lords and the Law in London.

'You have never been to London!'

'That's even further afield, my lady.' Mary Mark held Buttercup's reins up, and pushed the set of wooden steps closer to the horse. She helped Geraldine up into the saddle, making sure her right leg was safely hooked over the pommel and that the leaping horn did not pinch, and made the rider secure and comfortable. She arranged Geraldine's skirts over her legs much better than a male groom might.

Alone once more, standing on the cobbles between the stalls, Mary Mark watched her young mistress ride off, past the entry to the stables, taking the long way round to the mirror lake under clearing skies. It would take her about a quarter of an hour to reach the village at a steady clip, but the stable girl knew Geraldine often slowed or stopped to admire the trees, the fields, or some creature which dared to wander onto the path. She loved squirrels and jackdaws, and would often pause to observe a tiny fluttering butterfly happening to cross her path. The noises and scents of the countryside also caused Geraldine to slow. Mary Mark wondered whatever her mistress might find amusing in London, where she heard it was so built up and crowded not a single creature was left. Nothing there was natural.

'Rats!' She laughed as she returned to her tasks. 'There must be rats. There have to be rats. Where there's 'umans, there's rats!'

*

Ninian Crownrigg, Earl of Denisthorn, stood unseeing in front of the roaring fire in the hall. Behind him, the stairs were deserted. To one side, the library door stood ajar. He missed his son sorely, even though at this time of day the boy would be ensconced with the governess, conjugating verbs, reading pages of history, or adding rows of figures.

He also missed Athena, who at this time of day was generally in there, poring over whatever it was she pursued. He had no idea what she read, but decided he would make it a point to ask on her return. He stamped one foot, impatient, and looked once more at his fob watch, which told him Swinnart was a full five minutes late.

He turned to footsteps across from the library.

'I'm late, your lordship. I am very sorry. We are

moving a new family into the farmhouse up at Third Stream.'

'Is that right? What has happened to Waters and his family?'

'Waters found it hard to manage after his wife died, my lord. His oldest son moved off the land to work at the rope factory at Cheltenham, and both his daughters are now married. So he has moved to town and will work at the spa.'

'A farmer at the spa?'

'It will be a suitable occupation for a man in his fifties, I think.'

'So who shall we have at Third Stream?'

'They are called Davies, my lord – Nate Davies, his wife Bertha, and a clutch of small Davieses. He is good with sheep and knows a lot about the Leicester breed.'

'Our Blue-Faced Leicesters. That's good.'

'He has large herd and flock experience, in Tyne and Wear.'

'A good find, then – is he a nice enough fellow?'

'I found him a bit soft-spoken, but a look at his hands will tell you the kind of worker a man is. Nate Davies seems to be a knowledgeable shepherd with hardworking habits.'

They moved into the library, where the fire was hot but glimmering low. Ninian Crownrigg nodded and the agent threw a scoop of coal onto the embers, which caused a few sparks to rise.

Swinnart launched into a long and wordy account of what was happening with the tenants. Farm business followed, with the agent reeling off figures and dates, lacing the account with descriptions, anecdotes and explanations.

Lord Croukerne looked at the man's boots, which were slightly spattered with mud. The agent rode an enormous grey mare all over Denisthorn, wearing a large leather hooded cape which no doubt was now dripping, down in the mud room just inside the garden entrance at the back.

'Her ladyship, my mother the marchioness, is returning to Denisthorn and will stay with us for a few days, Swinnart. During that time, I shall be unavailable for the normal tours and inspections, so I expect you will take up the slack.'

'It will run smoothly as ever, Lord Croukerne.'

It was a remarkably brief statement for the voluble man, who saw a tacit dismissal in the earl's body language, but stood his ground.

'Is there anything else, Swinnart?'

'Will Lady Geraldine still ride out with ... um ... on Tuesdays and Thursdays she ... um ...'

Ninian Crownrigg rose and smiled. 'She rides out with us for my company, Swinnart. She will be ensconced indoors listening to her grandmother's account of the European trip, truncated as it was. I don't think you need worry about the role of riding companion to my daughter when I am unable to ride out.' Ninian Crownrigg thought he heard a subdued sigh of relief.

The agent shifted awkwardly.

'You fear she'll make you gallop, do you?' There was a smile in his master's voice.

'She's an enthusiastic rider. Lady Athena is still away, my lord?'

They walked out into the hall together.

'My oldest daughter is enjoying her time at Gallantrae. But she will no doubt come home soon, possibly simultaneously to the momentous arrival of her grandmother. It would not ... in any case, thank you for coming in, Swinnart.'

'My lord.' The agent gave a shallow bow and disappeared towards the back of the hall, swallowed up by the shadows underneath the elaborate carved gallery, which was the pride of the earls of Denisthorn.

The earl looked at his watch and saw there were a few minutes before the luncheon gong was likely to ring. He would join his wife and daughter.

Lady Geraldine, when the gong did sound, swept black flannel skirts around her and moved into the dining room, closely followed by the countess, in a dress that appeared to be in identical fabric, but fashioned in a more attractive mode.

'You come to luncheon without a veil, Geraldine.'

'No one wears a veil indoors now, Mama.' She looked at the small veil adorning her mother's coif, and the ebony comb neatly nestled there. 'You will be asking me to wear a bonnet next.'

'Married women used to wear a bonnet. The queen wears a bonnet.'

'I am sure the queen does a lot of things my humble position does not extend to.'

'A clever rebuttal, Geraldine, but those were better days, my dear. We all knew what to do, and we all knew what was expected of us. The times are moving too fast. Fashions change almost every month, and no one knows what is expected of them. The housemaids are showing reluctance to wear bonnets now! Or so Mrs Beste reports.'

'Don't they have those little caps now?'

'Exactly – starched to within an inch of their lives. Knots of froth! I feel they look ridiculous and serve no purpose. I half expect to find a maid's hair in my bed sheets, fallen there because the means of holding hair in place has disappeared.'

Geraldine shook her head in mock outrage. 'Whatever next! I wonder what the queen's maids wear?'

'Now do not be facetious. I'm sure no stray hairs ever appear in the queen's bedclothes.'

'They wear bonnets in the kitchen, do they not? Please say they do.' Ninian Crownrigg looked horrified.

'Indeed they do. And if they do not, they wear hair nets. Mrs Beste is not relinquishing our meals to chance, Ninian.'

'I suppose Athena wears a veil at Gallantrae.'

'Without a doubt. But she is due to return soon. Grand-mama would miss her if she were not present for her arrival.'

Ninian Crownrigg drew his mouth into a slit.

'What is it, Ninian?'

'I have had a note from Athena.'

Geraldine looked down at the lunch she had served herself from the sideboard. A small wedge of Cheshire cheese, a dollop of relish, and a tiny cut of apple pie were all she desired at that hour. Her smirk, she feared, would not go unnoticed.

'Well might you smile at the possible end of your brief reign, Geraldine, but Athena will return at some point.'

'I think she shows a great reluctance to come back to us, Mama.'

Her father nodded. 'Indeed. In her note, she asked me to ...'

'Asked *you*?'

'Yes. She's asked me for an extension to her sojourn at Gallantrae, saying Margery approves. And to excuse her absence to her grandmother.'

Lady Croukerne put her napkin aside and wrung her hands. 'What am I to do with these daughters!'

'She is a young woman enjoying a stay away from a household doused in grief, my dear.' The factual statement from Ninian Crownrigg was not welcome.

'It might be so. But decorum and appropriateness are a far cry from what she holds to be the truth, Ninian.' She held a handkerchief to the corner of an eye. 'Please respond that we want her home. And soon. And in plenty of time to settle before her Grand-mama arrives. And why does she address herself to you, when a note to me would have been more fitting?'

The earl did not give the answer that sprang to his mind. He looked at his younger daughter instead. A flash of rare understanding crossed the table.

'Could it be that there is someone there who has taken her interest?'

'Apart from Aunt Margery and Uncle Herbert, do you say? What? Like a ... Has she written to you, Geraldine?'

A forkful of pie hovered in the air. Geraldine's blank expression was an admission of sorts. Her silence was confirmation.

'What did she write, Geraldine? Why does everyone in this house think it is fine to leave me in ignorance? I am always the last to know.'

'She made no announcements, Mama.'

'But she confided in you?'

'Not exactly.'

Ninian Crownrigg was impatient. 'Really, my dear girl. Hurry up and tell us what - or *who* – your sister has found to be so absorbing at Gallantrae.'

'Has she sworn you to secrecy?'

'It is of no such enormity.' The pie and cheese lost attraction all of a sudden. She looked at her plate.

'So, please, tell your father and me.' Lady Croukerne put down her fork and stared at Geraldine.

'Edwina. I hardly think ...'

'My manners are not to be remarked on at table, Ninian. I can put them to one side when concern for my older daughter is paramount in my mind.'

He nodded. Then he watched Geraldine as she spoke slowly and clearly about what her sister might have found to be so entrancing at her aunt's house.

CHAPTER THIRTEEN

*In which Mr Herring pays a visit to Cheltenham House
and
the dowager marchioness ponders the future of the title*

The expression 'at sixes and sevens' was so often used below stairs at Denisthorn the week before the grand arrival, that there seemed no end to the confusion, which was more than just numerical.

Mr Herring even had reason to walk over to Cheltenham House himself, to speak to the butler there; old Mr Bann. He took along a small notebook and a fountain pen with a screw cap. The box it came in said it was guaranteed not to leak, since the pen's cap hid a close rubber sleeve that prevented ink from issuing through the nib.

Herring did not trust the invention, even though the newspaper article and advertisements that persuaded him to buy the pen guaranteed it. 'Mr Cross, inventor and devisor of writing implements, had better be right,' he muttered as he crossed the village, holding on to his bowler hat with the same hand that clutched the pen. It was not going in his breast pocket until he was absolutely sure it did not leak. The wind blew, his hat threatened to part company with his head, and his fist tightened around the pen.

Indeed, Alonzo Cross, inventor of the innovative rubber seal inside the pen cap, would have been amused to see how adroitly the butler avoided dogs, children playing with hoops and marbles, young ladies on those infernal bicycles, and women coming from market with heavily-laden baskets, not to mention one-horse gigs and tradesmen pushing handcarts.

'We are at sixes and sevens as it is. A large ink stain on my jacket will only add to the fuss.'

He took careful notes about the dowager marchioness's preferences and habits as Mr Bann spoke. His office was a great deal smaller than Mr Herring's own, and surprisingly, a great deal untidier.

'You have a smaller staff than mine, Mr Bann.'

'Indeed, Herring – but I do not cater to a whole family here, and we only have one carriage, housed at the tavern stable. No stableboys, and only one groom. Two house maids, who double as kitchen maids, one cook, and the housekeeper Mrs Conder, of course. She is rather new, and has had the good opportunity of her ladyship's absence to learn the ropes here at Cheltenham House.'

'And ...'

'And Mary Burgess, the lady's maid, is away with her ladyship.'

'Naturally.'

'Of course. She with the impenetrable Scottish accent. And the startlingly intense blue eyes.'

Herring was taken aback. 'I never noticed.'

'Which means she has never addressed you in anger, Herring. You are a lucky man indeed.'

Bann spoke at length about his mistress's present preferences, sometimes contradicting himself. 'So, a warm muffin in a covered dish on the breakfast tray, with blackberry jam.'

'You said marmalade before.'

'You can alternate. I believe you said four days?'

'Four nights, which means five breakfasts?' He started to count on his fingers.

'Whatever it is, I have tasted Mrs Jones's marmalade, and it will do splendidly well, for her ladyship's entire stay. And a tiny pat of butter, not a ball, she hates butterballs. Do not forget to instruct the footmen about her bedroom fireplace.'

'It's the first thing I noted.' Herring looked at the nib of his new pen. 'Why does she insist on a high fireguard?'

'It's ... ah ... a delicate topic, Herring. You do not remember his old lordship's um ... ways?'

'Let's be plain, Mr Bann. The fourth earl was a philanderer.'

'Hush.' The finger Bann held up to his lips shook a bit.

'And a hard taskmaster. But he is dead and can no longer give us trouble.' Herring tilted his head.

'Indeed not. Indeed not. The days are far easier now.'

Herring failed to see how any day could be easy with the dowager marchioness in the house. She was just as difficult, but for different reasons.

'When we were up at Denisthorn, Herring, and you were under-butler, and the old earl was still alive, and his present lordship was but a young man, we thought nothing would ever change.'

'And look at us now.'

'Are you content here at Cheltenham House, Mr Bann?'

'It's all I know now, Herring. Her elderly ladyship and her demands ... it's all I know.'

*

Back at Denisthorn, Herring read his notes and remarked to himself the *demands* had changed since early days at the house. The dowager marchioness was ageing, and with that came a list of unusual requirements. It was a good thing her lady's maid would be within easy reach for urgent consultation if need be; even if Burgess struck terror into the hearts of everyone as well.

Arrival was imminent, and tension in the house had increased. He noted the splendid flower arrangement on the central hall table, the penetrating scent of furniture wax, the swish of housemaids' skirts toing and froing on the stairs, bearing folded piles of linen and swinging work trugs. No cleaning was done when the family was about. Sorting, tidying and preparing were all that was in evidence at that hour. It was a matter of timing, and Mrs Beste and her head housemaid had timing down to the minute.

Standing in the splendid gallery, looking down over the hall, Lady Croukerne approved of all preparations. Her house was clean, ordered, well-maintained and attractive. Her family was attentive. A caring but firm letter had been sent to Athena, and she would arrive shortly before her grandmother. So the entire household would be standing, all present and correct, when the carriage from the station drew up on the gravel drive. In clement weather, they would all range just below the forecourt. If it was raining, Herring would take her down with a huge cricket gamp to greet her mother-in-law. She hoped for a break in the weather. Nothing was more depressing than a damp skirt hem from a dash out in a downpour.

Lady Croukerne imagined she could hear the clock on the mantelpiece below, ticking the seconds, each one closer to her daughter's return from Gallantrae.

She was joined by Geraldine, in her black flannel skirt and flounced silk blouse.

'Where did you ride this morning?'

'It was brief by necessity. Rain bucketed down and we turned back before reaching the first ridge.'

'Was Papa with you?'

'No, not Papa. I rode out with Mark from the stables.'

'Mind you do not get too friendly with the grooms, my dear. It won't do to give them ideas.'

'I doubt they will get delusions of grandeur from me, Mama. They work their fingers to the bone, shifting tons of muck, bales of straw, buckets of feed, cans of water ... their work never ends. They are too exhausted to have *ideas*. Their work never ends. Just so we can ride.'

Lady Croukerne blinked. 'If you know of any other way we might live, do suggest it to your Papa.' Her voice was prim and arch, full of the obvious sarcasm of the remark. 'Farms and estates will always have stables. There is no other way to get around but on horseback and horse-drawn vehicles. I cannot think what you might imagine as an alternative! You enjoy it so, my dear.'

'Of course I do. I'm just observing the hard work that is done by the staff to keep us going the way we do. I do hope they are paid well.'

'That is none of our business.' Her mother wagged a finger. 'Your father runs it all very well, with the help of Swinnart and a host of other people. They dole out *hundreds* of pounds every payday, in those small envelopes, and the servants all line up and sign for theirs.'

'Does it not make you wonder how they feel, receiving money in a *little envelope*?'

'I hate to change the subject, my dear girl, but your sister is very late. I did so want her to be here to greet Grand-mama.'

'Grand-mama might be so tired from her journey, and so full of anecdotes and commentary, and so detailed about the indisposition or complaint that has made her cut short her grand tour, that she might not notice Athena is missing.'

'Nonsense. Ah! I hear a carriage. This must be Athena. Let's hurry down. Do you hear a carriage?'

CHAPTER FOURTEEN

In which dissatisfaction and resentment build
and
an heir is found

Despite her diminutive stature, the look on the dowager marchioness's face when she saw Athena was enough to dishearten everyone in the hall. Neither seeing her son and his buxom but beautiful and capable wife again, nor the welcoming fire, blazing brilliantly in the hearth, nor the splendid flower arrangements, nor even the line of dutiful servants, all tidily turned out, were enough to gladden the heart of her elderly ladyship, who returned from abroad energized and in full fettle, despite her preceding news that said otherwise.

She took one look at her older granddaughter and held out a hand, as if to beseech support. It was not Athena, but Edwina Crownrigg who took her arm.

'Edwina! Edwina – is this how you allow your daughter to gallivant around the countryside in *merrie England*?'

'Athena, my girl.' Lady Croukerne had to be stern. 'Not only do you arrive quite disturbingly late, so as to be absent from the house welcoming party, but you appear like *this!*'

There was a titter from Geraldine, who so far had done her best not to attract any untoward attention. Her welcome had passed muster without undue comment and she drifted back to stand behind her father.

'What on earth has happened to your hem?' The dowager marchioness looked at her granddaughter Athena's skirts with a look so horrified it was more than just an overstatement. 'We can plainly see your boots, girl. You have not taken to riding one of those dreadful wheeled contraptions, have you?'

Athena looked around for a word of support, or a compassionate smile. She had no idea, before she alighted from the small carriage, that this would be part of her reception. 'A bicycle? No, Grand-mama.'

Her mother continued with the attack. 'All this on top of your news.'

What news? Athena had sent no news to be broadcast at Denisthorn. But she understood, and sent unspoken barbs of resentment towards her sister, who avoided her look. 'News?'

'Oh, my word. Do not answer in monosyllables, girl.'

Lord Croukerne could not take much more of what transpired. He stepped forward and shepherded his older daughter towards the dining room doors.

'The drawing room, I think, Ninian.'

He turned and guided Athena to those doors, where refreshment had been lain out by the footmen. He lowered his voice to a hoarse whisper. 'Athena my dear – have you had some sort of laundry mishap, or a sewing one, perhaps?'

'Oh, Papa! Aunt Margery took one look at my dreary mourning clothes and said my travelling ensemble at least could be brought into fashion by taking up the hems.'

Her father found a way to distract the rest of the family as they cruised in, like black ships all of them, a line of frightful faces. His mother held an enormous lacy handkerchief to her eyes. She sailed over to him, ignored Athena, and held out a hand.

'Mater.'

'How are you ever going to get over your loss, my son? Frederic was the world to you.'

'I distract myself with estate matters, Mater.'

Her gaze was gelid, erasing any trace of compassion that might have been there. 'Yes, the estate, the estate. Have you not thought at all about what is to become of

Denisthorn? What is to become of *the title*, Ninian?'

'I have given it fifteen minutes' thought, and then abandoned ...'

'Too difficult?'

'There is a lot going on.'

'A *lot*?'

'Do not make me apologize for modernizing my speech, Mater. I cannot be castigated more at this juncture.'

'Apart from speaking like a schoolboy, you seem to be ignoring the fact you will not live forever. Your father certainly did not. But he had you, thank goodness, for what it is worth.'

'Well, thank you.' He did not hide the irony in his tone.

'An only son, but you survived.'

'Evidently.'

'And now we are all in a quandary about your heir.'

'There is no heir.' Ninian Crownrigg stepped back before turning away to address someone else, not wanting to give his mother his back in too rude a stance. He did not hear the last four words she muttered under her breath.

Geraldine did. Moving up to her grandmother and taking her elbow to steer her towards the sofa near the fire, she nodded at the footman, who quickly poured a cup of tea to present to her the instant she was seated. Everyone had been briefed by Herring, so two thin half-moons of lemon accompanied the tea.

'How thoughtful.' She ignored the footman and thanked Geraldine.

'Welcome to Denisthorn, Grand-mama. We're all looking forward to having you with us for a few days.'

'Don't lie, dear. That footman looks like terror has struck his whole being. Your mother has dread written all over her face, and your father has abandoned all but hope. And there is no hope for Athena. Look at her *skirts*.'

'Fairley will have all her hems taken down.'

'Ah – you girls have an assigned personal maid?'

'Of course – Fairley. We used to call her Milly. She is Fairley now, since she comes upstairs.'

'*Something* is going right at Denisthorn.'

Geraldine took a silent breath. 'You just said something, Grand-mama. You just said *Of course there is*, when Papa remarked there is no heir.'

'My darling.' There was no warmth in the old lady's eyes despite the endearment. 'There is always an heir. Your grandfather's line came from somewhere, and will *go* somewhere. There are cousins.'

Geraldine wondered whether she should drop to sit on the sofa next to her Grandmother without an explicit invitation. She vaguely waved a hand. 'Cousins, Grand-mama?'

The dowager marchioness nodded and she sat. 'Two of your great-grandfather's siblings were rather prolific. And we never mention the *other* two.'

For a quiet moment, they both watched everyone else in the room, and Geraldine was afraid they might be interrupted before the old lady went on. But there was no real need for her to continue.

'I never thought of cousins. How little we know of our extended family.' She breathed something polite and rose again, making her way towards the bay window with an aspect over the lawn and parterre. It was a beautiful estate which, according to her father, kept them all going. Why did she never stop to wonder about family, about the world, about where the money came from to support them all in such a fashion? She had listened to the girl at the stables describe her narrow life. Tenants and workers obviously had no abundance of money.

How did Papa pay for all their staff? All their journeys? Their clothes? Their horses and carriages? Their London residence? Where did it all come from? She would have to put her father a few pertinent questions, though it was dubious whether he would give her accurate responses.

Cousins. Why did they never speak of cousins? Questions whirled through Geraldine's head as she stood with her back to the room, where everyone paid homage to the old lady, asking about her travels.

She listened as the conversation turned to Frederic's death, and then to the state of Athena's hemline, and then back to Grand-mama in Rhodes, or Grand-mama in Tuscany and the Apennines, or Grand-mama in Istanbul. But her mind stayed with the notion planted there by the word cousins. Cousins.

'Geraldine.' Athena stood behind her, a half-drunk cup of tea clattering in its saucer. 'How have you ...?'

'It's been lonely without you, Athena. I thought of you daily, enjoying company outside the family. Was the house party a great success?'

'I wished to stay at Aunt Margery's forever. Please do not resent me going.'

'I did for about a week.'

Athena winced at her sister's loneliness. 'There will be house parties and hunts and balls for you too.'

'Two years to wait seems like forever. Mama did not have to wait this long. Why are girls being made to wait and wait to be presented?'

'Perhaps it's because we have a very restrained queen.'

'Oh! You might be right. She's judicious, and understands a woman's predicament.'

'I don't know, but she has pulled and pushed fashions and customs quite to her own desires.'

Geraldine's eyes widened. 'Is that not disrespectful of our monarch?'

"I merely point out a fact. The queen insists on decorum and restraint. In Mama's day, girls were presented at court early, much earlier than now. They married at fifteen and were matrons with two or three children by the time they reached my age!' She paused and took a deep breath, wondering how it would be for her. 'They had a whirling social life and were much in demand. We live a cloistered life here at Denisthorn.'

'Oh, Athena - later this year you'll be more in demand when you come out. Did Aunt Margery's guests not find it strange to have your company a full four months before presentation?'

'No one said a word. Many of the guests were elderly, and used to young girls being introduced into society early. It was an eventful stay.'

Geraldine tilted her head and looked away. 'Your letters hinted at a lot, as if you could not say more.'

'There was a balloon flight. Baskets, with people in them, suspended from enormous balloons, up in the air, up in the sky, I say! Uncle Herbert called them *Montgolfiers*.'

'Oh! How exciting. Did you ... um ... fly?'

'No, it was for the gentlemen. And one of them sprained an ankle on descent. He leapt out of the basket too early, and shouted out in agony when he rolled on the grass in Grayson's Field.'

'My goodness.' Geraldine would have given her right arm to experience such excitement.

'He was ... I was ... He said I was most attentive when I sat by him and read from *Harper's Monthly*.'

Geraldine gasped. No such periodical ever found its way to Denisthorn.

Athena went on. 'I read something by a writer called George Du Maurier ... a serialized story called ... called ... something like the name of a hat.'

'*Really.*'

'We sat in Aunt Margery's sitting room, and she wafted in and out and in and out all afternoon, talking about the queen, but really desiring to be out in the carriage with the party. She could not, however, jolly well leave us alone, could she?' She smiled. 'Or ask her housekeeper to *watch* us.'

Geraldine laughed at the preposterous suggestion. 'Could you not join the party in the carriage? Where did they go?'

'Oh, I don't know. Up hill and down dale. I was quite happy reading to Mister Alastair Updike – his enormously swollen ankle elevated on a stool – who seemed to know a great deal about London society, and new books, and writers.'

Geraldine held a hand up to her lips. 'How exciting.' She did not dare say more. Something in her sister's eyes was so new, so unexpected, that her own inexperienced mind decided to ignore it and hold her tongue. Perhaps a confidence would slip out in time.

Oh, why could she not have all that herself? A pall descended on her spirit, a pall so close to dissatisfaction in sensation it made Geraldine want to march out into the hall and retreat to the stables to bury her face in Buttercup's neck. Only the sure consequence of a severe scolding from her mother and a memorable rebuke from her grandmother kept her in the room.

She left Athena at the window and wandered close to her parents, who seemed engaged in earnest conversation quite out of the dowager marchioness's earshot.

The earl seemed ruffled and red-faced. 'They live in Hawick.'

'Where on earth is Hawick?'

'Up near the border, Edwina. Very nearly in Scotland. And I do not feel the least inclination to go up and seek this man.'

'Your mother was very plain, Ninian. He is the apparent heir of Denisthorn.'

He stamped a foot, looking down at the beautiful Persian carpet he impacted, and up again into his wife's eyes. 'Not exactly Prince Bertie, is he? I'm not about to die next week, Edwina. The matter can rest until I gather my wits.'

'We won't forget.' She looked at his mother, who sipped fitfully from a fresh cup of tea. 'We should not be allowed to forget.'

'Forget! How could I forget the name Angus Crownrigg? *Mister* Angus Crownrigg? He does not even live the life of a landed gentleman. He is the governor of a bank. A bank!'

'Do not let it upset you, Ninian.' His wife's face was the image of tragedy.

'A money-changer ... a money-changer is the heir of Denisthorn. He is barely thirty. Or twenty-something. I don't know. I do not know how old he is. This is going to kill me.'

'It had better not kill you before a few decisions are made.' She handed him a fresh cup of tea, brought by the footman. 'Thank you, Formby.'

Looking across the room at her mother-in-law's sour face, it was plainly time for them all to retire to their rooms and dress for dinner.

CHAPTER FIFTEEN

In which a truce is drawn below stairs at Denisthorn
and a portrait is planned for the house

Mrs Beste thought some of the music on the sheets before her discordant, and some of it harmonious. She settled again on the stool in front of the piano and through her glasses perused the unmarked pages on the book rest, which had convenient brackets to keep the pages from folding upon themselves.

'I must say it was very generous of his lordship to send down this piano.' She caressed the polished brass of the candle sconces on the facing board, and gingerly tried two chords and an arpeggio, the ease and agility returning to her hands only very gradually.

'They have a big shiny black thing now, up in the hall. And we have sprained backs to prove it.'

'It's not a *thing*, Formby. It's a grand piano. Do not grumble, young man, it does not become you to constantly complain and exaggerate. The strength of oxen is in your arms alone.' She felt someone standing behind her and turned to spy Cook. 'When I think of my childhood, Mrs Jones, I am ridden with a rush of such different feelings.'

'You seem to think you have ...'

'Come down in life? No. No, no – it was not my father's fault that Mother died so early. Neither was it his fault I was youngest of four sisters. Luckily, the convent taught me a few things, and coming into service ... well, look at us. We really could not live and serve in a better house. It is ... it was a haven for me. And promotion came fast and regularly. It is a responsibility, but truly a haven.'

'Denisthorn is that. It is a haven. Play something.'

The housekeeper turned a page. 'Oh, we are lucky to

have this instrument now. We should send for some cheering song music.'

'Not *too* cheering. We are a house in mourning still.'

'Of course we are.' She looked at the sheet music and at her hands. 'Goodness, this is very hard.'

'What is it?'

'Something Russian, by Mr Borodin.'

'Oooh – *foreign*, then.'

'I shall entreat Mr Herring to send for the folk songs we played in convent, and some dance tunes. Oh, and *Fountain in the Park!*'

'Could you play that?'

'Indeed I might, if I had the music and if I practised a bit. But there are lists and lists of things I must attend to.'

'It will be quiet when the dowager marchioness returns to her own home.' Mrs Jones sighed. 'Do you know she sent down her breakfast again this morning?'

The housekeeper dismissed it with one wave of the hand. 'Surely you were prepared for that?'

'You know me too well, Mrs Beste.' She straightened the spectacles on her narrow nose. 'I exchanged her little pot of blackberry jam for one with marmalade, changed the posy of daisies with one of crocus – Marley from the garden is very obliging – and two dark brown pieces of hot toast instead of her muffin.'

'And ...'

'And Burgess took it up again. Now that woman Burgess is quite a scold herself. But she took it up after saying one tart sentence and giving one cold look.'

'And?'

'And it stuck upstairs, Mrs Beste. The sour old thing ate it.'

'*Mrs Jones!*'

'I mean ... *her elderly ladyship enjoyed her lovely breakfast in bed, so lovingly prepared by my kitchen.*' She moved away, chuckling as she went. 'I look forward to the music!'

Formby was back, mooching around by the long refectory table, pressing a finger down on crumbs to lift and flick them into the fire, where they sparked.

'Hadn't you better sweep those away properly, with a pan and brush? Is there nothing further needed upstairs?'

'That's right – work me to the bone, why don't you?'

She decided another rebuke would only send him scurrying away, even though it was no way for a footman to address the housekeeper herself. 'Formby ... Peter, what is eating you?'

'Mrs Beste, I do not mean to be nasty.'

'But you manage very well. You need to address concerns to Mr Herring. If you are unhappy, it makes life downstairs a bit uncomfortable for all of us.'

'I do not fancy being carpeted by Mr Herring.'

'If by that you mean standing on the carpet in front of his desk, perhaps that is the right place to discuss your predicament.'

He frowned and slouched. His face was a picture of disappointment. 'I'm sure I don't know what a perdick-what *that* is, Mrs Best, but I'm very un ... dis... un ...'

'Dissatisfied?'

'Unhappy.'

'Speak to Mr Herring.'

He slouched again. 'Or rather, let him speak to me. Because that's what will happen.'

'Something good is bound to come of it.'

'I could do that, you know.'

She sighed. 'I'm *telling* you to.'

'No, I mean – play the pianner. You could show me how. Would you? I could do that. I'd love to do that. Make music an' all.'

'I should like to show you a few chords, but only if you talk to Mr Herring. Go on now, ask him for a time. Do that, and after second sitting at dinner tonight, I'll show you.'

'It's complicated.'

'I have yet to see something more complicated than Mr Herring can solve.'

*

Sounds of a great to-do in the hall could be heard from one end of Denisthorn Hall to the other. Servants rushed about bearing portmanteaux and cases. Herring the butler wore the front steps going down and up, back and forth, back and forth, from the carriage to his seat under the stairs, and back, supervising the footmen, and forth, ticking things off the long list he held in his head. They all avoided Burgess, her elderly ladyship's personal maid, as she paced about wearing a sour expression.

The daughters of the house took the staircase, upward and downward, in an effort to calm their mother, and assuage the dowager marchioness, who stood in the gallery directing things; a veritable orchestra conductor. All she lacked was a baton.

'If this toing and froing were a piece of music, Grand-mama, it would be by Borodin.' Geraldine dared to jest with her, knowing it was only a matter of minutes before the house sank to a manageable tempo again.

'Borodin! That Russian – the laziest of them all?'

'You know him! How modern of you. So you do not like *Prince Igor*? I don't think it lazy at all. Some of it is quite rousing.'

'Bah. Where's Burgess? And where has your father gone? He's always good at vanishing when there were things to be done.'

'Herring sees to everything. Look – the carriage is almost ready to depart.'

They both looked down from their perch, through the glazed front door down there, which stood open, to the pool of watery sunshine that reflected rays upward, almost enough for them both to raise a hand to shade their eyes.

'Isn't it a glorious day?'

'I do not recall a *really* glorious day since about seven years ago, my dear girl.'

Geraldine did her best not to gasp. It was a cruel thing to hear. Her grandfather, the fourth earl, had died seven years before, which was when Ninian Crownrigg inherited the title and everyone's world was turned upside down. For it to be described as a happy day was shocking. She insisted on keeping the conversation with her grandmother to the weather. 'You will have quite a sunny enjoyable ride across to Cheltenham House.'

The dowager marchioness wheeled around and faced away, regarding a space on the wall where a large painting had been taken down. 'Well – I'm going to have to find wall space for that view of Denisthorn in my house. My stairwell is going to have to do.'

Geraldine wondered why the painting was changing hands, but did not ask. Questions, at a time like that, seemed superfluous.

'It will not be vacant for long. Your father's portrait will rightly hang in that prominent place, Geraldine.'

'A portrait of Papa!'

'Naturally. All the earls are on the wall. An artist will come to stay. Ninian is very reluctant, but he will sit still for a few hours.' It was like she spoke to herself. 'That agent will curtail his verbiage and do some real work for a change.'

'Swinnart?'

'Swinnart – more breath and gusts and talking than real work done.'

'There is refreshment in Mama's day room, Grand-mama. She says we cannot send you off without sustenance.'

'Oh, how I long to see my home now. I should like to embrace my old, long-abandoned routine. Mrs Conder will have the presence of mind to prepare things *exactly* the way

I like them.'

'I'm sure she will.'

After tea in the day room, they all watched and waved from the forecourt. All the servants looked delighted at the departure, their faces like bright moons as shadows lengthened around Denisthorn Hall. An expression of sheer relief adorned Lady Croukerne's face. There was a wide grin on Ninian Crownrigg's face as he returned to his pocket the large white handkerchief with which he waved his mother away. Geraldine took his arm when they turned to return indoors.

'It's not like she lives far away! What a send-off. It's only a short ride across the village to Cheltenham House.'

'So that is that, my dear girl. A visit that went surprisingly well, I feel.'

'Mama thinks so. Back to normal for us. Back to normal downstairs too, I should imagine, with Burgess gone.'

He laughed.

'I hear an artist is coming to the house, Papa.'

He turned, lips pursed, forehead corrugated with thought. 'Hm. Perhaps there is some sense in what your grandmother said about continuing the line of portraits on the wall.'

'But an artist in the house – that will be exciting.'

'I feel, however, that we might not afford Mr Joseph Gibbs, but we are sure to find someone suitable. Your grandmother insists on Gibbs, but I cannot see reason to drag him out here from Staffordshire. Besides, he is much in demand, and might not be available.'

'Unfortunately, we live in the depths of Gloucestershire, my lord.' She made it sound like a joke.

'Oh, how fortunate we are, in many ways, to live exactly where we do.'

'Yes, Papa. Only a train ride from the famous ancient spa town of Cheltenham. Any artist would jump at the chance of staying here for a few weeks.'

'If we find someone who does not charge like a raging bull, we might have the entire family ...' He stopped and swallowed. 'Too late. Too late, isn't it? Frederic is gone.' He swallowed. 'The chance for a complete family portrait has escaped us.' The earl released her arm and took the great staircase two at a time, and did not hear his younger daughter's remark that there were many perfectly clear photographs of the whole family, framed in silver, which had seemed quite magical when they were taken.

CHAPTER SIXTEEN

In which the family changes to grey
and
Athena applauds herself

There were seamstresses downstairs again, and the extra room in the female servants' corridor was occupied by three women whose only reason for living seemed to be hemming and stitching and piecing and trundling two treadle machines on stands, which they brought with them.

Great swathes of fabric were handled, and spools of thread, and packets of pins and the sharpest of needles. The man who came in from the village every second Thursday morning to sharpen knives was now occupied with scissors.

Lady Croukerne was having grey ensembles made up from a new book of patterns that had arrived from France. She and the girls pored over clothing illustrations for hours, debating, considering, and choosing.

'Aren't those sewing machines fast? We are so fortunate to live in these inventive times.'

'They are revolutionary! And the women so clever to work them, too.'

Their eyes lowered once more to the pattern book.

'Is that ruffle not too elaborate, do you think?'

'Those sleeves look far too tight and constricting.'

'I should need a corset twice as tight to consider such a waistline.'

'Oh, look at the cut of that skirt – how delicious!'

Not all were delighted at the prospect of turning to mourning clothes that were not a sea of black. 'So am I to come out in *grey*, Mama?'

'Look at this beautiful grosgrain, Athena. Please do not have an unhappy face while I show you these swatches.

Look – this is called Early Dawn, and is so very close to silver, or white!'

'And I suppose I shall drag a train behind me all over Buckingham Palace, and trip over a floor-length skirt.'

'I think you mean the court of St James. And you will not show your ankles and shock *everyone* at court, Athena!'

'Oh, stop it, Geraldine. You know I cannot stand to be teased so mercilessly. The fashion is changing.'

'Is it not a good thing, daughter of mine, that the patterns are French and so very on point?'

'Will not every girl in London have the same books, however, Mama? And choose the same dresses?'

'The fashion is the fashion. You must fit in with the general *fashion*.' She received a piercing look from Athena. 'Within reason. Showing one's ankles is not fashion. It's plain rebellion.'

Athena pulled a face.

'Then we shall contrive an exceptional look with blue peonies. I have Marley from the garden promising two or three sprays of peonies, which he will hang, dry, and *wire* with ivy, which will be very portable for us to take to London. And they will look both delightful and suitably muted for our circumstance. Don't you remember what he did with those beautiful hothouse sunflowers?'

'I should rather a sunflower than a *wreath* of peonies.'

'Or we could get the seamstresses to devise some silk flowers ... I do believe you can even order them now.' She flipped forward in the book. 'Look! But I still think that blue peonies from Denisthorn will be exceedingly beautiful.'

'They will all look at me and think of Frederic's passing.'

'Which is not unexpected, my dear, but your beauty will remind them instantly of your good bearing and that you are from Denisthorn Hall.'

'Because ...?'

Geraldine became impatient with her sister. 'Do you

not know that blue peonies are quite rare? Marley will exert a miracle *just for you*. He and his greenhouse. He and his tough leathery hands.'

It took a good three hours and copious notes and sketches, a bristling of paper bookmarks in the catalogue, and arguments about cut and length and bodices and necklines. Lady Croukerne was exhausted. 'I doubt I have the strength to go up and change for dinner.'

Both girls laughed. They had never experienced a day when the family did not dress for dinner, except possibly when Lady Croukerne was lying in around the birth of their little brother, but especially since the girls started to come down for the evening meal.

'So it's decided then. I shall have the pearl grey satin, the figured flannel, the spotted taffeta, and a three-quarter length wool jacket. In these designs.' Athena flattened four sheets of paper firmly on top of the book.

'I should like woollen britches and a riding jacket like Papa's.' Geraldine tried to make it sound like a joke but failed.

'I do believe you are serious.' Her mother put her finger down to mark a place in a pattern book.

'Papa looks very handsome in dark grey. Isn't it funny how mourning means different things for men and women? We are drowning in black weeds, wearing veils and jet necklaces, and going through the most detailed plans just to turn to grey. Except for a black armband, men must do little but ...'

'Geraldine!'

'I am serious this time. One day, men and women will not be directed along such different routes by the mores and demands of society.' She looked at her mother's concerned expression. 'It's true. The future will change women's lives.'

'Come now, Geraldine!'

Her daughter lost patience with the argument,

understanding she would never shift her mother from her opinions, which were so steadfastly supported by society. 'Look – I've decided on this jacket, two flannel skirts, two spotted shirts, and it would be nice if I could have a tie and two waistbands in this figured velvet.'

'A tie!'

'Many ladies in London are wearing shirts and ties with good effect. And in Paris as well – there are illustrations of them in this very book.' She leaved forward to show them.

'I should have known. No flounces or gathers for you.'

'No. Neither can I stand to wear lace or frills.'

Her mother decided not to embark on another argument. 'And how do you girls think I will look in the dark grey grosgrain, the dove grey velvet, this muslin for neckline trim, and this beautiful grey Belgian lace?'

'For a veil?'

'And for sleeve trim. Now – the most important pattern, Athena's coming out gown, with trim in that Early Dawn grosgrain.'

'It is very nearly white, isn't it? But am I tall enough to wear grosgrain? The swirls are so large.'

They looked at her without a word. Athena stood a good hand span over her sister and their mother.

'Good then – it's all decided.' Tired, but slightly relieved, Lady Croukerne closed the pattern book.

'Now, Mama, we must endure hours of measuring by the head seamstress. She breathes hard through her nostrils, with a mouth full of pins.'

'Mrs Dorning writes numbers like some ledger-keeper.' Geraldine and Athena agreed for once.

'Accuracy is everything in needlecraft, my darling girls. Be patient. We shall have a good day of it tomorrow. I think we should use my day sitting room for the measuring. I'll ask Mrs Beste to have something nice sent up from the kitchen with tea.'

The girls made a move to leave.

'Athena – stay.'

When Geraldine left, raising her eyebrows in jest at her sister, Athena prepared for the big lecture about coming out.

'You had a letter at breakfast, my dear.'

Athena merely looked down at the carpet whose pattern she now knew by heart and soul; every curl and angle, every figure and texture.

'After another two in yesterday's afternoon post.'

'It's correspondence, Mama. You receive many letters yourself.'

'Athena.'

'I correspond with Mr Alastair Updike. He was at Aunt Margery's house party.'

'And he writes without permission from ...'

'He hardly needs *permission from Papa*, Mama. There is nothing but an interest in modern short stories between us, and perhaps the occasional novel. We discuss modern novels.'

'Novels! Such as?'

'Such as *Trilby*, by Mr Du Maurier.'

Lady Croukerne raised a hand to her lips. 'Goodness! You have discussed such a subject with a young man?'

'Such a subject?'

'I've heard of the book, my girl. It treats subjects such as mysticism and *hypnotism*.'

'It is a fiction.'

Hands fluttered and eyelashes batted. Lady Croukerne was displeased. 'Yes, I do realize writers can make up any stories they like. Some of them, however, go beyond all that is reasonable and sensible and ... and *appropriate*. If your grandmother were to get wind of this, I should never hear the end of it.'

Athena stood her ground. 'I shall not breathe a word. If Grand-mama gets to know, it will not be from my lips.

Svengali will stay between the pages of the book.'

'Who?'

It was then plain to the girl that Lady Croukerne had no idea what lay within the pages of *Trilby*. 'I mean ... what fascinates me is the author's use of language. Mr Updike and I discuss matters of language. We speak of vocabulary, semantics, phrasing, metaphor, and symbolism.'

'If ...'

'And *if* we had governesses who understood these things, it would be so much easier for me to grasp.' There was no hint of sarcasm in her tone.

A spark of pride shone somewhere deep in the mother's eyes. 'I am more than certain of your ability to grasp metaphor and symbolism, Athena. Thank goodness for your future that your education was full and complete.'

The girl took the sentence as a blessing upon her literary pursuit, giving a little mock bob and flourishing her skirts before leaving the room, elated.

All her life she had listened to her mother stress the fact that a good education would eventually find for her a suitable match.

What she sought, however, was not a *match*. She looked for someone who would understand her as she was; a person in her own right with a mind and intellect worthy of note, and not merely a match. She did of course want to be a compliant and obedient wife, to dutifully run a house and raise a family; she wished for a settled, predictable and ordered life heartily. But she also wanted recognition as a person who could think for herself.

Silently applauding herself for the way she turned the conversation around, she saw the instance as an example of her skill with words. She had succeeded in turning the conversation from Mr Alastair Updike to Mr George Du Maurier and symbolism, so she had reason to congratulate herself.

CHAPTER SEVENTEEN

In which there is discord downstairs at Denisthorn
and
a decision is made about accommodation

Out of breath and with more than a shred of trepidation, Formby stood on the carpet in front of Mr Herring's desk. He looked down at the scuffed toes of his boots. He arrived there flustered, in a week-old shirt, waistcoat buttons undone, and needing a haircut.

'You must know, Formby, why I have summoned you here today and what I am about to give you.' The butler's sonorous voice filled the close room.

'A sound scolding, Mr Herring. And a severe warning to mend my ways and make sure I pull my weight when helping the housemaids upstairs in the mornings.'

'The character I have carefully written out for you ...'

'Character! A letter of recommendation? Surely you are not going to dismiss me out of hand. Mr Herring ... *sir* ...'

'Your behaviour of late, for a good three months, Formby, has been remarkable only for its lack of quality. You have ignored a number of warnings both from me and from Mrs Beste. Before the arrival of her ladyship the dowager marchioness, and after her departure, you have been slovenly of clothing and grooming, slow to respond, with a tendency to shirk work rather than do it with alacrity and enthusiasm. This is not the standard I have set for Denisthorn.'

'*Mr Herring.*'

'You have a week's notice to work out, after which I do suppose you will return to your family in ... are you not from outside Cirencester?'

'Mr Herring ...'

'Yes – you will return there.'

'I'll be on the streets. You're turning me out on the streets.'

'Nonsense.'

'I'll not have a roof over my head.'

'Nonsense. The letter shows a good enough character to get you a position in any household. You have been trained by the best. There is an entire column of situations vacant in the Gazette. I am willing to allow you a measure of time in which to apply yourself to writing some letters, Formby. Demonstrate some initiative. You have been trained by the best.' He waved a hand in the direction of his chest, turned his hand, and indicated the door.

'So that is that?'

'I'm afraid so. Please ask Mrs Beste to see me now.'

It was a relief to have the housekeeper in his office, even with such a stern face and stiff demeanour, than a recalcitrant and inflexible young man.

'The family will soon be off to London, Mrs Beste.'

'And on their return, after Lady Athena's court presentation, everything might resume a calmer plane.'

'Hm.' The butler widened his eyes meaningfully.

'You look as though you are about to announce some other disruptive event, Mr Herring.'

'I do not know how disruptive it might be to have an artist in the house.'

'An artist? How exciting. Of what kind? Oh, perhaps Lord Croukerne is thinking of having some musical soirees. Is a tenor coming to Denisthorn? Or a soprano, perhaps?' Her eyes widened too.

'Nothing the kind. Nothing the kind. The household will be in mourning for a full year, so the notion of musical soirees will be as far from his lordship's mind as it is possible to be. A Mr Joseph Gibbs ...'

'I have recently seen that name! While seeking sheet music. Mr Joseph Gibbs is a musician and composer. But he is long dead, I seem to remember. His quartets are ...'

'No, no ... nothing of the kind, I say. Her ladyship the dowager marchioness raised the subject of a portrait. His lordship is to have his portrait painted.' He consulted his notebook. '*Perhaps* a Mr Joseph Gibbs, and failing acceptance from him, some other gentleman.'

The housekeeper studied the butler's face. 'And there is a problem of some sort?'

'Well, Mrs Beste. He will be here for three weeks or longer. And there is the question of his accommodation.'

He had no need to say more.

'Ah. If he is a gentleman, travelling with a valet, and a member of the academy ...'

'You do mean the Royal Academy of Arts.'

'Just so. If he is a member, then I am sure her ladyship would not mind in the least if he were to be accommodated in the gentlemen's corridor in the house. His man can share with Thorn. And he will sit for meals with the family.'

'If not – if he is a mere artisan, neither gentleman ... nor servant ... then we must think hard about it.'

But the housekeeper's eyes were bright. She leaned forward. 'Miss Elphington-Brunt. Do you remember her?'

'Of course I do. She was governess to the two young ladies for a short while. French and elocution. And dancing, I think. Yes, yes – I do see what you mean. She was neither family nor a lady. Neither was she a servant.'

'And it presented no problem, because we put her in that suite of rooms in the south wing.'

'Not too distant from the main staircase, and not too close to the green baize door to cause her embarrassment.'

'And she ate her meals in that small sitting room. It is a very reasonable solution, with the sole consideration being ...' She looked at the butler.

'Yes?'

'... that there is no plumbed bathroom in that wing.'

'Oh – he would never know the difference.'

'We can run a footman up with hot water for shaving, and to attend to his fireplace, take up trays, and other chores.' She stood. 'If there's nothing else, Mr Herring ...?'

'I ... there's the matter of ...'

But Godwin the footman put his head around the door. 'His lordship would like to see you, Mr Herring. He says there are *two* things he would like to discuss.'

CHAPTER EIGHTEEN

*In which Mr Herring's past is discussed
and Formby forms a strategy*

Geo Herring glided into the library silently, hands clasped behind his back. With two fingers extended on his right hand, he dropped his arms in deference to etiquette long held in heart, mind and habituation. The two fingers would remind him his lordship needed to address more than just one matter.

'You need to see me, my lord.'

'Herring, I have discovered other cousins!'

'Is this the first matter you wanted to discuss with me, sir?'

Irritation at his servant's formality tightened Ninian Crownrigg's jaw. He mindfully relaxed his face, muscle by muscle. After a second, his eyebrows rose fractionally with the realization the butler had intentionally calmed him. He admitted to himself the butler had superlative perceptual skills, but he had to keep the upper hand. The man was after all his servant. 'This is serious, Herring.'

'I have no doubt it is, my lord, and I shall endeavour to help.'

'We have cousins up north. But, to my utter consternation, it happens that we have others – closer to home! It makes one wonder. Are there Crownriggs *everywhere*? And they take precedence over the northern family.'

'Precedence.'

'In matters of inheritance, yes. I have not yet disclosed my discovery to her ladyship, or to the rest of the family, but it was the dowager marchioness who hinted there was an estranged family of Crownriggs in London, of all places.'

'Which might prove convenient, my lord.'

'How infinitely optimistic of you, Herring. But yes, one should investigate why we have drawn out of touch with the London Crownriggs, and I should like you to ... I do not entirely know why I need you, now that I think of it.'

'You need me, if I might suggest, my lord, to consult my Debrett's Peerage, and perhaps pay a visit to the library at Cheltenham, which might elicit more detail, and make notes for you in this regard. It would save you time.' The butler did not say it would save his master the inopportune chance of being spotted leafing through telling tomes at the library himself.

'Excellent.'

'There was a second matter, my lord.'

'Was there? Ah, yes. Yes of course.'

The butler resisted the urge to shift, and kept still.

Lord Croukerne went on. 'Rather against my better judgement, I have engaged a portrait painter, a Mister Rupert Bottomley. He will travel from Cardiff ...'

The butler cleared his throat so softly he was surprised to see his lordship shift his gaze.

'Yes, Cardiff. I have no idea whether he is indeed Welsh. He might be there on a commission. It's not an extraordinarily long train journey, and ... and ...'

'Is Mr Bottomley um – ahem, my lord - I take it Mr Bottomley is a member of the Academy?'

'I took it upon myself to find someone good, even though I am not entirely vain and have no interest in the matter really. But a likeness is a likeness, and it must for the sake of the ... of the *future,* you see, it must be accurate. I like to think the portraits of the Earls of Denisthorn already hanging on our walls are accurate. I have faith in the fact they are true and perfect likenesses of my antecedents. I engaged Mr Bottomley because he comes warmly recommended by another member of the House of Lords. But I cannot remember whether the Royal Academy of the Arts was mentioned at all.' He looked at his butler.

The butler returned the look.

'You are quite right to inquire, Herring. I shall write to Lord Fewsbury with the question, forthwith.' He moved toward his desk.

'If it is accuracy you seek, my lord, then it is necessary. You might also hit upon an artist who will satisfy with artistic giftedness.'

'And then we should all be happy, including the dowager marchioness, whose idea this was.'

'It will not do now to have a blank space where the other painting used to hang.' Herring took a breath. 'For too long, that is.'

Ninian Crownrigg looked at his butler in silence. He took up a pen, and saw the man prepare to leave. 'You are a stickler for order and consistency, Herring.' He did not move his eyes from the pen and paper. He did not say it, but Herring was infinitely more useful a servant than his valet, Thorn.

The man turned, not wishing his master to address his back. 'And stability, my lord, and symmetry.'

'Both metaphorical and physical ...' he chuckled. 'Yes, yes. Thank you.'

The butler turned away.

'Ah – there was another thing.'

'We have discussed both, my lord.'

'Both? Ah, yes. Both. Both things.' He rubbed one eyebrow and looked out of the window. 'There is still the matter of Formby.'

Geo Herring's forehead became instantly corrugated. His thin brows narrowed above his nose. Was Formby that quick? He was not half an hour ago standing in front of the butler's desk. Was he that impudent and imprudent; to go above the butler's head?

'Formby, my lord. I am writing him a character.'

'So I hear. I beg you in this instance to demonstrate a touch more compassion. A touch more.' Dare he instruct the butler about staff matters? Ninian Crownrigg moved away from his desk, clasped hands behind back and moved to the window upon which his eyes were fixed, reluctant to meet those of the butler.

This then, was the main reason he was summoned. Herring's forehead stayed creased and his eyes stern. 'I have shown compassion several times. The young man resists all efforts on my part.'

'He has ...'

'May I interrupt your lordship, and also say Formby's impudence is affecting the running of some aspects of the household?'

There was a moment of silence. The faint sound of hooves could be heard in the distance. There was movement at the stables.

'I have no doubt, Herring, that your patience has been tried.'

''And he has now ...'

'He has resorted to asking to see me. I realize he has gone above ... that he has circumnavigated convention. It does not render your position in the least compromised, let me assure you.'

'My lord.' Herring gave the slightest of bows.

'I hear, however, that Formby's family has suffered yet another bereavement, and he is the only provider now, to his ailing mother. His oldest sister has ... childbirth, you see.'

'His sister expired while delivering ... while ...'

'Indeed, during a confinement. Perhaps it's not necessary to enter into the detail of the matter.'

The butler's eyes softened, and Ninian Crownrigg saw it.

'Perhaps we should allow the boy another chance.'

The pain of memory was all over the butler's face; a pain so deep he dared not admit to it.

'He will have it, my lord.'

'Very good, Mr Herring.'

The butler removed himself from the room and made towards the green baize door. He swallowed and thought immediately of the first two points discussed in the library, emptying his mind of the third with a stolid determination brought on by practice. He could not allow himself to be swallowed by grief over death in childbirth once again.

Cousins in London, and an artist to stay at the house. A portrait artist; it was an interesting development. A Welshman. He would have to discuss the matter of the artist with Mrs Beste.

But he glimpsed her neat form, her straight retreating back, outside the door of her ladyship's sitting room. Hurrying to catch up with her, his foot fumbled, and he stooped to examine the carpet. It would certainly not do to have a ruck in the landing carpet.

Mrs Beste stood not a foot away when he straightened up. 'You have discovered some flaw, Mr Herring.'

'I cannot spot it, but I almost tripped. Or rather, it was a small stumble.'

'Oh.'

They both regarded the carpet again, finding nothing.

'I have had an interesting conversation with his lordship. The artist has been engaged. His name is Mr Rupert Bottomley.'

'He could not be very famous.'

'Not a household name, or this household would surely be conversant with it.'

She laughed softly. 'I shall look with fresh eyes through some periodicals.'

'Thank you.'

*

Two footmen descended the stairs to the servants' hall. One pulled off his gloves, the other loosened his collar.

'How many rugs did we roll and straighten today?'

'I didn't count, my back is killing me. But I think of Maisie, doing all that sweeping, and I'm relieved.'

'I heard her talking to Fairley. She's been promoted.'

Formby, the one stuffing gloves into a pocket, pulled a face. 'Fairley has not been *promoted*. Hah! Just because she travelled to Gallantrae to be Lady Athena's personal maid does not mean she's any better than before. She's about as secure in her current position as I am, Godwin. As I am.'

'Surely you're safe as houses.'

'*Now* I am. All one needs to mention in this household is death. Plain and simple. Talk of death, and your future is assured.'

'Death?'

'You won't understand. One day you might.'

But Godwin was more interested in Fairley's status. 'So will she be a lady's maid or not?'

'Hard to say exactly. She certainly won't be gettin' more in her little envelope.'

'I think it's a betterment of sorts, looking after Lady Athena, like special.'

'Now that's a fancy word, betterment. You're gettin' fancy, like Glover, you are, Godwin. But listen.' Formby turned to face the other man as they neared the fireplace in the hall, and reached to the mantelpiece for a cigarette and matches. 'Fairley's too forgetful to do any more than comb a lady's hair.' He lit up and inhaled.

'That can't be right. Prudhomme says there are a hundred things to remember if you're a valet or lady's maid. A *hundred* things.'

'No, no – I don't mean duties. I don't mean lists of things to do. I don't mean pinning up hair, or sewing on buttons, or polishing shoes. I mean, Godwin, that she keeps forgetting important things.'

'Such as?'

'That Mrs Beste sometimes walks out with a shopkeeper. That one of the lads at the stables is really a girl, and that Mr Herring came back to live in the house, for example.'

'Came back? Was he ever gone? What happened?'

'It's just an example, Godwin! You weren't here, were you? You must have been a little nipper in skirts still.'

Godwin nudged him roughly with an elbow.

'Mr Herring ...'

'Mr Herring's a single man, so ...'

Formby blew smoke. 'No, no, no.' He picked a thread of golden tobacco from his lip. 'He's a widower. He was married, and he and his wife lived in one of the estate cottages round the way, past the stables.'

'Really.'

'He was married to a woman called Jessop. She was in service up at Cheltenham House.'

'What happened?'

'She died in childbirth. The baby died too, after a few days. It wasn't very jolly. Mr Herring got depressed on his own at the cottage, with no one to do for him. So his lordship asked him back to live up in his old room.'

'That was nice ...'

'He was back faster than his lordship could finish his sentence.'

'Very sad, I think.'

'Very sad, Godwin. Me mother nearly died with the last of my brothers, but she pulled through. She is hale and hearty now, years after. And if I ever had a sister ... hah!' He turned away. When he turned back there was something sinister in his eyes Godwin did not notice. 'If I ever had a sister, the likelihood she would die in childbirth would be very high. Very high indeed.'

There was a brief silence, in which Formby stubbed

his cigarette end on the fireguard and threw it into the flames.

'Funny that, how it nearly kills a person to give life.'

'That's how it works, Godwin – we'll never understand it. But we can still use the fact.'

'Use it?'

'One must use death for the *betterment* of life, I say. Good word, that.'

'So Mr Herring has neither wife nor bairn. How very grim. He must walk about his business ... the running of this house an' all ... all that we do ... all that the family upstairs does ... full of the thoughts that ...'

Formby swung an arm from side to side. 'Don't let it upset you. It was years and years ago. He's alright now.'

'Who's all right, Formby?' A female voice spoke from the doorway.

Formby and Godwin turned at once to see Mrs Beste standing, prim as ever, with two dark overcoats over one arm. She handed them to the men. 'Brushed ... properly, and returned to the coat cupboard in the hall. Now. This one might need a stitch in the cuff.' She looked Formby in the eye. 'Gossiping over a cigarette, eh? There's plenty to do down here.'

'Catchin' our breath, Mrs Beste. Catchin' our breath after rolling and layin' a thousand rugs.'

She laughed. 'That many.' Mirth did not reach her eyes.

CHAPTER NINETEEN

*In which amethysts cause a surprise; Lady Athena submits to
a gown fitting
and Lord Croukerne bears some bad news*

It was quiet above stairs at Denisthorn Hall, but busy and unsettled in the servants' hall, the afternoon Lady Athena had fittings for her coming-out gown. Mr Herring had an appointment in the village, which left the staff to their own devices, since Mrs Beste too was out. It rarely happened they were absent at the same time, but dentists and tailors could not be put off.

None of the quarrelling or bantering could be heard up in the sitting room of the lady of the house, where two seamstresses were installed, both armed with wrist-fastened pincushions and measuring tapes strung around their necks. One wore an apron, a definite indication of her lesser status, and the other wore steel-rimmed spectacles so thick it was obvious to everyone why she needed an assistant.

Miss Long, the woman in the apron, tended toward talkativeness, and received sharp but mute reproaches via her superior's eyebrows, which telegraphed disapproval as eloquently as words. The talk was all to do with fabrics, and bolt widths, and stitching, and how a gown ought to be hemmed; but woven and embroidered throughout were little hints about the presentation gowns of other young ladies travelling to London for the event.

'Pray tell, Miss Long, I am so interested in the gowns other debutantes might be wearing. Are this year's fashions much progressed compared to last?' Athena was quite curious as to what would be worn by all girls and whether they would all seem to be too uniform to distinguish one from another. 'Are we all selecting patterns from the same books?' Also, she wondered whether it was worth the bother to consult the latest French catalogues if they were so similar to those published on previous years.

Miss Long pulled two pins from between her lips and inhaled, ready to narrate and describe in typically long sentences that required much wind. 'Oh, much progressed, my ...'

A sharp look made her stop. Mrs Dorning put down a large pair of pinking shears, looked across at Lady Athena's face through her thick lenses, and nodded to Miss Long that she could continue.

'My lady, the fashions are progressing in the sense that waistlines are now more comfortable, and the silhouette is more vertical. Sleeves are no longer very elaborate – or absent altogether – such as in this gown of yours, where we have only a gathering on the shoulder, held together by a flounce.'

'And full-length satin gloves, I hope!'

'Indeed, my lady.'

The seamstress went on. 'Hems are also very slightly abbreviated, and there is much less of a bustle, so the train is ...'

'Abbreviated!' Lady Edwina sat forward, throwing a sharp shadow from the slant of window light that beamed across her. 'I should think carefully about abbreviating hems too much!' She looked at Athena so sternly it was no mean warning.

To keep the peace, some diplomatic phrase was required from the head seamstress. 'Rather than sweep the floor before and behind, my lady, hems are now just shy of the floor ... by perhaps an inch, but certainly not more than two.'

'So there will be no unsightly boots to be seen.'

'No ball slippers, either, which on the occasion would be the correct footwear.'

'Of course. Of course – how is one expected to remember all details, especially when things were so different in my day, and when ... it is one's first daughter!'

'It was an observation, my lady, also intended to point out that embroidery of the slippers will start at our rooms as soon as a suitable contrasting hue is chosen. Might I show you some thread samples?' Mrs Dorning approached with a cardboard folder holding rows of many knotted ends of coloured threads. She peered at them and squinted.

'Grey, grey ... and more grey, I suppose.'

'For your slippers, Lady Athena, I might recommend a very pale mauve embroidery thread which is only two shades different from the dove grey. We might ...' she looked at Athena's mother '... we might also consider a darker purple, which is also a suitable colour for coming out of mourning.'

Lady Croukerne sighed. 'If it's only for the slippers, which need to have a floral aspect of some sort, I suppose the consideration is a reasonable one.'

Athena smiled. 'Then it might not be out of the question to have a pale mauve stole.'

'Or to wear my amethysts.'

Her mother's unexpected offer made the young woman utter a little squeal. She hid a wide smile behind her hand.

'I can barely put up with your single-word responses, Athena. Screaming in surprise is not ... isn't ... can*not* be borne anywhere or at any time.'

Was it a scream? A rosy blush came to Athena's face, to be chastised in front of the working women. But it did not erase the delight in being able to wear some very pale colour for the court presentation. Her mother's pale amethyst parure, consisting of a tidy tiara, earrings, and matching bracelets were a gift from Lady Edwina's godparents when she was presented at court more than two decades earlier. Set in deep yellow gold and platinum, with a bevy of small diamonds, it was an envy-inducing sparkling set designed by a renowned Chester jeweller.

'Are we all finished then? We really should have had this session up in my dressing room, but there is not much space there for four of us. In any case, we should not be interrupted. The entire household knows of our preparations.' A fluttering weary hand rose to Lady Croukerne's breast.

'Is there no veil?'

'At another fitting, Lady Athena. Embroidery of the border is almost complete.'

'What about the train?'

'It should exceed three and a half yards, my lady. And the material for the entire ensemble is a happy choice, because the train is on the lighter side, and will not weigh Lady Athena down or tire her arm.'

'Or slow her progress up to the throne.'

'Will the queen be seated?'

'She was not, in my day. But many years have passed. We have been through this a thousand times, Athena.'

The young woman was helped out of the pinned gown and back into her day dress, which fastened at the back with pearl buttons and a wide sash, and it was over. She walked to a mirror, a narrow ornamental pair of which flanked the door, and adjusted her hair.

'Not in my sitting room, Athena.'

The dressmakers heard. Miss Long smiled, knowing it was a bit of a conceit to reprimand a grooming gesture after they had spent an entire afternoon seeing to her appearance, using the same mirrors. Her smile faded quickly when a semaphored message from her superior shot across the room.

*

Lord Croukerne, perturbed and agitated, was found pacing up and down the great hall. His wife glimpsed his figure as she emerged from her sitting room. She stood at the banister on the broad landing, which served as a gallery of family portraits, from wizened and wigged noblemen of the fifteenth century to Ninian's own father.

'I thought you would never emerge!' He stood below and looked up at Lady Edwina. 'I do believe you were ensconced in there with the seamstresses and Athena for what felt like half a year.' Around his legs, the two lurchers circled and circled, looking up with pointed snouts and wagging tails.

'It is a necessary retreat from other household matters, my dear. A lot was accomplished today.'

'Well – that's all well and good, but I have some terrible news.'

'Oh, Ninian – not more bad news. A person can hardly abide a sentence from you these days.'

'From me! You ...' In a trice, taking the stairs in twos, her husband was by Lady Croukerne's side, lowering his voice. 'We, I mean – we can hardly shout this all over the Denisthorn estate, for all and sundry to hear.'

'I doubt you have heard me raise my voice once in all our life together.' Her voice was prim.

'Humph.'

'Well, let us ring for tea, Ninian. And please get someone to take the dogs out. Oh, I am quite famished and parched after three hours locked away with a monosyllabic daughter and two voluble dressmakers.'

His dismayed face reddened. Could she think of nothing but food and drink, when he was bursting with his *bulletin of doom*, as she might call it?

Sure enough, Lady Edwina came out with the words. 'Come in and sit down, Ninian. What is your bulletin of doom?'

'Just when I thought we had found an heir ...' He watched her pull the bell. Soon, they would be interrupted by a servant. He had better get it all out quickly.

'Yes, Angus Crownrigg.'

'No, no, no!'

'*Not* Angus Crownrigg.' Edwina pulled a comical face. 'Ninian, let us calm down. You have worked yourself into a lather.' The door behind her opened. 'There you are, Godwin. What kept you? Please get Cook to send up some tea, and plenty of lemon.'

'My lady.' The footman gave a slight bow. He did not mention the chatter and comparative freedom of the servants' hall that afternoon.

'Let the dogs out, Godwin. Send them out with the stable boy.'

'Yes, your lordship.' He stood back, snapped a finger, and the lurchers bounded out before he pulled the door to.

'I discovered some Crownriggs in London. Joshua Crownrigg, a cousin who – for some ineffable reason – I had never heard of, lived in London.'

'Estranged. Things that happen in all families.'

What did Edwina know that escaped him? 'Well, Joshua Crownrigg was about as old as my father when he died two Christmases ago.'

'But he no doubt has four hale and robust sons.'

Ninian slapped his knee. 'Oh, I do wish you could take this a bit more seriously, Edwina.'

'My dear. I am exhausted. My ears buzz and I see stars. I have come out of a difficult cloister. But pray tell. I shall interject no further.' She folded hands and waited for her tea.

'I too am quite fatigued. Shattered, to put it bluntly.'

She put a hand on the seat next to her. 'Move closer, my dear, and tell me what it is all about.'

The door opened and a housemaid, whose cheeks were reddened and whose bright eyes looked as though she had been giggling, brought in a tray. No one noticed her jolly demeanour.

'Thank you, please leave it. We'll pour ourselves.'

'My lady.' She bobbed slightly and backed out.

'So, this Joshua Crownrigg is dead.' She gazed at her husband.

'He had one son, Horace.'

'Horace! The names some people choose for their children.'

'Horatio, then. I have no idea what they called him at home.'

'Horatio is better, don't you think?'

'Edwina ... Please, do listen to me. I thought the boy would present a better solution for Denisthorn.' Ninian Crownrigg buried his face in his hands.

'Does he not? Is he an invalid? Is he simple?'

'I had every intention of asking him here. Perhaps he would have taken up residence.'

Lady Edwina's face was nonplussed. 'Does he need you to offer a home?'

'It was a wild dream. I had every intention of considering adoption.'

'Adoption! Ninian! No one can ever take little Frederic's place.' She poured a cup of tea, floated a circle of lemon on top with a tiny pair of silver tongs, and handed it to her husband.

He watched in silence as she served herself.

'Did you hear what I said?'

'Of course, you are absolutely right. He is sorely missed. Oh, Frederic. How on earth are we going to survive this?' He looked away to the window for an instant. 'You know, whenever I look out of a window ...'

'Yes. Yes, it occurs to me as well.' Edwina extracted a lace handkerchief from somewhere about her person. 'It is a very, very sad loss.' Her lips tightened. 'How could you think of adopting this Horatio – whoever he is? It is an inconceivably miserable thing to consider.'

'Well, I can no longer consider it, Edwina. The boy has died.'

The cold plain words left Lady Edwina speechless and

still. The cup hovered between the saucer and her lips. Her eyes widened and no sound left her.

'It's a disaster.' Ninian Crownrigg softly slapped both hands to his sides. 'No sooner do I discover the family's existence, and the hope of an heir with at least a hint of a real connection, than I receive information, through the mail, that the boy succumbed to a riding accident, not a fortnight ago.'

'Really!'

'On Hampstead Heath. I know no details, but the long and the short of it is that he is gone.'

'And we are back to having to face the fact that Mr Angus Crownrigg, of Hawick, is to be your heir.'

'Indeed, Hawick, in Roxburghshire. To which place, on the Scottish borders, I should repair, as soon as possible, to try and salvage what is left of my wits, my endurance, and my peace of mind.'

Edwina looked at her husband in silence. He did not mention his misery, or his sorrow, or indeed his loneliness, in this house full of women, but she felt something in him that needed to be solved. And salved.

*

Because of her sore mouth, Mrs Beste longed to return to her rooms at Denisthorn, but it was urgent to take a spell. She sat on an empty bench under a tree in the village square, not many yards from the church and small cemetery. Three dogs barked at a passing duck and her little troop of ducklings, but did not touch the birds. She watched, with jaw cradled in palm and the disgusting taste of blood still in her mouth. She should have asked one of the girls to accompany her. Prudhomme would have been more than happy to come out, even though there were three of Lady Croukerne's dresses to attend to, and many pairs of shoes to clean.

The bench was hard and uncomfortable, but the housekeeper sat here, nursing her painful jaw.

'You seem distressed, Mrs Beste.'

She turned to the male voice, unwilling to speak for fear of a shot of agony from the site of her extraction. Nodding in silence, she blinked, hoping he would understand. Mr Pillow, the grocer, was usually rather understanding.

He looked at her hand, saw the pain in her eyes, and nodded too. 'I see. Have you just had a visit to Mr Mason's clinic?'

She nodded again.

'Please come with me. There's nothing a cup of tea at Florence's Tearoom cannot soothe.' He held out a hand.

Mrs Beste took it.

Together, they entered the tearoom and took a corner table. In minutes, they had a large brown teapot, cups and saucers, and a little jug of fresh milk before them.

'I shall pour you a nice cup, Mrs Beste. Oh no, no – let me do it. And there is no need at all to talk. I shall converse for both of us, for I have a bit of news.'

All she could do was nod again. Sipping guardedly from the cup, she kept the liquid away from the exposed site of the missing tooth, which the dentist said would hurt much less out than in. She was starting to doubt him.

'You will be better tomorrow.' The grocer repeated what the dentist said, but having two people attest to something she doubted did not render it true for Mrs Beste. 'All you need do is swish a little salt water around in your mouth when you get home.'

She knew. She nodded.

'And brandy.'

She nodded again.

'Now listen to this bit of good fortune. I have been made an offer by a large company in Cheltenham. They have offered me great benefits if I join them ... join what they call their *chain*. And what does it involve, do you ask?'

The question hung on his tilted head.

Mrs Beste nodded to concur it was what she would ask.

Another sip of tea, and the mythical healing properties of the infusion could be felt to work their spell.

'Well, I'd have to hang their sign above my shop. I'd have to employ two more counter hands, and I must stock many of their branded products, including butter, sugar, and flour.'

His companion's raised eyebrows said it all.

'Branded, yes, *branded*. Yes, I know, I know – the local dairy does supply me with butter. It is something to consider, however. It will mean much more business.'

She shook her head.

'Ah – you think the customers I have now are the customers I shall always have. Well, not so, when you hear the other part of the news.'

She raised a shoulder.

'I see you are curious. You want the other part of the news. Which is that up at Gallantrae, the master has sectioned off and titled a sizeable tract of land, and there is to be a new estate of cottages and *houses*!'

Her eyebrows almost met over her nose.

'You do not believe it? I've had it from one of the footmen up at Gallantrae! It will increase the population of people needing a shop by a considerable number, don't you think?'

Mrs Beste half nodded.

'And it will not happen overnight, you tell me. I know that. But by the time we have more people milling around, I will be ready to serve them. Can you imagine the business?'

A reluctant nod inclined her head.

'Of course you can imagine it. I see you can. In any case, expansion is on the cards, Mrs Beste. And I shall expand as needs must.'

She blinked a slow blink. Mrs Beste was very tired.

Mr Pillow was no fool, he knew when to stop talking about himself, and he saw her exhaustion. 'Now, how are you going to get home? Shall I ask at Mulberry's for the small gig?'

Mrs Beste refused quite adamantly by shaking her head and rising.

'That was a good cuppa, wasn't it?'

'Thank you,' she whispered.

'See? You will be fully restored by tomorrow. Shall I walk you part of the way then?'

They came out into the sun, only to see a dark figure marching across the square, past the bench, past the church and its yard, and past Mulberry's.

'Is that not Mr Herring? Things must be very quiet at Denisthorn for you to be about the village at once. Stand there just a moment.' He stepped away. 'Mr Herring! Mr Herring!' He ran a few paces, waving his hat in the air.

The butler was startled to be hailed so loudly in the middle of the small village. He stopped and turned slowly, trying to muster as much elegant surprise as he could.

'Ah, yes. Splendid afternoon, is it not?' He gave a shallow bow, and raised a hand to his hat when he saw Mrs Beste in the doorway of the tearoom.

'Mr Herring, you must be heading to the Hall.'

'Mr Pillow, is it not? Good afternoon. Indeed I am bound to Denisthorn Hall. My fitting at the tailor only took half an hour.'

'Well, it is fortuitous, because Mrs Beste is in some discomfort after a visit to the dentist, and she would benefit from some company and an arm to help her home.'

'It would be a pleasure, if not only a duty.'

'Ah.' The grocer did not know how to decipher a meaning in the sentence. He gave the butler the benefit of the doubt.

Mrs Beste was at their side.

'I shall leave you to your walk home, then. Take his

arm, Mrs Beste – it would not do at all to have you stumble when your ordeal is all over and finished, and all that's left is the walk home.' Pillow beamed and turned away.

'Indeed.' Mr Herring crooked his elbow and the housekeeper placed her hand in it.

Together, in silence, they walked away from the square towards the slight inclination which would put them on the road towards Denisthorn Hall.

CHAPTER TWENTY

*In which Lady Edwina contemplates Athena's future
and the London season is reviewed*

'It was a beautiful ceremony, and Queen Victoria looked in
fine form. It was so exciting to be there, to see her, to be in
her presence. Do tell us what she said to you, Athena.' Lady
Croukerne fidgeted with a long glove, attempting to smooth
two wrist wrinkles of grey satin.

'I cannot remember, Mama.'

'Surely it is the most memorable moment of your life
so far! It was for me, so many years ago – I still remember
each waking second.'

'What happened to your presentation gown, Mama?'

'Oh – I seem to remember it was kept for a year or so.
And then ... and then it was refigured and given to one of
the cousins. Yes – that's what I think became of it.'

'So you never wore it again?'

'A presentation gown is rather distinct and special, my
darling girl. How can one be seen twice in such a striking
design? A white gown! It's rather more special than any ball
gown. And much more spectacular than a wedding outfit,
which is usually remodelled and re-worn a number of times
afterwards. I did love my wedding ensemble, which was a
suit of lightly embroidered skirt and jacket – both practical
and elegant. I wore it to travel, so many times. Such a
delightful blue shade.' She mused about her younger days
for a moment, then turned to Athena again. 'Surely you
must remember the words of the queen on the most
important instance in your young life!'

The contrite daughter rose from a hard chair in the
Belgrave house sitting room and wandered over to the

window, from which she could just glimpse the tops of a number of cabs and carriages down in the street, whose gas lamps had halos of greyish yellow light. Would the excitement and movement never stop? It was well past midnight, and her mother showed no signs of wanting to retire. The streets showed no signs of clearing. Returning from St James was a harrowing kind of drive, when they could hear every word the coachman uttered, or shouted. The streets were crowded with horse-drawn vehicles of all kinds, and everyone was tired and excitable at the same time. She would never forget the constant sound of hooves on hard London cobbles.

But she could not remember a word Queen Victoria said as she approached, curtseyed, and remained poised in a semblance of decorum in an awkward huddle or crouch before the monarch. She remembered her calves aching, and her back protesting, and her stays digging into her sides, but she could not remember the queen's words. As the daughter of an earl, she would not merely kneel and kiss the queen's hand, but had to lean forward for the queen to kiss her on the forehead. Fear of losing her balance accompanied her to that moment. She could not remember rising from that crouch.

Aware of all eyes upon her in the crowded stifling palace drawing room, she was conscious of the fact that in the sea of white gowns, hers was the only one trimmed in pale grey. In the sea of ivory, she was the only silver bird in sight. Supremely glad of the touches of mauve, and the fact she was allowed white gloves, and not black satin ones for deep mourning, she had held her breath for long moments at a time, nervousness eating at her like acid.

At least she wore an enviable parure of amethysts. Her tiara alone was conspicuous for its restrained beauty. There was a sea of diamonds – all the tiaras in the room seemed to be made entirely of diamonds, with the occasional small sparkle of emerald, or sapphire, or garnet –

but hers were the only purple stones there.

'All the veils seemed to be exactly the same! And the court official did not fold my train properly – it weighed on my arm in a very tiring way.'

'Can you imagine trailing it up those stairs behind you? Three and a half yards of satin and grosgrain. Folded any way – correctly or not – is a necessity!'

'And why is it obligatory to wear white ostrich feathers?'

'It's the fashion, my dear. It is also a requirement of the queen's. Could you even think of meeting your monarch, and not wearing a fine feathered headdress? It's unthinkable. Now what did Her Majesty say?'

Athena turned to the window once more. Outside, carriage lights, lampposts, the shiny black tops of cabs and gigs, were a blur. Everything was a blur. She was too intent on remembering what to do, when she was in the drawing room of the palace, for anything else to register in her mind. She thought of something plausible to say. '*You are Lord Croukerne's girl*, I think her majesty said.'

'Well, yes. You were announced, and Papa was up with the Peers. And I watched from a distance behind you.'

'Yes.'

'You are one of very few words, my dear.'

'But I shall remember this for a long time, as you say, Mama. The queen has piercing eyes and a very direct gaze.'

'You will go to bed happy. Fairley has waited up ever so long.'

So, at last, it was bedtime on the long-awaited day, which seemed, in retrospect, a blur of getting ready, waiting, waiting, waiting, and dressing, pinning and fussing and brushing and plumping and smoothing.

Relinquishing her cloak that afternoon to a court housemaid, after the interminable drive which took hours, had made her think she would never see it again. There were so many similar cloaks.

And outside, the crowd was dizzying; they pressed in on their carriage windows, peering at her face, her dress, and her hair.

'Isn't this a fine one!'

'Ooh, her dress isn't pure white.'

'Can one wear grey in the presence of royalty?'

'Look at this one, I say – isn't she pretty?'

'Isn't she unusual?'

'Look at those purple stones!'

'Has she got an embroidered stole?'

'Are those not lilies on her cloak?'

All that confusion Athena remembered, but she could not recall a single word that came out of the queen's mouth.

'Do you remember who was ahead of you? And who brought up behind you?

'No, Mama – I did not know a single one of the other girls. We were presented in order of arrival, of course. The line of carriages was incredibly long. We moved at a mile an hour.'

'So many young girls. It's like *anyone* can fill out a presentation card these days.'

'Not anyone. We do know that only daughters of ladies who have been presented can apply, Mama. It cannot be very many.'

'Too many – far too many, these days. Hundreds.'

Her mother's words were quickly forgotten too. Athena was exhausted. She had barely eaten a mouthful all day, for fear of marking her dress. Even in the carriage, when everyone partook of the portable luncheon, and sipped out of flasks, she did not dare eat too much.

And afterwards, as she was fussed over and plumped and pinned and smoothed all over again to sit for a photograph, with her miraculously returned cloak, the last thing on anyone's mind was food.

Luckily, Fairley had been instructed by Mrs Beste to take up a tray. Finally alone with her lady's maid in a room that seemed just as ablaze with lamps and candles as the palace of St James, she spied a small plate of salmon sandwiches and a tiny eared covered bowl of bouillon.

'Oh, Fairley, what a lifesaver you are.'

'It is my pleasure, Lady Athena. A girl will come up with tea in a minute.' The young servant, who could not have been much older than Athena, gave a little bob. 'Congratulations, Lady Athena. The day went very well.'

'And so I am now out, and an adult.'

And so she was divested of that day's finery, and the parure of amethysts was placed back in its velvet case and returned to her mother's room.

*

The next few days were unremarkable. Athena longed to return home, but the London season went on and on. In the absence of Ninian Crownrigg, Earl of Croukerne, Baron of Brockworth, life in London proceeded along the customs laid down through the years. There were visits and soirees, readings and card parties, dances and concerts, plays and recitals.

'If I must sit through one more evening of Mr Blanc's piano trios, I should surely die of boredom, Geraldine.'

'Oh, if only I could go in your place – but I have two more seasons of sitting out as a *child*. I do so miss riding with Papa. I cannot wait to return to Denisthorn Hall.'

'Where has Papa gone, exactly?'

'To the Scottish borders, to a place called Hawick.'

'And what for, right in the middle of the season?'

'He is obsessed with finding an heir. He's says it can wait, but pursues it regardless. And he thinks it a good time, seeing we are all so occupied with the activities here in London. He seeks a man, a cousin of ours, it seems, by the name of Angus Crownrigg.'

'And all you can think about is riding, Geraldine. You

do ride down here too.'

'There's precious little to be done here in London that I have not done a thousand times before. I know the parks backwards. And all the people are interested in is viewing each other's riding habits and hats. And bicycles! A bicycle in the park is not the same as taking Buttercup out on the estate, at a fair clip, even though it's side saddle and rather tame.'

'In Mama's day even bicycles were out of the question. She still thinks they are the height of inapt modernity.'

Geraldine threw an arm up with impatience. 'Why are we expected to conform to everything in our parents' minds, even though they are generations behind and so dreadfully out of the picture? Modern ways are pushing everything out of the way ...'

'... too rapidly for them, I'm afraid. I glimpsed one young lady pull off a glove *in the presence of the queen*.'

'Oh – was she shot at dawn, or garrotted in the afternoon?'

'Geraldine! Rough speech does not become you.'

The younger sister pulled a face and swirled her grey flannel skirts. 'You need to pull yourself out of the dark ages, darling sister. The entire world is changing. And it is *women* who are changing it. Is the work of Mrs Pankhurst all for nought?'

'She is a storekeeper, Geraldine, or the wife of one, at any rate, and will never be presented at court.'

'I am starting to think this emphasis placed on the court and all things noble and regal are a bit of an obstacle to normal life.'

'Geraldine!'

'Athena! Do not be an old lady before you turn twenty!'

The older girl stamped a foot. 'All this is fearful nonsense. But thankfully, we should no longer need to think of anything when we marry.'

Geraldine's eyes widened. 'What! Because our husbands will do our thinking for us? Are you willing to leave everything ... relinquish all your rights and powers ... to a man?'

Athena had a nonplussed expression on her face. She was evidently confused by conflicting messages from society, her mother, and now, her sister. 'It will be a relief, don't you think, to let everything happen and simply organize a lovely house, support and help a husband, do charitable works, and raise a family? Surely that is what we are perfectly cut out to do?'

'As women? What absolute bosh. We can do everything and anything a man can – and better! I should prefer not to marry.'

'Whereas I cannot wait. What nonsense you speak. What else could you possibly do, Geraldine?'

'Cannot wait? Oh, I do think you are considering Mr ... the man with whom you discuss literary matters.'

'If you mean Alastair Updike, I really do not know. We are mere correspondents. We share a common interest. There is no suggestion of any other attention, let alone of the romantic kind.'

'But you have said many times that it is impossible to have a friendship with a gentleman without it leading to romance. You think men and woman are different. *You think everything leads to marriage and babies!*'

'It is what I used to think. We have heard – and experienced – so much about infant death and childhood illnesses of late, that I must say it has scared me and pushed me out of line. I no longer know with certainty what it is I do think.'

Geraldine came to sit next to her sister. She took her hand. 'Well – that at least is the pure truth, my dear Athena.'

They both turned to greet the countess into the room.

'It was a good idea, dear daughters, to resist the call

and beckon of invitations today, and take a well-deserved rest from our wild social whirl. I have called for tea to be served up here. We should have a lovely intimate chat.'

'How wonderfully propitious, Mama.'

'We should talk about you, Athena dear. Have you made any new and welcome acquaintances?'

'I think Mama means, Athena, have you, while being paraded and shown off and exhibited like a prize as a marriageable object, *fallen in love*?'

'Geraldine!' Mother and daughter exclaimed at once.

'Oh – I apologize. I am not supposed to talk of love for another two years or so. I am not supposed to vote until and unless I own land as an independent woman. I am not supposed to work or consider a university degree. I am not supposed to talk politics, lest I stumble upon an argument I fail to understand. I am not supposed to think of anything except marriage and a family, but *only* after I am presented at court.'

Lady Athena and her mother stared at Lady Geraldine without a word when she rattled off her diatribe.

'I have decided to ignore that discourse, Geraldine.'

'I should ignore you too.' Athena raised her chin.

'Papa would not ignore me.'

Lady Edwina laughed. 'You are a touch too vociferous for your father. I have heard from him, by the way. He is returning by Wednesday's afternoon train to Kings Cross from Edinburgh.'

'Ah, it will be very pleasant to have him back.'

'Come and sit by me, Athena dear. Tell me about last night's ball.'

Athena settled on the long sofa next to her mother. They waited while a maid came in with a laden trolley.

'This looks nice.'

'Oh – is this a new kind of cake?'

'I do believe it is called *Bienenstich*, and its recipe comes from Munich.'

'In Germany? Does that mean what I think it does – *Bee Sting*? Goodness, Mama – the cook in this London house is far more advanced than our staff in the Denisthorn kitchen.'

'London is so much closer to communication, my dear. Trains make everything so much speedier. And there are establishments in town that take on foreign cooking methods and recipes the *instant* they are ah ... invented.'

'Who knows what Papa has tasted in Scotland.'

'Goodness knows. I cannot wait for his return. Tell us about the ball, Athena.'

'With Lady Greyspeck as my chaperone, I was required to keep to the one room. But the dancing was lively.'

'Were you introduced to many people?'

Athena laughed. 'So many that I cannot remember any names but four.'

'And they are?'

'Lady Cynthia Howarth, who wore a gown embroidered with orange flowers. Orange! Sir Dorian Clews, who must be a hundred and four if he is a day. The Misses Shantleby, of Doncaster, who had very little to say, and Captain Charles FitzSimon, or FitzSaul, or some such name.'

'His regiment?'

'From his uniform, I knew it was the First Middlesex Rifle Volunteer Corps. Rather modern.'

'How interesting.'

'Not at all. Not one bit interesting. It was an effort not to grow thoroughly bored with it all, except the gavotte, of course.'

'What was Captain FitzSimon like, my dear? Did you have him down for the gavotte?'

'He was portly, and short, and did not dance. He talked only of engineering and running bridges over *vast bodies of water*.'

'Really!' Geraldine was very amused. 'Nothing about rifles or war?'

'No, only of steel and reinforced concrete – whatever that might be – and of expeditions to far-flung lands such as New Zealand, where, apparently, it's always winter.'

'You must have misheard that.'

It was Athena's turn to laugh. 'Oh no – I heard it correctly. Captain FitzSimon must have mis-said it! He was full of facts and figures, and even mentioned the enormous cost of building bridges.'

'A gentleman? Discussing money?'

'Unheard of in your day, Mama.'

'Don't be facetious, Geraldine.'

'And was Mr Alastair Updike, who you met at Aunt Margery's, nowhere to be seen?'

Athena lowered her eyes, annoyed her sister was such a tease. 'He was at the concert at Almack's on Friday night.'

'Where you renewed your acquaintance?'

'Yes.'

'And you discussed ...'

'The music being played.'

Her mother sighed with impatience. 'And?'

'... a new novel by ...'

Lady Croukerne sat bolt upright on the sofa. 'Something appropriate, I hope.'

'By Mister Thomas Hardy, Mama – it's called *Tess of the d'Urbervilles*.'

'Oh, what a lovely title.'

'It's about a young woman who goes out seeking an inheritance that is rightfully hers.'

Geraldine clapped hands. 'Interesting. It must have made you question why Papa goes over great distances, to Scotland even, seeking an heir, when he has two perfectly good heiresses at home. If you were male, Athena ...'

'Hush, Geraldine. Do not stir her so.'

'But it's true, Mama.'

'The law is the law. Custom is custom.'

'If there were no need to change laws, there would be

no need for a parliament.'

The other two women were confused by Geraldine's truism. They all sipped tea in silence, until Athena remarked how delicious the new cake was.

'I did read that this is one of London's most highly attended seasons of all time.'

'Well, we are here. It's only memorable because of Athena's coming out, and only remarkable for the fact I utterly refused to attend the juvenile ball.'

Her mother was prim and adamant. 'I could not face dragging you there against your will, Geraldine. Sometimes you can be rather headstrong.'

'Sometimes?'

'Always.'

'And neither of us will ever regret it. I'm sure I was not missed in the least, by anyone.'

The double doors opened, and Herring the butler stood there, holding a small silver salver on which reposed the unmistakeable yellow envelope of a telegram. 'A telegram, my lady.'

'You bring it with your own hands, Herring.'

'Seeing it's from Scotland, my lady.'

He retreated, and the girls' mother pulled the single sheet from the slit envelope.

'Oh, listen to this! *Returning forthwith*, stop. *Accompanied by Angus Crownrigg*, stop. *With us for a week at Belgrave*, stop. *Regards, Ninian.*'

'Well!'

'He must have liked him.'

'Like him or not, he is the heir, my darlings.'

'And like it or not, he will be spending some time with us here in London.'

CHAPTER TWENTY-ONE

In which the Glorious Twelfth is observed at Denisthorn,
deep dislike works its way into the family
and
Fairley learns a lesson

With the London season behind them, and a rapid return by
train to Cheltenham, and then by carriage – and the wagon
for boxes, bags and trunks – back home to Denisthorn Hall,
the family of Earl Croukerne prepared in some haste for the
hunt.

It was always that way. Easter was spent preparing for
London, and London sent them rushing toward a hectic
month at home, where they hosted a number of house
guests for what the Crownriggs always termed 'the little
hunt'. November would then bring them a busier, chillier
fox hunt, which took them to Christmas.

This year, accompanied by a closed box in the form of
Mr Angus Crownrigg, the family journeyed in comparative
unease in a reserved train carriage that seemed more
uncomfortable than usual. Met at long last at Cheltenham
station by two grooms, who transferred all manner of
luggage with high alacrity from train to wagon, they piled
into the more comfortable but narrow horse-drawn coach,
exhausted and full of the desire to have at least two days of
rest before the first guests started to arrive.

'Who will arrive for the hunt first, do you think?'

'Who are we having? I doubt the Marquess of Ripon
will venture to our neck of the woods again, after last year's
mishap with his dog.'

'Which was no fault of our grooms'.'

'But he thought it was. Blame had to be placed
somewhere.'

'Aunt Margery and Uncle Herbert will come.'

Lady Croukerne smiled. 'My sister will not miss an event at Denisthorn. She loves you girls.'

'Did she never ...?' Geraldine was about to ask about her aunt's childlessness, only to receive a sharp look from her mother, who would not discuss family matters in front of a perfect stranger.

'Reverend Sir Michael Littlejohn will be first to arrive. He always is. And this year he brings his ward – his orphaned niece, who has attained majority, and is now nineteen. She was presented at court this season, with you, Athena.'

'I do not know her.'

'Lady Octavia Littlejohn, the poor girl. Sir Michael's brother and his wife perished in a carriage accident while touring in Italy.'

The addition of a guest was good news to Lady Edwina, who always strove, and sometimes found it difficult, to keep the numbers of ladies and gentlemen even. This cousin from Hawick might have perfect manners, but he did threaten to skew the numbers towards too many men. She shot a searching glance under the rim of her hat.

Angus Crownrigg sat on the left with his back to the horses, his head held straight and alert, next to his distant cousin Ninian on the right, because although it was a trip home, for which the coachman needed no instruction, it was his rightful place. His lordship was the last to enter, after making sure the coachman saw to it there were no protruding skirts or scarves. Finally in his seat, Ninian looked fixedly out of the window at the passing countryside, listening to the sound of hooves and the vague whistle of wind around the carriage top.

'Did she never miss a hunt at our house?' Geraldine rephrased her question, to gain a sweet smile.

'Never, my dear girl. And I must say she rides extremely well.' Lady Croukerne appreciated the tact.

Geraldine had to agree. 'I have learned from her through observation and imitation. But ...'

'... But you would much rather ride like Uncle Herbert.' Athena's tongue would one fine day get her into trouble, but she knew the presence of their new cousin would avoid her a scolding. Sitting with Geraldine between them, she could not exactly gauge the expression on her mother's face, so felt safe. She saw the ghost of a smile cross their new cousin's face. 'Do you ride, Mr Crownrigg?'

'Cousin Angus, please.' He looked across at Lady Croukerne, who tucked a shawl around her, appearing to feel a draught around her shoulders. She wore a bland face. He waited until it looked as though she was listening to him. 'After the very pleasant week I have had with your family at Belgrave, I should dearly like to be addressed by your daughters as a cousin, if they may, Lady Croukerne.'

There seemed to be no country reticence or modern negligence in this man. He moved, spoke, and comported himself like an equal. Perhaps noble blood could not, after all, be erased, diluted, or forgotten. Nothing was known about his parents, both of whom had departed this life. No one knew about his education. But he dressed well, had come down to dinner in evening dress in London, and showed himself every inch a gentleman.

Still, she divulged no gratuitous warmth. 'Just the girls,' she replied. There was no chance she would ever risk being addressed as *Cousin Edwina* by this man. He had better address Ninian correctly, too.

The man turned to look at the older daughter. His profile was rather pleasing, and there were minute similarities to the Crownrigg chin. His eyes, after all, were of the requisite lightness, and he also wore reading glasses when offered a newspaper.

His voice was modulated. 'Yes, I do, Cousin Athena. I do ride. My haunts in London are Green Park, and Hyde Park of course.'

'Oh, you spend time in London.'

'Most certainly, it's essential. We have a small townhouse in Holborn, which allows us to do important business and banking several times a year. I travel from Scotland with a clerk.'

'And a valet?' This was a test; it was obvious to Lady Croukerne's daughters, and her husband, who looked across at her with a subtle mark of bemusement in his eyes.

'And a valet.'

There was a collective breath taken in the carriage, and a few minutes of silence.

'Herring has sent word ahead that we are bringing a guest. No doubt everyone will be accommodated to my satisfaction.'

'No doubt at all, my dear.' The earl threw his wife a knowing glance. 'The grouse hunt brings us many guests and their staff.' He addressed his cousin. 'And my man Thorn will be more than happy to look after you, as he did for the four days in London, Cousin Angus.'

The cousin nodded.

The family had had plenty of time to observe the man, the way he carried himself, his apparel, and his speech when they all got back to the house. They disgorged themselves from the coach to be met by a line of servants, and half tumbled up the front steps to tea in the drawing room, where the gentlemen soon retired to the earl's small library.

No one could find fault with him except Athena. 'He's much older than I thought. And surely he must have better stock somewhere in his luggage. We have seen an entire week's worth of gaudy ties.'

'Neckties are changing in fashion too, Athena. You will find that the more he realizes his position as the next earl, the less flamboyant his necktie will become.'

She was surprised her mother had jumped to his defence, even in his absence. But it was true noblemen and the gentry wore subdued neck adornment, sometimes a mere narrow black tie, as worn by Prince Bertie, and people in the village often wore brightly-coloured cravats knotted in fancy fashion.

When asked if he hunted, while being quizzed by Lady Croukerne in the carriage home, the newly-found cousin said he was a firm follower of the Glorious Twelfth near the Borders, which came close to surprising everyone.

'Why is it called the Glorious Twelfth, Papa?'

'It's self-explanatory, Geraldine. The twelfth of August can only be described as glorious, because it opens the grouse season!' Her father gave a broad smile. His love of the hunt was obvious.

*

Four days into the week of the hunt, a happy but exhausted Geraldine swept through the garden entrance at the sound of the hounds baying in the early morning. Her riding habit was not the freshest it could be, but it was understandable after many days of hard riding. She shunned a new habit of very dark grey velvet because it hindered her riding, and trapped her legs, which she liked to swing free.

'You are in brown again, Geraldine.' Her mother was quick to criticize at breakfast. She spotted a black armband on her daughter's sleeve, which she thought the height of impudence.

The hunt was one of the few occasions the lady of the house appeared out of her rooms before eleven, so it was an event where custom was put aside to a certain extent. But wearing a male form of mourning, or one a servant would wear, was very untoward.

'I cannot abide my new grey habit. It chafes so. I also cannot abide our new cousin, if the truth were to be heard.'

'Hush! If he is not about, one of the servants is sure to hear. He is a very pleasant man, with excellent manners, and he would be hurt by such a comment.'

'I care little about his feelings. He does not pay enough attention to Lady Octavia. She is shy and a bit out of her depth.'

'Her riding leaves a lot to be desired, I hear.'

'Perhaps now she is the Reverend's ward he might see to some instruction. But she is miserable and lonely.'

'Oh! Poor dear. Surely Cousin Angus can sense she needs compassion and company.'

'He is a man, Mama.'

'That is not the only thing you hold against him, I feel.'

'I do resent the fact he will inherit all this one day, and I, who have lived here most of my life, will have to find residence elsewhere.'

'You will enjoy an estate of your own when you marry, Geraldine, like I did. Lady Octavia will one day find happiness in marriage and children. Like all ladies. I love Denisthorn Hall with all my heart, as you do, you must know that.'

Geraldine uttered a huff. 'And you will no doubt be dispatched to Cheltenham House when the time comes, just like Grand-mama was. I find that a deplorable state of affairs. She must have felt it sorely.'

'Your Grand-mama is no stranger to the laws and norms and customs of England, my darling girl. She is very happy at Cheltenham House. When your Papa inherited the title and all that came with it, Denisthorn became his ... ours. Remember she lived here for two full years more after your grandfather, the fourth earl, passed away.'

Geraldine remembered it only vaguely, and wondered whether her grandmother was ever truly happy, but said nothing in response. She pulled on gloves, grasped her whip, adjusted her veiled hat, and was ready to join the crowd for the stirrup cup.

'Are you not riding today, Mama?'

'Three days are sufficient for me. I did promise your

father, but I do rather wish to get out of this outfit, after all, and spend some time organizing things at my desk. I shall ring for Prudhomme and have a restful day instead. I sent out word to Lady Octavia. She will join me for an informal luncheon on the terrace if it's still sunny then.'

*

Fairley and Prudhomme had similar jobs divided by time and place. The former had only recently been placed in a position of importance, looking after Lady Athena as her personal maid. Prudhomme, on the other hand, was for many years Lady Croukerne's lady's maid, although the passage of time did not show on either her face or her figure. Indeed, if seen trotting about dutifully in the corridors of Denisthorn, she presented a youthful spry and active form.

Tending to plumpness, Fairley often wondered why that was, seeing they all ate more or less from the same table. It was the consistent, almost unvarying, servants' hall fare; a diet they all partook of, whether they liked it or not. Fairley did like it; pancakes, toast, stews, soups, fried mackerel, boiled cabbage, and stodgy custards. And the occasional sliver of cake leftover from upstairs.

She liked it all. It was generous and tasty and clean compared to what she was raised on in a pauper's cottage without running water outside Cheltenham. Her father was the kind of workhorse whose long hours and exhaustion did little to improve their lot despite his intentions, and her mother bore eight children who surprisingly all survived, despite the conditions. So it was not an unusual thing to have a breakfast of bread singed on long forks held to the grate on cold mornings, or to scramble and fight over a bony kipper on a cracked plate, or to wonder what to do with the windfall of a small pig's head that would soon go off if not immediately boiled. But they were a healthy lot, who rarely caught the diseases rampant in the slums, and if they did, they recovered stronger than before. But survival on porridge, bone broth, and bread and dripping left them seedy and sallow.

Her mother's dream came true; all her girls went into service, starting at the very bottom as skivvies, carrying buckets of fireplace ash; mopping, scrubbing, beating rugs, and sweeping, sweeping, sweeping. But meals were regular, clothes were provided and more or less clean, and she slept on a bed with a horsehair mattress. Only rarely did she have to head-to-toe with another servant; it happened when there was a house party and all the ladies brought a maid. The house skivvies would then all crowd in together to free beds for guest maids, who were all addressed by their mistresses' surnames and acted like they were royalty.

Fairley was living her mother's dream, and loved every minute of her service, promoted the instant she understood how to do a chore to perfection, to one she had to learn anew. Finding herself in charge of Lady Athena was again a learning stage, but she asked, asked, asked Prudhomme about each hairpin she inserted into the young lady's hair, each lace she adjusted on her corset, each skirt and blouse she bore away to clean.

'You had toast and marmalade, and I had toast and marmalade, Miss Prudhomme. And yet you remain shapely, and I turn to fat.'

'If you hurry along the corridors, and take the stairs at a fair trot, you might stay lean.' Prudhomme smiled. 'But some women just have big bones.'

'I must indeed.'

'You must check that Godwin does your lady's shoes correctly, now. The hunt brings a considerable amount of dirt into that boot room.'

'Yes, Miss Prudhomme. And I must mend a ladder in a stocking, and fear I won't find matching thread.'

Lady Croukerne's maid looked about them, nodded,

pulled Fairley to one side and closed the scullery door. 'You were chosen for this position, rather than a trained girl through an advertisement, Fairley. Mrs Beste thought it would suit you, and I see why. You are a superior kind of girl, you are clean, and you might turn out to be clever.'

'Really, Miss Prudhomme? Yes, Miss Prudhomme.'

'So keep your wits about you – you do know how to learn or you'd never have found yourself wearing that lacy cap. You must speak cordially at all times, even when you are ruffled. Never gossip. Your mistress will ask questions of you, because maids see much more than ladies do. Learn how to be tactful as well as truthful. Never be caught in a lie or you'll lose both trust ... and your position.' The older maid took a breath.

'My goodness.'

'Listen to me. I like you, Fairley, so I do not mind the odd question, but observation is the key. Look at everything I do. What do I mend stockings with, eh? Be observant and resourceful. You learned some of that below stairs. Resourcefulness is a lady's maid greatest asset. I do hope you read and write properly because it is necessary, to leave clearly legible notes for tradesmen and the lower servants. So practise at night.'

'Yes.'

A kind look shone in her eyes. 'There are several books in the hall bookcase. Some are rather old, and a few are not appropriate. Look – I shall choose a few useful ones for you. And remember there is a second dictionary on the cook book shelf in the kitchen.'

'Thank you!'

'Be neat in your person – I note that you are clean, but your fingernails need attention. You must become tolerably quick with your needle, and you must keep a tidy sewing box. You may look inside mine to see how things ought to be done.'

'Really!'

'Yes, have a look. As for stocking thread ...' She looked behind the door to see if anyone was listening. '... use a hair from your head. It is strong as silk. That will match closely enough, and you will never run out.'

'A hair!'

'If it is long and strong enough, and *clean*. When the footmen and kitchen maids go to the village on Friday nights, to let their hair down, so to speak, where am I to be found, Fairley?'

'Indeed I have no idea.'

'Letting my own hair down, but not quite in the same way. I am in one of the stair cupboards, with a strong and steady chair, a copper jug of hot water, two towels, and one of the old washstands ... and I'm *washing* my hair. You would do well to observe the same practice instead of drinking ale and spending your money, and sharing a rowdy time in a public place.' The lady's maid with the superior position and more extensive knowledge stopped for breath.

The younger one was speechless.

'What is it you do, Fairley? I hope it is something intended to improve yourself.'

'To improve is my full intention. Of course. And I save money to send home, miss.'

'There you go. I knew you had sense. Now add hair-washing on a Friday.' She smiled. 'Whether you need it or not.'

'All the stockings return from being cleaned on Fridays.'

'They arrive paired and rolled, but you must check your lady's pairs, and set aside time to repair them properly. Learn through experience which part of your lady's stocking foot gets most wear.'

'Yes, Miss Prudhomme.' She already knew it was the lower part of the heel.

The older maid opened the scullery door. 'One last thing ... although nothing is 'last' in this occupation – there is always more to learn.'

'And what is that?'

'Discretion, discretion, discretion. You must never fail in that. Your position will immediately be forfeited if you forget your place. Your eyes might see things that will startle you; what happens upstairs can often be surprising and even shocking, but your tongue must be still and silent. Even with me. I do not desire to know what you might see. Understood?'

The girl nodded. Rather than scared off by all the warnings, her heart filled with satisfaction and happiness that she had landed such an enviable position without having to apply. As Prudhomme said, it was extremely unusual and incredibly fortunate. She would never forfeit it. She had learned another thing, and her own dictionary upstairs, in the attics of the house, would confirm that night what it might mean. *Forfeit*.

CHAPTER TWENTY-TWO

In which a footman learns a little Latin
and
Angus Crownrigg proves curious and knowledgeable

A handkerchief with a beautifully embroidered motto was found lying underneath one of the armchairs in the drawing room, by a working footman.

'*Memor esto*. What does that mean?' The young footman fingered the lawn fabric of the handkerchief. 'What do these words mean, Godwin?'

The other footman shook his head. 'Where did you get that?'

The man pointed at the spot on the figured carpet from where he had picked the kerchief.

'That must belong to the dowager marchioness. Let me see. Yes. It is her elderly ladyship's. She has dropped belongings here before. Once, an earring. Another time, a fan. This must be taken down to be laundered, and when it's fresh and pressed, it will be returned to her ladyship's maid.'

'What! Is someone to make the journey to Cheltenham House simply to return a hankie?'

Godwin smiled. 'It is not merely a hankie, my man. It belongs to someone venerable and special, and as you say, the embroidered motto alone makes it valuable.'

The other man laughed. 'I said no such thing. I asked what it meant, and you obviously don't know.'

'I know precious little Latin.' He laughed again at his own words.

'Is that what it is? Does the lady dowager speak *Latin*, then?'

Godwin had reason to laugh again. 'I don't think

anyone speaks Latin, except Papist priests.'

'Oh, *that* Latin. I hear the people at Gallantrae are Roman Catholics.'

Godwin signalled with a hand, and together, the two men lifted and moved a sofa, three armchairs, and a huge ottoman while Maisie and another housemaid swept underneath them.

'It is none of our business what they are, Timmy.'

'Tim. I tell you every day my name is Tim.'

'Your name is Foster, young fellow me lad. Let that be printed on your brain, if you have one.'

They moved to an oval marble table, and removed a number of heavy silver frames, in which were held likenesses of the Crownrigg family. One of the maids dusted the marble, and wiped it down with an oiled cloth, and the men returned the frames to the exact places they had stood before.

'How much dust could have fallen on this table since Wednesday?'

'If you are critical now, Timmy Foster, you'll be critical and unhappy forever if you stay in service. There is perhaps some dark and secret reason why certain chores are done on certain days, and it's not for the likes of us to debate it.'

The younger boy laughed. 'Debate it! It's buried in the dark and secret mind of Mrs Beste, no doubt.'

'Hush. That kind of disrespect is the fastest way to find yourself delivering sausages for the village butcher.'

'Which you think is inferior to lifting sofas, Godwin.'

'What does your old man do, young man?'

'Don't *young man* me ... he hauls coals for the smithy near the railway in Cheltenham.'

'What did your *grandfather* do?'

'Haul coals at the mine.'

'See? We all need to better ourselves.' Godwin spent his days watching Formby and Glover, and knew very well what and what not to do. 'Remember thy ancestors.'

'What?'

'*Memor esto*. That's what that embroidered motto means. *Remember thy ancestors.*'

*

Ninian Crownrigg, Earl of Croukerne, gritted his teeth through another meeting with Swinnart, the agent. He sifted mentally through the man's words, over and over, trying to reach the meaning of what he said; the import of his descriptions and narrations, to get to the crux.

'So, Swinnart – what are we discussing here? Another change in one of the cottages?'

'Not so much a change as the necessity for repairs and maintenance, my lord. In more than just one, I'm afraid. I have carried out, together with a manager, a very detailed inspection of each and every cottage on the estate, indoors and out, and we have, together, come up with inventory, condition, and requirements.'

The earl flapped the sheet of paper handed to him by the agent. 'And does this list ...' He looked at it again. 'Good heavens. This list goes over both sides of the sheet! I must ask you to accompany this list of requirements with an approximation of what each item might cost. In *brief*.' He took the paper to the direct light of a window.

The agent shifted on the carpet while he waited, looking as if his feet hurt.

'Because, Swinnart ...'

The agent showed signs of starting to talk again.

'Just a minute, just a minute. I beg your silence for a minute, Swinnart.'

'Yes, your lordship.'

'Because it does not look as though there is a single cottage that does not require some sort of attention. Not a single one! We have ... what is this? Broken windowpanes, chimneys that do not draw, inefficient water pumps, missing roof shingles, missing coal scuttles, precarious ceilings, broken ... ah, I see ... broken door hinges ...' He looked up.

'My lord.'

'Surely all these items do not require a great deal of ... of ... resources.'

'The resources of which you speak, and quite rightly, my lord, are – in the main – time and manpower.'

The earl thought he was going to say money. 'Time and manpower?'

'Because, as is exceedingly plain and evident, in all practicality, and in weather fair and foul, there are twenty-five cottages, my lord.' The agent forced lips together in an effort not to say more.

'I do know how many cottages we have up there, Swinnart.'

'Indeed, my lord.' He pressed lips hard once more.

It was the moment chosen by Mr Angus Crownrigg to enter the room. 'Ah, I do apologize, my lord.'

'It's all right, Cousin Angus. We are finished here.' He waved the piece of paper again. 'Like I said, Swinnart. Kindly furnish me with another list: an approximation of the cost of each item.'

'My lord.' The man gave a shallow bow.

'As you say, Swinnart ...' He glanced sideways at the Hawick cousin, who would one day inherit Denisthorn. '... an indication of um ... *time and manpower*.' He hoisted himself up by his own lapels.

When the agent left the room, Ninian Crownrigg slumped onto an armchair and regarded his distant cousin, who still stood, dutifully waiting to be invited to join the earl.

'You have no idea, Cousin Angus, the amount of time and trouble that must go into running an operation of this size and quality.'

The cousin hovered.

'Take a seat, dear man. Please join me and please sit down.'

'How many farms are in the subdivision? Is there a home farm?'

Ninian Crownrigg raised an eyebrow at his relative. Was this sincere curiosity or pecuniary interest? He supposed only further conversation might reveal the answer to the question. Eventually, this heir would show qualities that would either worry him more or, given some good fortune, reassure him.

'You seem perturbed.'

The earl drew a hand over his forehead. 'Grain prices are so damnably low that we are finding it hard to cover even the basic costs. Even keeping grain for replanting – even such a basic aspect of running a farm – is becoming a problem.'

'So there is a home farm.'

Another look from one man to the other passed in silence. In the distance, the sound of horses' hooves could be heard, as well as the calling of many birds.

'Look, if you are sincerely interested, Cousin Angus, I think we should set aside a morning ... or two ... for a tour of the estate. Your questions will be ... um ... do not mistake my meaning, my dear man, your questions are welcome, but I must gather my wits and try to figure a way to cover the costs of repairs to the estate cottages.'

'Of which there are several?'

'Twenty-five on the hill we call Grayson's Mound ... you see, generations ago a duke called Eftfeld owned these large tracts of land. He had a man called Grayson, who was a legendary agent. After subdivision in 1870 – you know, when the laws changed – Grayson's Mound and Grayson's Field as it is still known, fell into different divisions. Her ladyship's sister and her husband now own Gallantrae, where Grayson's *Field* is.' His forehead corrugated into horizontal lines. 'I must tell you that it is excellent wheat-growing land ... but they run cattle, leave some of it fallow, and hold *excursions and picnics* on the rest.'

'I see. And it's called *Gallantrae*.'

'My sister-in-law's husband is Sir Herbert, of Gallantrae.'

'They are quite well-known. Is he not the very um ... successful investor?'

'He is. When Lady Margery's first husband, who was a marquess, died, she married Herbert Fanshaw, and he thought it made perfect sense to take the larger holding and build a country house on the ridge, giving it his name.'

'I see,' he said again.

'But we were talking about *cottages*. There are another twelve or so of ours – better ones – between the back of the house and what we call Better Meadow. They are staff cottages. The part called Lesser Meadow, over the hill a bit, to the east, is now part of Gallantrae too.'

'All occupied?'

'The cottages? Oh – that's something we must ask Swinnart. He will have a roll. So what do you say to riding out for a few hours with him this week?'

'I should like that very much, my lord.'

'Cousin Ninian, please call me Cousin Ninian. We have stood on ceremony too long. My wife is a stickler for good form.'

'I admire her ladyship's grace and wisdom, Cousin Ninian.'

The earl looked up. 'Ah. Good, good.'

*

It would have been lonely at Cheltenham House if it were not for the dowager marchioness's luncheons with her daughter-in-law and granddaughters on Wednesdays. When he was alive, it was one of the visits to which Frederic, even at so young an age, could accompany them.

A small brougham was used, since it only needed one coachman, usually a groom with little to do on Wednesdays, and one horse; and it was good in all weathers.

The pattern was resumed whenever the family was in residence at Denisthorn, so it was with unusual anticipation that Lady Croukerne summoned her daughters on their return from London, and after the hunt was over.

'We take luncheon with Grand-mama tomorrow, my darling girls. We have not been for a very long time. So much has happened since she returned from her tour.'

'And there does not seem to be much wrong with her, Mama. Do you not remember how we feared she was unwell?'

'No sign of any malaise, thank goodness. Now, because it will very soon be autumn, we might think of including another shade or two to our wardrobes. Geraldine wore brown to the hunt every day, after all.'

'Really, Mama!' Geraldine uttered an impatient interjection.

Her mother took it literally, on purpose, and smoothed that wave. 'Yes, really. I did meet you on your way through the garden entrance every single morning. Even Lady Octavia, who does not ride well and who I could sense detested the hunt, had two perfectly beautiful riding habits.'

'Her uncle must have bestowed upon her a splendid wardrobe stipend. Did you see the evening dress she wore on the last night? Her seamstress is excellent.'

'Anyone would look beautiful in that figured lutestring. And she knows how to select her colours. Ashes of roses is a divine hue.' Lady Croukerne sighed. 'You looked a bit dull and dishevelled out riding, Geraldine. They could not deny if they watched you, though, that you are a fine horsewoman. A bit brown, that's all!' She smiled. 'But that is behind us now. We are all three of us thoroughly tired of dark grey, light grey, dove grey, charcoal grey, gunmetal grey, and all other shades and hues of grey, grey, grey.'

'So I shall soon go back to my pastels and become thoroughly tired again.' Athena folded hands in lap and looked out of her mother's sitting room window.

'For tomorrow, we can make do with shawls and hats and gloves of whatever colour you like, Athena. Then it might be time to have the seamstresses back.'

The older daughter sighed. 'I do not think I have the patience to go through the catalogues again, or stand still to be measured and pinned and turned this way and that, and looked at for hours on end. The seamstresses have enough patterns made out to my size. Can I not just have similar dresses to my mourning clothes, but in different fabrics, cut out on the same patterns?'

Her mother clapped hands. 'What a capital idea! It would save so much time and bother. What do you think, Geraldine?'

'I cannot bear to be talking about calico and taffeta, and shalloon and wild-bore and gauze and dimity for hours on end. I should be happy with a few coloured ties and lengths of material ... of *whatever* kind ... to decorate my hats. It does not take a milliner to re-do a hat. Perhaps Fairley will be good enough to re-style my hats.'

'Fairley is my maid!' Athena half rose from her seat. 'Why is it that you must always usurp my progress? We do not have to share Fairley ... do we, Mama?'

Geraldine placed a hand to her lips. 'Goodness! I don't believe I do hinder you in any way. What makes you say *always*? And what progress could you possibly mean?'

Athena's eyes were bright and wide. 'I am no longer a girl now, and I have ...'

Their mother laughed. 'My darlings!' She turned to Athena. 'What is it you think you have, my dear? You need to marry before you *have* anything.'

'And that can only happen if Papa endows me with a fortune.'

Geraldine shook her head. 'We are stuck in the Middle Ages, and require dowries before anyone will lay eyes on us.'

'Oh, pray do not be so inelegant.'

'Of course Papa will endow both of you with fortunes.'

'Such covetable glittering prizes for two lucky suitors!'

'Geraldine, dear.'

'A husband takes control of everything – his wife, and her fortune.'

Her mother looked at Geraldine with a sore scowl. 'Well, not always, I must admit.'

'No?'

'Most ladies desire to be rid of concerns about the inelegant question of *money*, Geraldine. It's coarse and sordid. Men do all of that so much better. But if a girl so wishes, her fortune can be secured in an estate trust, controlled by the Chancery Court. Few do it, because word gets about, but it is perfectly possible. In that way, with a legal trust, a lady does not feel her husband would benefit from the sum in any way.'

'Can husbands not run off with the money?'

Calmer now, Lady Croukerne sighed and continued. 'No. You will find that husbands greatly benefit from having wives, and do not usually *run off!* If need be, when a lady encounters some emergency, she can access the fund, or indeed its interest, but no husband can touch an estate trust.'

Geraldine beamed. 'I like that.'

'If a husband outlives his wife, it is then all his of course.'

'Her money, perhaps, but not her property!'

'How do you know that, Geraldine?'

'There was something about a law passed, in one of

Papa's newspapers. A woman can have, and safeguard, her own property, separately from her husband's.'

'I think you are right, daughter dear. It was a law passed a few years ago.'

'Do you hold any property, Mama?'

'Being legally allowed to dispense with it as I saw fit, I also made use of the law that let me pass it all onto Papa to administer. In any case, it's only a couple of tenements in Chester.'

'What sort of a law is that? Don't answer, I know. One written by men. It's obvious.'

The countess smiled, a touch condescendingly. 'None of this conversation tomorrow at Cheltenham House, please girls.'

'Of course not.' Athena sat back. 'The last thing Grand-mama is interested in is the marriage and property laws of our country. We shall talk of pleasant things. And I shall carry my pink parasol and wear a pink sash.'

'If you like.'

'I'll be in my brown habit, after my ride with Papa.'

The countess looked up. 'No, Geraldine, not tomorrow – you can miss the outing for once. Papa will be riding out with Cousin Angus and Swinnart, to inspect the estate.'

'Is he never going to leave?'

'Who, Cousin Angus? Goodness, Geraldine, surely you have got over your dislike of him? Or is it resentment? There is no hurry at all for him to leave.'

'Isn't there a bank he should be running? Does it run at all well in his absence? Are people not banging on his bank's doors, demanding their money? Is there not any important *business* to be done? I should have thought his family might miss him, if husbands are so desperately needed by wives.'

Lady Croukerne's wide eyes showed her own dislike of the younger daughter's choice of subject. 'What a panoply of questions! I don't know about such things, and I do not see why you should be interested.'

Geraldine was stung. 'I am not in the least bit interested in what he owns or what he does.'

Athena smiled. 'You did ask.'

'He is getting Denisthorn when Papa dies.' Her voice was aggrieved.

'Could we not be a bit more jovial, Geraldine? Papa has a long way to go yet – a long life to live.'

'No. Neither can I be jovial to think that unless I remain a spinster, everything I ever own will be under the jurisdiction of a husband, trust or no trust. I have no doubt the Chancery Court is run by men.'

'It's the law.'

'It's bosh, and I shall stay unmarried, and live at Cheltenham House with Grand-mama.'

'Geraldine, it is highly unlikely your grandmother will out-live Papa.'

The girl turned to look at her mother, whose head was tilted in a kind of compassion.

'You don't fully understand, daughter of mine.'

'I do. I shall stay and live with you then, Mama, when you go to Cheltenham House as a widow and Angus Crownrigg inherits Denisthorn ... and everything else with it and around it.'

Athena laughed. 'Someone will sweep you off your feet when you come out at court, and the romance will soon make you forget *money*.'

'Have *you* not been swept off your feet, Athena? The London season is behind us and you do not seem to be swooning with love.'

Athena had to have the last word after that. 'I would rather sense than swooning. And you would rather fall in love with a horse, Geraldine.'

*

Luncheon with the dowager marchioness on Wednesday was uneventful. They ate in the small intimate dining room, served by Mrs Conder and one maid.

'We shall continue on our own, thank you Elsie.'

It was clear to Athena her grandmother had something to say. But it was only about dear Frederic and her memories of him.

'I never thought I should miss the little lad so very much. Whenever I go out in my walled garden, I picture him on that swing.' She touched a lace handkerchief to the corner of an eye.

'Perhaps you can have it taken down.'

'Never!'

'Perhaps you can have ...' The countess looked at her mother-in-law.

She interjected. 'Yes! I shall have a little memorial erected for my dear little Frederic. You know, I was going to bestow the title upon him. He would have been the next Marquess of Harpensted. It will never happen now. I shall have a statue ... a boy on a swing. Capital. How sad, and yet what a lovely idea. I shall engage a sculptor. A boy on a swing. Oh! A boy on a swing.' Once more, she dabbed at a tear.

'Oh – your handkerchief, Grand-mama!'

The old lady looked at the fancy scrap of material in her hand. 'What about it, Athena?'

'Prudhomme said she was given one of your hankies to have laundered. It was found in our drawing room.'

'Have her send it on to Burgess. She looks after all that.' Her gaze turned inward, and she shook her head. 'I shall have a sculpture in the garden, and little Frederic will be forever remembered as the boy on a swing.'

In the brougham on the way back to Denisthorn, Geraldine brought it up. 'Frederic did not spend much time on swings, though, did he Mama?'

'Oh, when he was very little, I suppose he did.'

'Not an inordinate time, though.'

Athena huffed and turned to look at the countryside and the village outskirts through the window. 'Oh, let Grand-mama remember Frederic as she likes, Geraldine.'

'It's not for me to *let* her.'

'Girls!' Their mother raised a vexed hand. 'Of course she is going to remember little Frederic in her own way.'

'Did you not think it was rather strange of her, though?'

Lady Croukerne did not acknowledge the thought with either a nod or a word, but it did cross her mind that her mother-in-law was starting to act a little distracted. Just a trifle unfocussed.

*

The sound of piano playing resounded along the downstairs passage, up the stairs, and could momentarily be heard when someone pushed the baize door open. The door was an effective sound barrier; when it thumped shut again, the sound was lost.

Below stairs, however, the servants gathered around Mrs Beste as she played and sang. Some of the girls took up the refrain and sang along.

> *And I never shall forget that lovely afternoon*
> *when I met her at*
> *The fountain in the park*

Everyone clapped and asked for more.

'Oh, let's do that again, Mrs Beste!'

'Yes, play it again.'

She stood and smoothed her skirt. 'No indeed. It's time we all looked after our evening chores and got ourselves to bed. Come now!' She rolled the embroidered felt cover snugly over the keys and lowered the lid. 'It's time. I'm sure Mr Herring has already done his rounds, and sent Godwin to check all the doors.'

'I watched your hands, Mrs Beste. I'd love to learn.'

'We already agreed, Formby. Finish your tasks early on Thursdays, and you'll get thirty minutes at the keys.'

Glover, the under butler, glowered at them. 'What? Learning to play the pianner, are ye now? How about you first learn to do up buttons, or remove stains from your own waistcoat?'

'I can and do look after my own weskit, thank you very much, Jack Glover.'

'Mister Glover to you, Peter Formby. *Mister* Glover.'

CHAPTER TWENTY-THREE

*In which an artist takes up residence
and
a chandelier is described in detail*

Rupert Bottomley was met by the earl all on his own when the carriage in which he was brought from the station crunched up the driveway at Denisthorn three weeks before Christmas.

His pending arrival and accommodation was treated with great bewilderment by Lady Croukerne who, although she agreed with Mrs Beste's solution, now had on her hands the tricky situation of two male visitors in the household, which set numbers awry.

'Who should I invite to stay for Christmas? We sorely require a lovely lady guest to make up the numbers.'

Ninian Crownrigg marked his place in the newspaper with a finger and looked up. 'We have two perfectly lovely daughters, Edwina my dear.'

'Ninian *my dear* ... we cannot be thought or seen to be keeping the gentlemen for our daughters!'

'Ah.'

'We had no idea, had we, at the time, that Cousin Angus was a widower! I thought he would be off, back to his family for Christmas. I thought he was a married man who left his family behind in Hawick for a brief time. But no – there is no family waiting against his return – so he will be with us indefinitely.'

'Indeed.'

'And now we have the artist Mr Rupert Bottomley, who arrives with a valet ... who by the way, also serves as his artistic assistant –'

'Well, we do not know what to make of that, do we?' The earl's voice was full of mirth.

'I'm serious, Ninian. Mr Bottomley might be a member of the Academy and a gentleman, but he is also single. A bachelor. I really think we need someone to fill out our dinner table. Balance, I have always thought, is an admirable concept, because even if we ask Captain Kirksduff from across the ...'

'Is he not back in Australia?'

'I do not know! What about equilibrium? We need to institute a kind of balance.'

'Admirable. I agree.'

Lady Croukerne inhaled deeply. 'Can we not take this a touch more seriously?'

'Lady Agatha Fiennes.'

His wife shook her head. 'Not after that fuss at our little hunt she made, about *preserving species*. She fancies herself as some kind of evangelic animal protector.'

'Hm – I can imagine how she would regale the gentlemen at dinner with arguments against shooting and fishing.'

'As she did one of the evenings over cards!'

'Lady Octavia, of course.

'Sir Michael is giving her a tour of the Low Countries. They are now in Belgium. She has written to Geraldine.'

'What about the eldest daughter of the Blockley's? Sir Adrian's daughter, Miss Blockley, whose name I can never remember?'

'Oh! They are only in Minsterworth!'

'Yes – infinitely convenient. Surely they would run their daughter out here, from their little estate – quite easily, if she received an invitation she could not possibly refuse, my dear.'

'I cannot remember her name either. Would she be old enough, do you think? Oh, she would make a great companion for Athena. Yes.' The countess became suddenly quite excited. 'Oh, she can have Byron. No one has stayed in that room for months upon months.'

The earl watched as his wife prepared to rise and make her way to her lovely little desk, where she would write the invitation.

'It would have to go in the mail, I suppose.'

'Yes.'

'If only I could recall her name.'

Her husband sighed patiently and his finger marked a place in his newspaper once more. 'Mrs Beste would have it down somewhere. I'm sure we had the entire family here at one time.'

He too thought balance would be redressed if a young lady were to swell their numbers in the house. When the artist arrived, he was surprised. Rupert Bottomley was a very handsome young man whose deportment and apparel announced him as a gentleman of some means, even at such an early age. Perhaps portrait painting was taking a popular bent and he was doing well. Better than one would think for an artist.

The man had sprung out of the carriage and stood in front of Denisthorn Hall, looking up at the façade, hat in hand and shading his eyes, and then turning to admire the mirror lake and surrounding bosky landscape.

'A very pretty wooded location, Lord Croukerne.'

'Yes. Sheltered, in a picturesque valley, and nicely designed, I have always felt.'

'Without any Georgian additions.'

His host laughed. 'Neither my grandfather, the third earl, nor my father were ones to remodel a façade or add a wing purely for aesthetic reasons. The place is large enough to accommodate a family and guests, and all the necessary servants, quite comfortably.'

'Excellent. It retains all its original beauty.'

'And costs a fortune to run and maintain. But thank you. I think you will find the interior just as pleasant and comfortable. We have found you a room, near the gallery up there ...' he pointed upward at the third storey. The early afternoon sun turned the stonework aloft into gold and he admired the sight. 'It has plenty of natural light and might serve well as a studio.'

'How kind.'

'After you are suitably refreshed, we should go up together. Perhaps you might like to meet the family first. There's tea in the drawing room.'

They entered the massive hall, where fires blazed in the matching hearths on either side. A central table held a bowl of cabbagey roses. Over their heads, the renowned chandelier tinkled slightly to the draught from the front door, which Herring closed behind them.

They all waited in the drawing room for the artist to return after Herring took him up to the south wing, where rooms had been prepared for him. His man disappeared downstairs, and would presently also go to the wing to unpack his master's big trunk.

The drawing room was warm and welcoming, and Ninian Crownrigg enjoyed the surprise on both his daughters' faces when Mr Bottomley entered the double doors. His handsome demeanour was not what they had thought an artist might present. Like their mother, perhaps, they were anticipating a boring afternoon with a stuffy old portraitist. In their minds, *eminent* meant *elderly*. Athena had looked his name up and found the word *eminent* in one of the descriptions of a portrait of two members of the House of Lords. Introductions and cordial conversation over tea were remarkably pleasant because of the surprise.

Lady Croukerne had expected awkwardness. They had never hosted an artist. She did not know whether to treat him like a gentleman guest, or a servant, or an artisan. A discussion with Mrs Beste gave her the solution. He was more on the level of a gentleman tutor, which they had accommodated, together with governesses of good social standing, in the past. Or perhaps at the level of a famous violinist, who had performed two soirees at Denisthorn. He had eaten his meals with the family, just as it was planned Mr Bottomley would.

'I was expecting someone like Mister Arthur Hamlin, who was a maestro of the piano, and who stayed with us for a few seasons to instruct the girls, Mr Bottomley. But I find you are much younger.' She regarded him with a tilted head. He was clean-shaven, suitably tall, and wore a muted tie and narrow shoes.

He bowed, smiled and pursued the conversation without a moment of awkwardness or reticence. This was a man used to moving among the nobility, addressing everyone correctly and oozing confidence and poise. Lady Croukerne glowed with approval and delight.

'I much admire the architecture of Denisthorn Hall, Lord Croukerne, and also how it sits in the landscape. It suggests genius, although it must have been built a long time after Inigo Jones.'

'Correct, but my grandfather reliably held that the architect of this place, and the landscape designer, endorsed the principles of Inigo Jones highly, and emulated them in this design. We had occasion only recently, at our daughter Athena's coming out, to see the great man's work at the palace of St James. You can see his influence in our mirror lake.'

'Indeed I have noted it. You must also tell me about your chandelier. Its reputation precedes it. I heard of your famous chandelier in London.'

'Well, it caused a stir in its day, when it was installed by my father, after his grand tour of Europe. Made of soda glass, it was handmade – mouth-blown, as a matter of fact – in Murano, Venice. It is an exact replica of the twin chandeliers hanging in the Ca' Rezzonico palace in Venice, took over a year to make, and weighs nearly a ton. There was another stir when it was converted to electricity, just over a year ago.'

'How interesting. Is that not ...'

'Frightfully risky – no. Costly? Yes – we have what is called a generator, and a man employed who understands such ... ah ... modern technology. It was not always reliable at first, unfortunately. But the bulbs I am told, are greatly improved now.'

'*Technology.*'

'Yes. That is the word for it. And we call the man our technician, or *electrician*! My father would have been delighted to see it in its splendour now. In his younger days, you understand – was quite particular, and wanted a pure glass chandelier of note. Two Venetian artisans came by train from Italy, to safeguard the individual pieces, which travelled in crates, within the same carriage with them. It was then assembled over a fortnight, piece by piece. Mr Bann, the butler of the time, was displeased about how long it took! I think I was told as a child I should remember it being hauled into place. But I am afraid I do not.'

'The stories that go with such pieces are sometimes as valuable as the artefacts themselves.'

Lady Croukerne smiled at the artist's gracious compliment. 'I agree. The chandelier that hung there previously came a long way too, chosen by a previous Lady Croukerne in Prague. Very tiny in comparison. It's a very beautiful seven-arm Bohemian glass chandelier, with hundreds of crystal drops and brilliant cup sconces. I must say I do admire it. That one too is now *electric,* and now hangs in the hall at Cheltenham House.'

'Many possessions and effects and *things* that rightly belong here are at Cheltenham House.' Lady Geraldine's arch remark went ignored by her mother.

Her father gave her a silent mystified look. His eyes then turned to look at his wife, who in turn watched Geraldine, who escaped rudeness by peering at the artist in intense bursts, falling just short of staring.

Rupert Bottomley's man was being introduced below stairs just as his master got to know the family up in the drawing room. Although both meetings happened over tea, the conversation, proceedings and topics were vastly different; as was the food consumed.

His name was Richard White, but according to the etiquette of the house, the valet was called 'Mister Bottomley', after his master. The custom came from having a mass of valets and ladies' maids to stay, and sorting out who looked after whom during big hunts and large house parties. Some said it avoided confusion, others swore it added to it.

'Since Mr Angus Crownrigg is travelling without a valet, you are the only visitor below stairs, at the moment, Mr Bottomley. You will be sharing with Thorn, his lordship's valet. Godwin has taken up your bag.' Herring indicated a chair, and sat in his place at the head of the long table in the servants' hall.

'Thank you.' He nodded when a kitchen girl poured him tea.

'So you must unpack that enormous trunk. It took three footmen to get it off the cart.'

'Yes. But it's awkward rather than unreasonably heavy. It contains two floor easels, a table easel, a collapsible mixing table,' he paused and looked at the ceiling. '... A number of oil cloths, a number of drop sheets, and several boxes of paints, knives, palettes, and brushes. Not to mention a drum of linseed oil and ah, a larger one of turpentine. Then there are several smocks and a number of aprons.'

'My goodness.'

'It is a very difficult, detailed and laborious art.'

'Many fear it might be overtaken by photography.'

'Never. When one has the use of colour, one wins over

photography. Oil paint and canvas will long outlive mere pieces of paper. And portraiture demands a very specific relationship, though perhaps not overly long, between the artist and the sitter. One must divine the character, through intimate but tactful conversations, and make it appear, like magic, in the finished picture.'

'You know a lot about it.'

'I am not only Mr Bottomley's valet. I serve also as his artistic assistant. I grind minerals, and mix paint, look after his expensive brushes, remember poses, and a number of other tasks.'

Mrs Beste came in to listen. She dropped silently into a chair.

The butler nodded at her in greeting.

The artist nodded too and continued. 'His lordship will have a number of decisions to make about the painting as well.'

Herring stroked his chin. 'Really! Decisions ... such as?'

'Oh – full length or half? Life-size or three-quarter scale? Daylight or lamplight? Indoors or out? Rectangle, square, or round? And there are many more questions, about the background, the palette, and what his lordship should wear, whether he should shave, which side to part his hair, and so forth.'

'It is much more complicated than we supposed. We just know it will probably match the other portraits in size and style.'

'Ah – other portraits. There is that aspect too. Many noble families commission portraits to ah, continue a line ... such as in this case. But when it comes to style, each artist has his own.'

'Or hers.'

The artist's valet smiled. '*Hers*. Hm ... I do not know of any travelling portrait artists who are women.' He looked querulously at the woman who asked.

'This is our housekeeper, Mrs Beste.' Mr Herring quickly jumped in with a belated introduction, trying to deflect an argument.

'... but the Royal Academy of Art has had many female exhibitors, such as Harriet Gouldsmith, who also exhibited at the Water Colour Society.'

Mr Herring needed to stop the man before he went on too long. 'We could sit here discussing art all evening, couldn't we, Mr Bottomley, Mrs Beste ...? But we all have work to do.'

There were cordial smiles all round.

Formby stood at the door, smoking and smirking. 'It is also highly unlikely that any of us down here would have our portrait painted.'

There was a meaningful silence, when Mrs Jones took a deep breath and tilted her birdlike head. 'There was a photograph taken a while ago of all of us, out on the steps of the garden entrance. We all remember that. I wonder what became of it.'

CHAPTER TWENTY-FOUR

In which Lady Geraldine discovers direction
and
Lady Athena fends off attention

There was outrage in Lady Geraldine's eyes, plainly visible to her mother and father. Despite the gelid silence in the room, there was a buzz of tension.

The young woman took up her cup and set it down again, having only worked the teaspoon back and forth twice. 'I cannot believe you did not notice Cosmo was limping!'

'You speak at last.'

A sharp glance from her daughter silenced Lady Croukerne. 'For all you say about loving animals, Mama, I see precious little to confirm the sentiment.'

'I shall not have you address your mother with such rudeness, Geraldine. And they are my dogs after all.'

She inclined her head towards her mother. 'I apologize, Mama.'

Lady Croukerne nodded in acknowledgement, but a look of unease still shielded her eyes.

'I apologize, and yes, they are your dogs, Papa, and you are very busy. Perhaps I should take over some of ... perhaps I could ... perhaps ...'

'Do you suggest you should take charge of the lurchers, Geraldine?' Lord Croukerne's astonished gaze was like a physical barrier between them.

'Only to keep an eye on Cosmo and Damian's welfare. And to take them off for a bit of a run sometimes.' She hung her head, took up her cup again and this time, sipped her tea. 'It's a small thing, and not something Athena would even think of. It would not occur to her. Not in a *month* of Sundays.'

Silence once more settled on the room.

'Papa ...'

'My dear, I am so taken up in my time these days.'

'It's that stupid portrait. Mama will agree with me that you spend an inordinate time up in that wing with Mr Bottomley, who really must be the slowest portraitist in the entire British Isles.'

Lady Croukerne responded mutely, turning her head towards one of the windows, and then to the small Christmas decoration on a corner table. The enormous Christmas tree in the hall had been lit with candles the previous night, but she did not feel at all in the spirit this year. She neither nodded nor spoke, but agreement was plain in her eyes.

'It will soon be finished.' Lord Croukerne stood and paced.

'Someone will be in to draw the curtains soon. Hadn't we better all dress for dinner? Where on earth is Athena? And where is Cousin Angus?'

Lady Geraldine gave a lopsided smile, which she guarded by looking down into her now empty cup.

But her father saw what it was she hinted at. 'Goodness, Geraldine.' He turned to his wife. 'Goodness, my dear.'

Lady Croukerne rose, just as a footman entered and made his way to the windows to draw their beautiful damask curtains. 'Nothing of the sort, Ninian. Let's not jump to needless conclusions. Athena is spending more and more time at her desk, writing thousands of words, and has little interest in our cousin from Hawick. As a matter of fact, she rather ...'

A rustle of skirts announced Geraldine's movement towards the door. 'You are right, Mama. We really should be dressing for dinner if we are not to miss the gong.' There was a small frown over the bridge of her long delicate nose.

*

At the dinner table, cordial conversation was started by Rupert Bottomley, who mentioned the Christmas tree and the little candles on it, which for safety's sake had to be extinguished each night and relit the following evening. 'I do believe this is the third or fourth Christmas tree I have ever seen.'

'We saw an engraving of the queen and the royal family gathered around the Christmas tree at Balmoral.'

'And it was a simple thing to ride out and choose a tree to be brought indoors, last year.'

'A simple thing!'

'And we did it again this year!' Athena nodded at her father's words. It was not clear from her expression whether she liked the seasonal decoration or not.

'It was I who rode out with Papa to choose it.' Geraldine made sure her part in it was not omitted.

'When Mrs Beste consulted me about Christmas this year, she did have ... she did ask ... we did decide to proceed as we did last year, despite ... despite ...' Lady Croukerne struggled to keep emotion from her voice.

'Frederic did rather like the excitement of having a large tree brought indoors for Christmas, didn't he?' Lord Croukerne noted how his wife and daughters averted their sad eyes. 'And expressly because of that, it was rather brilliantly thoughtful of you to continue in the same vein, my dear.'

'Yes, well ...'

'It is a beautiful tree, my lord,' the artist intervened. 'It fills your grand hall with a respectfully festive atmosphere which is at once elegant and restrained.'

All the ladies looked at him. He had managed to find exactly the right words. 'In two of the houses I have visited to paint portraits in, they had soirees of carol-singing under the tree. Most enjoyable.'

Geraldine's eyes widened. Her eyes had followed the artist all evening, and she hung on every word he spoke. 'Might we not have that too, Mama? After all, we do have a new grand piano.'

Lady Croukerne thought for a minute, put down her napkin and nodded slowly. 'If it is not too raucous an event, of course. If it is ahem ... restrained and elegant, as Mr Bottomley says the tree is, then we might have some singing. Of appropriate hymns and carols.'

'Do you sing, Cousin Angus?' Athena turned to her left, only to catch a sharp look from her sister. 'What is it, Geraldine?'

Geraldine paused, her pudding spoon poised between plate and mouth. 'I'm sure I do not know what you mean, sister dear.'

It was very plain to all at the table, however, that every time Athena addressed Angus Crownrigg, her sister's eyes blazed.

Lady Croukerne sensed something, but could not put a finger on the precise feeling that assailed her, especially not when it was the pudding course and the temptation of indulging in every last morsel, except perhaps the polite remnant of a smear of cream, took her. She addressed her gentlemen guests. 'Well, we can all look forward to the dowager marchioness from Cheltenham House here for dinner tomorrow. She has a visitor, and would like to introduce him to us all.'

So the subject was changed, but not before Angus Crownrigg could utter a soft response to his cousin. 'Yes, Cousin Athena, I do sing.'

Ninian Croukerne sat back from his pudding. 'And might I ask who that guest could be?'

'My dear, Neville Robarts is in Cheltenham for some reason or other ...'

'... concerning trains? Robarts? Wasn't his name Gerald or Jeremy or something like that? What is he doing, visiting my mother?'

'You must be thinking of his father, and the name was Jonathan, Sir Jonathan Robarts.'

'Ah – was he knighted, then?'

'It is *Sir* Neville, as well.'

A comment from across the table was just audible. Athena too put down her spoon. 'Everyone is getting knighted, aren't they? For simple things like laying railways, owning a newspaper, or setting up a chain of *shops*.'

'Oh, darling daughter – Mr Robarts did not lay a railway. He is an engineer with an enterprise of considerable size, which manufactures rolling stock. And it's hardly simple.'

'*Rolling stock?*'

'That is the name, I take it Athena, for train carriages and cars and such, which are drawn along by the steam locomotive. I think they might construct locomotives as well. As for knighthoods ... we live in interesting times. The entire country is opening up, thanks to these enterprising individuals and their firms, and it is now possible to reach places as far-flung as Edinburgh, as I recently found, with no difficulty whatsoever, in a mere matter of *hours*. They are rewarded for enterprise and service to the empire, not for family lines or nobility.'

'So what these men, these engineers do, is important?'

'Without a doubt, Edwina. Without a doubt.'

'So this Sir ... what did you say his name was?'

'Neville. Sir Neville, the son and heir of the Robarts enterprise, and fortune.'

'Can one use the word *heir* for such a situation, Papa?'

'One can, Geraldine.' He caught the spark of humour in her eyes. 'One can.' And he smiled behind his napkin at the differences between his daughters.

When the ladies rose to leave the gentlemen to their port, cigars, and brandy, Angus gave a shallow bow. 'Might we make up four for cards, Cousin Athena?'

Her skirts swished and her fist tightened around her fan. Bringing a fan to a dinner at home at Christmastime was perhaps a bit of an exaggerated addition, but Athena wanted to out-do her younger sister. 'I might go up early, Cousin Angus.'

Geraldine, who was decidedly easy to out-do in matters of dress, was socially more adept and far more eager to please. 'If Mr Bottomley will play, Cousin Angus, I'm sure Mama will enjoy a few rounds of napoleon.'

*

Formby dusted down his trouser fronts after rising from table in the servants' hall.

'Dying for a cigarette, are you, Formby?'

'More eager to get my fingers on the pianner keys, I am.'

'What – more eager than dallying around in the courtyard outside? I hear Elsie from Cheltenham House was here earlier. She might still be chattering with Alice and the others.'

'It's after dark, Glover. She'd be long gone down the road through the village. And Mrs Beste is willing to teach me, so I'm going to make the most of the next thirty minutes.' He glanced up at the clock on the mantelpiece, and sure enough, Mrs Beste was back after having risen from dinner. With a key from her belt, she unlocked the piano lid and rolled up the felt cover.

'After you, Mrs Beste.'

'Well, Formby – we should need another stool, and you had better sit here.' She indicated the seat, and smiled when Prudhomme brought another stool. 'There won't be much musicality tonight, I'm afraid, everyone. This young man must learn to flex those fingers.' She looked with raised eyebrows at Formby's hands, which had more blisters, bumps and scratches than she expected. 'For someone who does not have to do yard work any longer, young man, you have workman's hands.'

'I still help to split firewood, Mrs Beste. I still roll carpets. And I'm running enough buckets up and down to the rooms near the gallery to sink an ocean liner.'

'With gentlemen guests there, and no plumbed bathroom on that landing, yes – I grant you there's a lot to be done at the moment.' Her eyes smiled. 'Are you sure you have time for this?'

'You said thirty minutes, mam. I have thirty minutes, and then I'll do t'boots'n'shoes.'

Despite the lack of what the housekeeper termed musicality, many of the staff stood around listening. Music was so rarely heard below stairs, and was such a novelty still, that they simply loved the sound.

'You'll be playing *Fountain in the Park* before long, you will, young fellow.' Mrs Beste was surprised at the footman's ability to put what she showed him to memory. 'You have a good head for chords, Formby.'

'It's just A-B-C, like you said, Mrs Beste.'

'I suppose it is.'

He flexed fingers and held them level with his eyes when they finished. 'Music hall, Mrs Beste. That's me ambition.'

'You've a long way to go yet, son.' Her words were whispered, but there was no doubt in her tone. 'And you might want to choose something a bit less inelegant and raucous than music halls.' Her eyelids drooped in a discreet way.

'What are you saying, Mrs Beste?'

'Only what I've heard. I've not set foot in such a place, but their reputation is – you might say – wild, noisy, full of smoke, and intemperance. Music halls are not genteel places. There is free mixing of the sexes ...'

'They are diverting places! Fun places! And a great deal of money changes hands.'

The housekeeper's lips formed a thin straight line. 'I do not doubt that for a minute.'

'And I can become a –'

'Learn how to play first, Peter. *Then* make your plans.'

His voice went down an octave with disappointment. '– a professional entertainer.'

They heard a high laugh from the kitchen door. 'Hah ha! There's a name for it? Getting fiddler's pay for being a brother of the string?'

'What does that mean, Mrs Jones?' Formby was offended, but he raised his chin a touch.

'Fiddler's pay means getting paid in gin, or ale. And brother of the string means ... come on, son – that means musician, surely you know that.'

'But no fiddles for me. I'll play the pianner.'

The housekeeper turned as she left the room. 'I can just imagine glasses of drink lined up on top. It's a string instrument too, Formby.'

'No it ain't. Pianner? String? What strings?'

'Yes, as a matter of fact it is.' And that was Mrs Beste's last word.

CHAPTER TWENTY-FIVE

*In which Ninian, Lord Croukerne's, life changes forever
and
There is an unexpected turn of events*

The silence in the garden entrance, a lofty, light-filled space where two lurchers circled and circled, their paw nails making clicking sounds on the black-and-white tiled marble floor, was quite complete, except for the retreating sound of hooves in the distance.

'Geraldine, you cannot be serious.'

It was unusual for both her mother and father to occupy that space at once. It was not like the hall, or the gallery, or the drawing room. No one met there to talk. It was a space where people and servants came and went, almost always in a hurry, from one location in the house to another, or from the hall to the garden, or from one demanding task to some arduous duty, if it was a footman or a maid. It was nevertheless a beautiful part of the house, where the single fireplace at one end competed with the draught from opening and closing doors. It was furnished sparsely with a long mahogany table and a few chairs, three dark upholstered benches and two long rows of hooks for capes and coats, umbrellas, and other outdoor coverings. Even now, Geraldine's whip and gloves lay on a chair, and her riding hat and veil on the table.

'Might we not speak about this in my sitting room, my dear girl?' Lady Croukerne did not know whether to smile widely, break into tears, sigh, laugh, or fall in a faint from the unexpected news.

'Geraldine, how could you have allowed such a thing

to happen? Really, my girl. Really!' Lord Croukerne turned, as if to depart in a sudden flurry of temper. But he stayed, took a deep breath and took his hands – which were until that moment clasped behind his back – apart, and clapped them together smartly but silently. 'Geraldine. I'll start again. I apologize. Fathers wait decades for this moment, and hardly recognize it when it arrives.'

'Oh, Papa!'

'Are you happy, my darling girl?'

'I do not know, Papa.'

Her mother placed a hand on top of the head of one of the dogs. 'Sit, Cosmo!'

The lurcher ignored her.

'*Sit, Cosmo.*' Lord Croukerne was obeyed. The other dog circled and circled. 'We should repair forthwith to your mother's sitting room, and discuss this in peace and quiet.' He looked at his wife. 'What do you say, my dear Edwina?'

'I am dumbfounded. I am struck dumb. I am tongue-tied.' But she smiled.

'Stay!' Ninian held up a finger and both dogs held back.

Father, mother and daughter walked across, through the large double doors, underneath the gallery, and out onto the superb Turkey carpets, where pine needles had already fallen from the Christmas tree. They did not stop to admire it.

Ninian Crownrigg stopped to allow his wife and daughter through the door of the library, and then through to the small sitting room.

His wife made straight for the bell. 'I could not possibly do this without sustenance of some sort.'

Glover appeared at the door.

'Tea, Glover. Please. It's rather urgent. And something small to go with it.'

'Your ladyship.' The under butler bowed and left the room backwards, pulling the doors to behind him.

'Let's sit and ...'

'Take a deep breath, Edwina. It's not the end of the world.'

'I don't know what it is. No doubt Geraldine feels it's the beginning of hers. Geraldine?' Lady Croukerne could hardly admit surprise when she had watched Geraldine almost stare at Rupert Bottomley every time he was in the same room with her.

'How *did* this happen, Geraldine?'

'Oh, Papa. I don't honestly know.'

'And did you give a response?'

She frowned at the thought he would think her so impolite. 'Well, of course I did!'

'*What did you say?*' Mother and father uttered the words together in almost exactly the same intonation.

Geraldine turned and turned again, moving to a settee and perching lightly on its tight rounded damask seat. 'We were preparing to go riding. The groom, Jenkins, was at the door. And Cousin Angus was pulling on his gloves and talking about Lady Octavia, of all people.'

'*Cousin Angus!*' The parents exclaimed together once more.

Geraldine almost rose, but she exhaled fitfully and sat back, looking exhausted. 'Who did you think asked me to marry him then, *Rupert Bottomley?*'

Mother and father looked at each other and nodded.

'Yes, darling girl. I think we both thought that.'

Geraldine held a hand to her mouth and tittered almost as she had as a child. 'An artist?'

'A gentleman artist, of considerable means.'

Lady Croukerne took her fifth deep breath inside a minute. 'What did you *say*?'

The doors opened and Glover came in pushing a tea trolley.

'Thank you, Glover. We'll do it.'

They waited. In the silence that followed, interrupted

by the slow sough of air as the under butler closed the doors again, they listened to a sudden downpour of rain beyond the dull grey windowpanes.

Edwina poured herself a cup of tea, leaving her daughter to serve Ninian.

'I agreed that he should talk to you, Papa.'

'What did you think, my darling girl? I suppose it was the best way to turn. Were you expecting such a proposal? Did you give um ... did you give the man reason?'

'What has been going on? We had absolutely no idea.'

'Neither did I, Mama. I hardly ... I mean ... I hardly ... When he asked if he could talk to you, Papa, I saw exactly what he sought permission for.'

'I didn't think you liked him.'

'Well, I don't. I didn't. I don't *know*.' Geraldine opened hands, palms upward. 'I don't know. He did go around it in a strange way. But in hindsight, in a good way. Don't you think?' She frowned. 'Athena is going to be livid. Outraged. I haven't even come out. What does one do?'

'You are the younger sister. You are still so very young. Mind you, your mother was not much older. Times are changing. If one can get from London to Edinburgh in a few hours, is it so unreasonable to find marriage proposals do not occur to sisters in birth order?'

'What will Athena think?'

'About what?'

They all turned.

The older daughter stood in the doorway, dressed in pale pink, a new merino shawl draped about her shoulders.

An air of gelid expectation and trepidation fell on the room.

'What do I think about what?' She looked at the three faces in turn. 'Papa? Mama?' She went to the tea trolley and poured herself a cup, placing a thin slice of lemon on the surface. 'You tell me, Geraldine. Both our parents are tongue-tied. Has something happened?'

'Cousin Angus has asked me to marry him.'

Athena took a sip of tea. And then she laughed. 'What did you say?' She took another sip. 'Goodness, he's years older than you are.'

'Not too many. Five. Seven? Not more than seven, surely.'

'He's a widower.'

'Yes, Mama, he is. I don't know what to make of that.'

Geraldine's hand shook as she placed her cup back on the trolley. 'Are you not upset, Athena?'

'Upset? At this surprising turn of events? Hardly. Are you happy, Geraldine?'

'I don't know what to ...'

'... Think of it? It's the perfect solution for Denisthorn Hall.' She tilted her head at her father. 'Is that not so, Papa?'

'What a question. What a thought.'

Athena insisted. 'Is that not so?' The look of relief on her face started to put a bloom on her cheeks. 'Geraldine can marry Cousin Angus, Denisthorn will be hers, and we'll all live happily ever after. After you die, that is, Papa.'

'Oh!'

'How can you be so cool and callous, Athena?'

'In this instance, I think it's lack of competitive spirit, rather than callousness. No, no, think of it, Mama. Think of it. I'm being practical. Geraldine will be ... when the time comes, I grant you ... the new Lady Croukerne. Practical!'

'And reasonable. Yes, darling Athena. You must be right.' Lord Croukerne looked at his younger daughter. 'What would you like me to say when I am approached by Cousin Angus, Geraldine?'

'Will this mean I can spend my life at Denisthorn, and never have to move away to Cheltenham House?'

No one answered the young woman. A rumble of thunder was heard, which preceded another loud shower. Rain, falling diagonally, could be seen through the window.

'Aren't you glad you weren't caught riding out in

that?'

Geraldine gave a small wry smile. 'It's scarcely a worse problem than the one that stopped me going out there. And I have no idea where Cousin Angus disappeared to.'

Athena looked at her mother.

Lady Croukerne nodded. 'Yes, Athena. Do not look so stunned. Apparently it's just happened. Cousin Angus was pulling on his gloves in the garden entrance.'

'In the garden entrance. Do not try to persuade me that is not the most romantic proposal of the year.' She looked at her father, who glared at her.

'Athena!' Lady Croukerne's face was a picture.

'Oh, Mama, allow me a tiny juncture of humour, at this momentous time. Geraldine understands.' She looked at her sister. 'Don't you?'

Silence from the younger girl and the distraught look on her face brought Lord Croukerne to the rescue. 'Geraldine does not know what to think at this moment.'

Athena swept past, stood at the window, and then turned in. 'Geraldine is most fortunate. *Most* fortunate. And, if I think of it, so am I. Now I am free.'

Her parents exclaimed at once. *'Free?'*

The older girl held out a hand, and tugged a bit at the merino shawl. 'Well, I thought the responsibility for Denisthorn, because I am older, fell to me. I would worry and worry about the future, not knowing what it would bring for us all, but especially Mama. Not knowing whether I would find a suitable match. Not knowing whether you all *expected* me to fall in love with Cousin Angus.' She adjusted the shawl again.

Whether they were struck with her unwonted wordiness or with the meaningfulness of her words was not clear. No one said a word.

'Because that would have solved all dilemmas, would it not?' she went on. 'I thought I was trapped, between wanting to be dutiful, and wanting ... Now I can sleep well, in the comfort that it has less to do with me than before.' There seemed to be something else, but she stopped, and shot an inquiring glance at her sister. 'Geraldine?'

'I don't know, Athena. I don't know if I am happy. I was so mortified and scared you would be upset.'

Athena gave a small laugh. 'I am relieved. And I wish you well. I ...' At last, she seemed lost for words, as was her wont. 'I ... Cousin Angus ... This ... this is not a small enterprise, Denisthorn is hard to run, Papa never misses an opportunity to state the obvious, so I hope our cousin from Scotland knows that.'

Her father grimaced. 'Perhaps you think, Athena ...'

'I do not only think, Papa. I *see*. And Cousin Angus seems to consider, looking at this turnaround, that he needs help from someone who understands the estate. And goodness knows Geraldine knows this place like the back of her hand ... learned from the back of a horse, what's more. He would not have found that in me.'

'But we never thought ...'

'Of course you *did* think it would be propitious if Cousin Angus and I liked each other, Mama! We have been thrown together often enough for me to see that very clearly. Only it turned out ... not to be an issue.' Athena laughed again.

'All this maturity and insight, my darling girl.'

'Did you not expect that either, Papa?'

'At last ...'

'My true colours? Yes, well – a tiny bit of sarcasm never goes amiss *en famille*, is what I've always thought.' With those words, Athena swept out of the room, trailing the shawl, which had come loose again, behind her like a train.

She left behind an astounded family.

*

Mr Herring folded a sheet of paper, straightened the items on his desk, and joined fingers in a pinnacle. He breathed through them, blew and blew again, softly and pensively, then seemed to make a decision and rose. Adjusting the angle of a pen, and touching the sheet of paper on which he had been making a rough list when he was interrupted, he made to leave the room. But questions buzzed in his head. And possible answers. And problems to solve. And the choice of a handful of solutions.

He put his head out of his office door and looked upon a spotless passage floor, a spotless wainscot, and a clear space, just as he liked it, at the bottom of the stairs. Not a soul in sight. Not a voice to be heard. In the distance, somewhere above his head and to the right, the hushed swish of rain and rumble of thunder made him grateful he stood where he did.

'Denisthorn is a haven,' he mumbled to himself. 'I hope it is a haven with well-tended fires and occupants who are warm enough. Where the devil are those footmen?'

It was not his habit to invoke the devil, but the conversation he had not five minutes before had rattled him. The surprise was great enough for the butler to utter the monosyllable he always exhorted his staff never to say on its own. *What?*

'*What?*'

'Begging your pardon, Mr Herring.'

The butler looked at the visiting valet and shook his head. 'Mr Bottomley, are you absolutely sure? We do not look favourably upon gossip here at Denisthorn Hall.'

'It is not gossip, Mr Herring. I have it from the source itself that Mr Crownrigg ...'

'... who will one day inherit the title and estate ...'

'The very same. The other gentleman guest.'

'Go on. I must hear it again if I'm to believe a word of it.'

The artist's valet nodded. 'Mr Crownrigg and my master spoke at length upstairs in the atelier, where the portrait of his lordship is all but complete.'

'What – Lord Croukerne's picture finished in such a short time? I was told it would take weeks.'

'His lordship is a good patient sitter, who has generously made himself available, and with very amenable features.'

'Are you saying the master of Denisthorn has a simple face? Plain features which are easy to copy?'

The valet laughed. 'Nothing of the sort. And portraiture is not *copying*. But I think Mr Bottomley found him a good subject to paint, that is all. I think he enjoyed it more than some other portraits, and he worked on it long and hard.'

'Perhaps. Yes. Of course. Naturally. Now – speak of that conversation, the one you think so expedient as to bring its import to me. I should not, should not, I say, suffer gossip.' The butler poised his fingers in a triangle.

'My master conversed in depth and personally with Mr Angus Crownrigg, late of Hawick, where apparently, he had no consolation but his work at the bank, and where he was lonely and bereft in his widowhood.'

'Yes. So far none of this is new to us.'

'Like I said – they spoke of a proposal. He um, put the question, let us say, to Lady Geraldine, and she advised him that he may speak to her father.'

'A proposal. To Lady Geraldine! How on earth is Lady Athena going to feel?'

'That, sir, I do not know.'

The old experienced butler set his hands flat on the desk, looking as though he was making a decision. 'No, no, no – this is not right.'

'Not right, Mr Herring?'

'Every time someone mentions Lady Geraldine, we are inclined to think of, or mention, or praise, or feel sorry for her sister Lady Athena. It's as if neither of them can exist without the other.' He drummed the fingers of one hand. And then drummed the others. 'Or rather, it's Lady Geraldine who always plays second fiddle.'

'She is the second daughter.'

'Well – it might seem an obvious thing to sticklers to convention and custom. But I was a second son, Bottomley, and I never liked being treated as an afterthought, or having my big brother mentioned every time I made a decision or bought a cloth cap or joined a club!' His eyes bulged on the thin face.

The visitor sat there, immobile and silent.

Herring went on. 'It's time we gave Lady Geraldine her due.'

'Has she come out yet?'

'It's not important!'

'Not important? Whole households revolve around the coming out and presentation of their daughters.'

'What is it, really? A rite of passage. It is merely a date. One day! The wearing of a white dress and a kiss from the queen. It does nothing, says nothing, about their abilities, their character, their nature and skills.' The butler took a breath. He had more to say. 'This year in April, young man, there was a royal wedding. Does no one remember? Princess Victoria, our monarch's granddaughter, was married.'

'Yes, I know that.'

'To her first cousin – also a grandchild of the queen, which you will grant was a momentous event. And yet some titled ladies still find *their* presentation at court, something that happens as a matter of course every year, as a more important event! I find it astonishing.'

'But Mr Herring ...'

'Our Lady Geraldine is a young woman of talent and intelligence, and understands the importance – or lack of it – of a coming-out. She has skills and assets that outshine mere social standing. For one thing, she can out-ride and out-manoeuvre anyone you care to mention. Except perhaps her father. She knows the layout of the estate far better than anyone. A single day in an impressive dress and three feathers in her hair will not change her. Or make her less, or more, accomplished.'

'Out-ride, you say!'

'She is a very capable horsewoman. From the terrace of the garden entrance, it is possible to see her take the hill, at a fair clip, up the profile of the ridge to the woods.' His hands now waved in the air. 'No one can catch her. No one would *dare*.'

'You observe your ... you have stopped to watch her, Mr Herring.'

'We servants here at Denisthorn love our family, Mr Bottomley. I'm sure you have had opportunity in your work to have seen this strange phenomenon before.'

The visiting valet stood. 'Not like here, Mr Herring. Not like here. Denisthorn is a very unusual household.' He stood.

'That it is cleaner and more ordered than any other ... of that I am quite certain.'

Richard White, valet to Mr Bottomley, could not disagree. He nodded in silence.

'Well, we shall deal with the news when it is made known. If there is an engagement in the air, there will be a dinner,' the butler continued. 'And possibly also a soiree of some sort. And visitors from Edinburgh, of course. It might be a very happy Christmas indeed.' The stamp of anticipation was plain on his face. It took years off him, brightening his eyes and lifting the creases on either side of his mouth.

'No doubt we shall meet at dinner, Mr Herring.'

'Yes, yes. And mind that nothing gets out to anyone else.'

'Not a word.'

Minutes after the valet left, Mr Herring stood in the passage, looking at but not seeing the space below the stairs. It was filled soon enough by two chattering housemaids, one carrying what looked like a petticoat, and the other a coal scuttle. They scurried off in different directions when they saw the butler, who seemed in a brown study; fingering chin in deep thought, pacing slowly and deliberately.

If Lady Geraldine were indeed to marry the heir to Denisthorn, Mr Angus Crownrigg, the future that extended out ahead of them all at the house would not seem so mysterious or so bleak after all.

Fast footsteps thundered and clattered down the stairs.

'Who's that? Please do not rattle and bump down the stairs! Think of others. What could possibly force you into a run, for heavens' sake?'

'Mr Herring, Mr Herring! Come quickly.'

'Formby, please slow down. You're losing control, young man.'

'The master, sir. His lordship, sir.'

'Now you are babbling. His lordship is out riding in the company of one of the gentlemen visitors, I think. Stop! Slow *down*, Formby!'

The footman gasped and spluttered. 'Yes, exactly. Exactly. He ... they ...'

'And they should soon be returned to the stables, for it is coming down cats and dogs outside. Thunder, even. And lightening.'

'He ... they ... the storm ...'

The butler slapped his sides in exasperation. 'What has happened, Formby? Take a breath, man.'

'There's been an incident, Mr Herring. You must come quickly.'

The butler stiffened.

'There's been an accident. It's his lordship, sir. His

lordship has been thrown from his horse.'

The area at the foot of the stairs was suddenly peopled by a dozen servants, all talking and gesticulating at once. They were dispersed just as swiftly by Mrs Beste, who arrived on the scene breathless.

'We are needed upstairs, Mr Herring.'

'Is his lordship injured, Mrs Beste?'

They climbed the stairs together.

'No one knows. They have sent out the head groom and two stableboys with the wagon. Or the cart. I don't know. It's very stormy out there.' Her face was pleated into lines of concern.

Out in the deserted hall, the fires blazed and the Christmas tree glimmered, deserted and cold.

'I think we should expect an arrival at the garden entrance.'

'Well, I hope the fire there has been tended. This one needs attention.'

'We shall see, Mrs Beste. Come on.'

They strode together across the hall through the arched doorway, under the gallery and into the garden entrance.

They were coming up the external stairs. Doctor Gable was surprisingly already there. Men from the stables brought Ninian Crownrigg up on what looked like a wooden door, a plank, a straight and rigid article that held the unconscious master horizontal and still.

'Good heavens!'

'Clear a space, please give us room. His lordship is unconscious. I need to tend to him immediately.'

'Here? Surely we ...'

The doctor was abrupt and almost rude with concern. 'Here, Mr Herring. *Here.*' He directed the men to set the plank on two chairs. In an instant a kind of makeshift bed was made out of the makeshift stretcher. 'Whatever you do, please keep the family and the female servants out of this space. Keep everyone away, do you hear? And send for the surgeon from Cheltenham. Now! Now!'

'The surgeon!'

'Don't question everything I say. Now!'

'Yes. Yes, Dr Gable.'

An ashen and dishevelled Rupert Bottomley hung behind all the men, sodden from the rain, arms crossed high against his chest, as if to defend himself from something. He did not know what to do, or to whom to address himself, but he was hesitant, and did not want to retrace steps back out onto the rear forecourt and the inclement weather. Mrs Beste approached him, and he took a small step forward.

'It was so rapid. So sudden. I really do not know what hit him.'

'Come and take a seat, sir. They will bring towels. Someone might see to you when his lordship's urgency lessens.' She did not sound either reassuring or certain it would happen.

'Look, look, he still does not stir.'

'What happened?' She helped him to one of the long benches, took his hat and whip, his cape and gloves, and hung what she could of the drenched items on hooks. 'What happened?

'I think it was a branch. Yes, the branch of a tree. A sizeable limb. It came crashing down on both of us, but it got his lordship across the shoulders, on the head I think. On the head!'

'Mr Bottomley. You're home and safe now.'

'We thought we caught a break in the weather, see? We thought we could outride the approaching storm. His lordship thought ... we thought it would be exhilarating.' His own face was scratched, and there was a small gash on his chin which had already clotted and stopped bleeding. He had not had the presence of mind to try to stop it, and blood had dribbled down his neck to stain his stiff collar.

'Your chin has stopped bleeding.'

'My chin!' He raised fingers to explore his face and neck.

Footmen bearing towels, hot and cold water in basins and buckets, and all manner of restorative items appeared, and Mrs Beste signalled with a hand held high. 'Here, Glover.' She left the under butler to look after their guest, and went to stand as close as she could to the small crowd that worked around Lord Croukerne. They were joined just at that instant by Thorn, the earl's valet.

The doctor had placed an ear to the chest, and then a listening horn, and had turned his lordship onto his side. 'He is breathing. He's taking shallow breaths. His heart still beats. Beats regularly. Regularly, but slowly.' The words were intended to reassure himself, more than those who stood around him.

'Thorn – stand here, just behind his lordship. Make sure he does not move or roll backwards.'

'Of course, Doctor.'

Mrs Beste looked toward the doors, and knew Lady Croukerne and her daughters must be out there, distraught and panicked. She made her way to the edge of the small crowd, opened one side of the double doors and slipped through. And there they were, the three of them, in the company of a young woman in travelling clothes, who had apparently just arrived and was greeted by no one except the family. They were all silent and pale in the face.

'His lordship seems to be um ... breathing well, my lady.'

'Oh Mrs Beste. Thank goodness you were there to see. How is he?'

What could she tell them?

'My lady ... he ... they ... he ... his lordship is lying on his side. Quite comfortable. Thorn is there. Doctor Gable is busy ... um ... examining his lordship. He should be ready to tell us something, as soon as he knows it himself.' She said the weak words of comfort automatically, as if she had learned them, set them to memory. 'Apparently the surgeon has been sent for. His lordship will be given ... um ... the best of care.' How did she know? She knew nothing. But it was as necessary to comfort the ladies of the house as it was to restore his lordship.

'Do you know what happened, Mrs Beste? Why is it that we cannot go through?'

'Doctor Gable requires as much room and quiet as he can get. Mr Bottomley said the storm was terrible. They could not see for the driving rain. And a tree ... part of a tree crashed down upon them as they were riding.'

Lady Athena was heard to utter a cry. 'Oh, poor Papa.'

'Is Mr Bottomley injured? Is his lordship injured?'

'I could not see to tell, my lady. Mr Bottomley is conscious and sitting down. His lordship is lying down in the care of Dr Gable.'

Lady Croukerne dabbed a handkerchief to her eyes. 'Lying down! Prone or supine?'

Mrs Beste was taken aback. She did just say he was lying on his side. 'I do not know, my lady.'

'Oh, I do so want to be close.'

'He is being seen to – Thorn is by his side. And Mr Bottomley has a few scratches to his face and chin. Glover is with him. Mr Herring is seeing to everything else. It's ... it's quite in hand, my lady.'

'What of the horses?' Lady Geraldine's skirts swished as she approached the closed doors. She stopped short of opening them, then turned and hurried out under the gallery and through the great hall.

'Where is she going?'

Mrs Beste guessed Lady Geraldine would head out the front of the house to make her way to the stables, where she would learn more of what happened from the stable boys, and see what had happened to the mounts the men had taken out onto the hill that stormy day.

Lady Athena and her mother sat to one side and

waited, in the company of Miss Blockley, newly arrived from Minsterworth and still in hat and travelling cape.

'I am so very sorry ...'

'Miss Blockley is quite shocked, Mrs Beste. We have not received her properly.'

The young woman shook her head. 'It is of no great concern. There is a household crisis.' She started to shrug out of her outer garment. 'How I was received is of no great importance in the circumstances.'

Mrs Beste took her cape. 'I shall get one of the girls ... have your bags ...? *Oh dear!*' Mrs Beste was troubled, but it was not the end of the world, and she had to keep her wits about her. With Miss Blockley's cape over one arm, she hurried towards the back of the house to the baize door, and in a flash two maids were summoned to take over. One of them showed Miss Blockley to her room upstairs, where her bags had still not been carried up, and set about helping her charge get settled. The other was sent to the kitchen to arrange preparation of something restorative and have it brought up.

*

Not all household servants were in the garden entrance seeing to Lord Croukerne. A few, mostly female, still ran things under the emergency leadership of Cook, Mrs Jones, who directed operations standing at the kitchen threshold, from where she eventually moved to her small wall-mounted kitchen desk, which had been temporarily cleared of cookery books. 'Relieving Mrs Beste during a crisis is my responsibility,' she told herself.

Her cool steady head and thin capable hands were called into action for a couple of heart-stopping instances, and she was equal to the task. Denisthorn Hall rose to the occasion, and it was a matter of an hour, or perhaps ninety minutes, before sanity and order were restored. Mrs Beste and Prudhomme looked after the ladies, including the new guest, who had arrived without a lady's maid.

'Fairley is going to have to manage.'

'I know she will.'

'His lordship is now settled in his own bed.'

'What – in his dressing room?' Prudhomme looked at the housekeeper, wondering about the sanity or otherwise of the arrangements. 'Surely Thorn let them know it is far too narrow in there.'

'If they think the dressing room is the best place, then so be it.'

'No, Mrs Beste. Thorn and Mr Bottomley's man have installed him in the blue suite.'

'Not in Byron. Miss Blockley is in Byron.'

'No – Wordsworth.'

'Ah. So her ladyship ...'

'... will not be disturbed, and everything will proceed much the same as usual.'

'Our new lady guest ...'

Mrs Beste bridled and set about restoring her position as head of the female household staff. 'Is in Byron. Do not make me repeat myself, please. She has a name, Prudhomme, she is Miss Blockley, and hopefully she will not prove to be too much work for Fairley or you.'

'Indeed not. Fairley has helped her settle.' Prudhomme perched for a minute on a fireside chair in the servants' hall. Her feet ached and she showed signs of tiredness. 'She apparently does her own hair, and is even capable of choosing her own gowns and matching her jewellery, such as it might be.'

'Do I detect a note of disdain, even in this circumstance, Prudhomme?'

'Indeed not, Mrs Beste. It is surprise. Plain surprise.'

'I see.'

'If today's ladies are not so helpless, and can do just

about anything for themselves, where does that leave the future of ladies' maids? Will we be done out of our employment ... women like Fairley, who is new as a lady's maid, and myself? I have been one for years. I often wonder what is happening to the world.'

'Well, the world of service is changing, I grant you that.'

'We stagger from thinking we should never cope if every daughter of every successful newly-knighted businessman is to be a *lady* ... ladies without titles, through whose hair we must trail brushes and combs ... to wondering if work will dry up if and when all ladies learn to manage themselves in all respects.'

'Aspects, aspects. Respects, respects.'

'You seem to think it is droll.' Prudhomme folded her arms and sat back, easing her legs.

'There is nothing funny to be found in it. Deeper thought would make us all run to the towns, wouldn't it now?'

'My cousins have *run for the towns*. There is much to be done in London, for example. From Cheltenham and Stroud to London, as fast as a train could take them. One works as a milliner, in a new hat factory, and two have found work making confectionary, in another establishment. So their letters tell us. Is it going to be nothing but factories, factories, factories now?'

'Who is buying all those hats and all those sweets?'

'Well, they themselves, I would imagine.' Prudhomme gave a wry laugh. 'My hat-making cousin can afford as many sweetmeats as she feels inclined to eat, and my sweet-boiling and chocolate-bar-forming cousins can wear a number of fetching hats each.'

'While we are content here with trimming the same old hats differently, using cheap ribbon, year after year.' Mrs Beste pulled herself up. 'No, no, what am I saying? It's my own frugality that makes me do that. I can easily have that lovely new blue hat I spied in Mrs Cartwel's village shopwindow last month. *Easily*, I do suppose.'

'See? We are all improving our stations. Where will it all end?' She lifted a hand to indicate the arrival of Formby, who had just trotted rapidly down the service stairs.

Mrs Beste turned. 'Formby! Slow down.'

'That's all I've heard today. *Slow down, Formby*. There's a lot of comin' and goin' People to be met, things to carry. Furniture to move. I've helped Godwin move two beds already.'

'Have Miss Blockley's bags reached Byron?'

'Fully an hour ago.'

'What's happening upstairs?'

'The surgeon is here. Mr Herring has just taken him up. His lordship is apparently awake now, but I do not know if he's speaking or anything like that.'

'Oh, thank goodness. What relief. Surely he will be as right as rain soon.'

'I'm sure.'

'Good.'

'Good? It was the devil moving the bed away from the window in the blue suite.'

CHAPTER TWENTY-SIX

In which Christmas at Denisthorn is celebrated
and
a celebration of a different kind is in order

Lady Geraldine emerged from the stables, shoulders still drenched and rounded in anguish of a kind she never thought would assault her. This was almost as bad as Frederic's death. Different, but strangely similar. Different, and heart-breaking.

Someone's running footsteps rang out from the cobbles of the breezeway between stable ranks. 'My lady! Lady Geraldine.'

She was half-pulled, half-guided back under cover, firmly but gently. 'Oh, Mark, it's you.'

Mary Mark hastily and clumsily pulled a stable cape over Geraldine's shoulders. 'You cannot go back out in that, my lady. You will be blown clean away. In a little while, when it relents, Tom and I will walk you back to the house, with a stout umbrella.'

Geraldine's only response was a sob.

'His lordship will be better soon, I am sure.'

'What have you heard, Mark? Come on, Mary – tell me what you know.' Her shoulders rounded and she allowed the girl to embrace her. Tears flowed down her cheeks.

'You will make yourself sick, my lady. Do not weep so. His lordship will improve.'

'I am sure of that. But *Buttercup!*'

Mary Mark pulled Geraldine closer. 'It was unfortunate that his lordship chose Buttercup today, my lady.'

'Both her hind legs!'

'She could not take the ordeal, my lady.' The stable girl lowered her own head. Whether it was one hind leg or both, the mare was irretrievably injured and had to be shot by her father, the head groom, who had returned to the stables sullen and silent, long wet hair blown about by the four winds, shotgun broken over one arm and brown cape darkened by the bad weather. When the storm abated, the men would be sent out to deal with the carcase. The details of course, were kept from Geraldine, who knew only that her favourite mount was no more. And that her father was upstairs at the house, surrounded by doctors and a surgeon.

'Do I only ever come to the stables to cry?' Shades of the days when Frederic had sickened and died were still fresh in both their minds.

'You have had many many happy days here, my lady.'

'Yes.' She nodded and cried more. 'We have ridden out so happily. Oh, Mark. Oh *Buttercup*.'

'Everything will be fine by Christmas, my lady.'

Geraldine raised her head. 'How could it? Christmas is in little more than a week. I am utterly distraught and wretched. I have a decision to make – one that no one can help me unravel. And now I have lost Buttercup.'

Mary Mark did not know what to say.

'It is the most confusing week of my life, Mary. You must help me through it. You must.'

How could she do that? In her breeches and red scarf, in her tenuous position as a stable 'boy', Mary Mark was possibly more confused than her mistress. 'I shall.' There was determination she felt was utterly false in her voice, and yet she fully intended to do what she could. 'Another mount will be found. There is a new foal up at Gallantrae, I am told. Perhaps ... You must come down to the stables at every possible interval, my lady.'

'I wish I could bunk down here with you.'

Astonishment assaulted them both: the girl who made

the statement, and the one who listened. It was as unlikely as anything. It would never happen, of course, but the saying of it was a memory created that could never be unmade.

*

Lord Croukerne spent Christmas Day sitting up in a Bath chair, which someone had found for him in Cheltenham. The surgeon had approved his transfer from bed to bedroom fauteuil to wheeled chair only hesitantly, and only reluctantly, but the earl insisted on joining the family.

The chair was an old three-wheeled contraption whose cane was under attack from woodworm. It wobbled and creaked, and could not be properly controlled, so a man had to be sent up from an estate cottage on the day before Christmas Eve, to help restore it to usefulness.

Godwin helped oil the wheels, and applied a generous coating of beeswax to the seat and arms, after which he polished hard, so that the chair looked serviceable, if not new or even comfortable.

'It would be better, and aid your convalescence, if you were to have bed rest for a full month ... or even two, my lord.' With an appealing look, Dr Gable sought concurrence from the surgeon, who would travel from Cheltenham every other day by brougham, to make sure his lordship was not worsening his injury.

The moustached man, grave and taciturn, did agree. He removed his monocle and replaced it. 'Your back must be ... one must think ...'

'I *am* thinking of my back! Indeed – it will not brook me ignoring it. It hurts like the devil, sir.' But he would not spend Christmas in bed.

Instead, Ninian Crownrigg, Lord Croukerne, fifth earl of Denisthorn, was placed in the Bath chair by Thorn, with help from a footman, each morning, and eternally bemoaned the fact it was dreadfully uncomfortable.

'Is there no handyman or furniture-maker in the village who can help? Or perhaps an upholsterer? What I need is support for my legs. I can neither feel my legs, nor control or move them. So ... can you see? Can you see what I mean? I need them supported somehow.'

'My lord.' The surgeon stepped forward. The expression on his face spoke louder than words. 'A temporary ...'

'I am not a fool, Doctor.' Lord Croukerne lowered his voice. 'I am far from stupid. I can feel where the pain ends and where *nothingness* starts. Do not tell me it will pass soon, and that there will be an end to this, for I know – and feel – otherwise.'

Both doctors tried to appease the patient.

'Otherwise. Do you hear? Otherwise. I do feel my legs will be useless forever.'

'It is Christmas Eve, and ...'

'I know what day it is. I *fully* understand why our Christmas Eve gathering had to be cancelled. I *fully* appreciate the household is tiptoeing around me and my lambent infirmity. I *fully* intend to be in the dining room tomorrow, with everyone else, to celebrate the day, and to congratulate my daughter on her engagement. Is anyone listening to me?'

'Of course we are, your lordship.'

'Certainly.'

'Yes.'

'Then send me Thorn, and Mr Herring. Yes, together, together. We must hatch a plan of some sort.'

'Not her ladyship, my lord?'

'Especially not her ladyship. We are expecting the dowager marchioness over from Cheltenham House from moment to moment. I want some peace before that ... before my mother descends upon us to repeat everything about my legs and back that I have been told a thousand times already!'

*

The gathering around the Christmas dinner table on the twenty-fourth of December 1894 was animated and some smiles, at least, were in evidence. But a new grumpiness had seized his lordship since the accident, which marked his forehead with ridges even deeper than those inflicted by the impossibility of running the Denisthorn estate on diminishing resources.

'Now, you see, incapacitated in this way,' he gave an almost-silent groan and gasp, 'I cannot ride around on a svelte mount, like a mad fellow shaking everyone up to fulfil whatever tasks they are supposed to do.'

On his left, Miss Blockley merely nodded, unwontedly at a loss for a relevant response. It was despite of her fine upbringing and coaching from her mother and a Swiss governess as to the importance of saying at least one appropriate sentence about topics addressed to her. What showed on her face was a realization of his pain.

To his right, when it was time to turn again, Ninian was faced by the stolid expression of his mother, who regarded him with lowered eyelids and a slight inebriation brought on by a too-attentive footman, a bit too loose with the sweet wine during the sorbet and dessert courses.

'What? Is there to be no pudding? I mean – plum pudding, drenched in brandy and set alight? Has Edwina not seen that things be done right?'

'Mater – Edwina and Mrs Beste sat over this menu for days on end. No one else was allowed in that sitting room for hours. I should know. I now need someone to wheel me around in this infernal thing. I cannot just storm in ...'

'You would never dare storm into a meeting of your wife's with her housekeeper, Ninian.' She was blunt and even-toned, the agreeable modulation in her voice negating the scolding. She shot a glance at the young lady on her son's left, and broke convention by asking her a question. 'Is it not a very curious fact, Miss Blockley, that there is no such thing as a single plum in plum pudding?'

It was the choice of ignoring the question and raising the ire of the dowager marchioness, or responding across the chest of her host. The guest chose the latter. 'I do suppose it is because the ancient name for raisins ... or any large dried grape really ... was *plum*. Which could have been an abbreviation for *plump raisin*.'

'Oh – you clever little thing.'

Miss Blockley was not little, either in age or dimension. Compared to the Croukerne daughters, she could be observed to be quite plump, herself much like a pudding raisin. But agreeable; she was gifted in diplomacy and tact. Lady Croukerne wondered why they had not thought to have her more often at Denisthorn, as a companion for Athena and Geraldine, as she was vastly more agreeable than Lady Octavia.

It was also noted, at this festive dinner, after which there was all expectation of toasts and speeches, that the young guest shot more than just half a dozen pointed glances at the artist, Mr Rupert Bottomley. The observation made Lord Croukerne edgy. 'Are you at all interested in art, Miss Blockley, might I ask?'

The young woman put down her fork and spoon, delicately picked up her napkin, and fluttered her eyelids at her host. 'A great deal interested. I have read all the Vasari, in the original Italian, and also some of Mr John Ruskin's works on modern painting.'

'Really! She is a pretty clever little thing, Ninian.'

'Mr Ruskin is a controversial figure, I am given to believe.' Lord Croukerne shifted shoulders uncomfortably, and uttered a small groan. Since he no longer had a son for whom to seek an appropriate wife, whether Miss Blockley was clever, or little, or pretty, was far from personally relevant.

'He has written a number of interesting works, and is an authority on art. He knows the continent backwards.'

'Well, he has spent enough time away from Britain, that is true. You must spend many a fascinating moment discussing the fine matters of art with Mr Rupert Bottomley.' Ninian indicated the other side of the table, where Mr Bottomley sat between Lady Geraldine and Lady Athena. On the other side of Athena sat Angus Crownrigg, who hardly cast his eyes on Geraldine all night.

'As a matter of fact I do.' There was no point in denying it, and it showed in her eyes, which were neither stolid nor empty, unlike those of the lady on the other side of the earl, which were showing the signs of venerable age, over-indulgence, and the lateness of the hour. 'But I am looking forward to speeches.' She was clever in nudging proceedings along, too.

The earl nodded at Herring, who in turn directed the footmen to change wines. From the double doors, Glover emerged holding – not quite aloft, so everyone could see the contents of the dish, and admire – a very large plum pudding, in all its flaming glory.

'This is the point at which, if I have everyone's attention, I might beg your permission to say a few words. You will all also forgive me for not rising to my feet.' Ninian paused. 'We celebrate the fact tomorrow is Christmas, and we humbly express gratitude for yet another year passing. It had its incidents, one of which especially was profoundly sad.'

There was a moment's silence as they all remembered young Frederic.

'Let us raise glasses to the memory of my absent son.'

During the pause that followed, all eyes lowered.

The earl continued, his voice bravely holding up. 'Now we must raise glasses and drink for a special reason. I have every happiness in announcing the engagement of our daughter Geraldine to Angus Crownrigg, our distant cousin from Haw ... from Edinburgh.'

Voices rumbled and expressions of congratulation crossed and recrossed the table.

'To the happy couple!'

'When can we expect a wedding?'

'Oh, may the new year bring you good things!'

'Dear Geraldine, congratulations.'

'Best wishes, Angus!'

'We discovered Cousin Angus only recently. We lost Frederic, and found an heir for the estate, and the happiness is redoubled by the fact that Geraldine will – many years ahead, of course – one day become mistress of Denisthorn.'

The old Lady Croukerne, at her son's elbow, gave something between a nod and a shake of the head. When conversation resumed, she hissed at him. 'She is only a child still, Ninian. Whatever are you thinking? What about Athena? And where are his people?'

'She will be eighteen in the new year, Mater. Edwina was only just twenty when Athena was born.'

'Tut, tut. I know. I was a few months short of twenty when you were born. But the queen is trying to knock sense into all of us. Look at her brood! She says she does not enjoy hearing of child-brides, or little girls in white dresses presented to her before they are eighteen.'

Lord Croukerne shifted slightly, wishing perhaps for his bed. But he met his mother's hooded eyes and had to agree with her. 'Still, Geraldine has a lot of sense. She is vastly more worldly and intelligent than Athena, who is more than a year older.'

'And practical, I am hopeful that she is practical, because she will have to involve herself far more than Edwina has ever been involved in the running of Denisthorn.'

'All that is still in the future. While I am alive and well

...' Ninian stopped. He regarded his hands, now knotted in his lap. His napkin lay in a creased muddle on the table. 'I do not know. I don't know at all. It's going to be incredibly difficult doing it from a wheelchair.'

'Is that what that contraption is called?'

'I have a man coming up from London in the new year. Apparently there are now some remarkable wheeled chairs on the market, in which one can propel oneself. A new invention.'

'If one can fly in the air supported by nothing but a huge balloon full of hot air, Ninian, I suppose it is possible to conceive of a chair one can move oneself. But how it is done I cannot for the life of me determine.'

From the other side of Lord Croukerne, Miss Blockley's voice was heard, clear and without hesitation. 'The new chairs have very large side wheels, much larger than yours, Lord Croukerne. They also have what one could call an extra rim, which one grips and pushes, with both hands, to turn the wheels. I think there are two rear wheels, rather than one, for stability. And they are upholstered much like an armchair, instead of that cane, which must be supplemented with cushions if one is going to be at all comfortable.'

'You seem to know a lot about wheelchairs, Miss Blockley.'

'I read a lot, that is all. It is a solitary state of affairs, being one of just two children. My brother has been away at school since he was nine, so I am for all intents and purposes an only child. One with her nose forever in a book.' There was a weight of regret and loneliness in her voice.

The marchioness's eyes widened. 'You are not short of a word, either. You make an eminent conversationalist, my dear.'

CHAPTER TWENTY-SEVEN

*In which Lord Croukerne comes to depend on others
and
Lady Geraldine cannot think of the future*

Rupert Bottomley stood, hat in hand, at the bottom of the grand staircase in the hall at Denisthorn. Above his head, the great chandelier he had admired on arrival weeks before tinkled in the draught from the front door, which stood open to brilliant sunshine from the most beautifully clement weather any January in anyone's memory had provided. It occurred to him that had it not been for the exorbitantly expensive luxury of electricity in this privileged household, lighting for the portrait he painted would have been a lot different. Light bulbs and lamps with magical 'switches' helped him work into the night quite often, and sped completion of the work considerably.

He heard the creaking of the wheeled chair, looked down, and turned. 'So your dog no longer limps, Lord Croukerne.'

'This is the other one. This is Damian. I do not know where Cosmo is. But no, he no longer limps, thanks to the intervention of my daughter Geraldine and the boys at the stables.'

Looking down to speak to the earl was slightly bothersome; it made the artist stoop despite his intentions. The master of Denisthorn sat in the tight cane Bath chair, looking very uncomfortable, and doubtless was in unbearable pain the entire time he was out of his bed.

'I enjoyed my stay here, my lord.'

'And I am delighted with the portrait.' He looked past the artist, who stood with his back to the stairs and the gallery, where the painting, framed to match the rest, now hung among the portraits of previous earls of the estate. 'I find it fits in very well with everything. And it serves as a subtle inclusion for descendants, without being too gaudy or exceptionally conspicuous.'

'I think I ...'

'You understood your brief, sir, and for that I thank you.' He gave a sharp nod of the head. 'Let me tell you what I enjoyed most.'

The artist was surprised. 'Yes, please do.'

'Briefly then. I do not want you to lose any of that lovely warmth and sunshine on the drive to the station.' He went on. 'I enjoyed coming up to the room you turned into a studio.'

'Into an atelier, yes.'

'And I was quite surprised to see how much equipment and supplies you need to paint a picture. You protected the floor and furniture from paint, similarly to when decorators paint walls! I admired your numerous smocks and aprons.'

'Very observant, my lord.'

'Well – there was a lot of sitting still, in the quiet. Part of the enjoyment was not being dragged unwillingly into conversation for the sake of politeness. I liked the quiet. I sat still, and you painted. I noted that your assistant very gently adjusted my hands or head, in order to achieve the same position. And you waited for the right light to fill the windows. I liked that. I liked it when you said *We might wait a couple of hours for the shadows to bend our way.*'

The artist laughed. 'Mostly they do.'

'It was an opportunity to escape everything that happens at Denisthorn, the long descriptions from my agent, the trouble with tenants, lame dogs, the problems with sheep diseases and broken fences. And yes, I appreciated not being accompanied by the family. It was private, quiet, and I shall not forget it. Every time I walk past my portrait, I shall look at it not in vanity, but in gratitude. Thank you.'

This was a temporary resumption of the earl's natural temperament, marred by moods brought on by the discomfort of his new predicament. He did not mention the word *commission*, neither that a huge payment had exchanged hands. To discuss money at that juncture would have been the height of tastelessness.

'As I say, my stay here was most enjoyable. I liked meeting your other guests, my lord, namely Miss Blockley, who has since returned to Minsterworth, I think, and Sir Neville, who was very interesting to talk to.'

'About trains and fishing, fishing and trains.' Ninian not only found Sir Neville slightly repetitive, but also very ugly. He could not understand how someone with such ordinary looks could start his own train-building dynasty and accumulate such extraordinary wealth. His clients could not look too closely at his bulbous nose or asymmetrical cheekbones. He did have piercing blue eyes, but they did little to offset the striking bad looks. He looked older than his years.

'I found him fascinating on trains. There is a lot I did not know about gauges, and carriage furnishing, and how the interior lamps are lit, for example.'

'Indeed.' Ninian was not about to be drawn into another boring conversation about something in which he had no interest at all.

'And I enjoyed cards with Lady Croukerne and Lady Geraldine, and also what little conversation I had with Lady Athena.' There – he had mentioned them all. 'Perhaps it would have been pleasant to have seen more of her ladyship the dowager marchioness.'

'Cheltenham House is not that far away, but she finds a lot to occupy her there. My daughter Athena is making herself scarce these days. She repairs to her desk to write, apparently.'

'Well – you never know. We might see a published work from her pen one day.'

'Hrumph.' The earl changed the subject. 'Most of all, I think you enjoyed conversing with Miss Blockley. I spotted you down by the back terrace a number of times.'

The artist looked slightly embarrassed. 'Ha ha, caught out!' He pretended it was a joke.

'No doubt there will be occasion to converse once more when the season comes round.'

'Please do not feel you must see me down to the carriage, Lord Croukerne.'

The earl raised a hand, and Godwin was promptly behind him, ready to push. Everyone was getting used to the chair. 'I shall stand – so to speak – at the top of the stairs. The family is already gathered down on the forecourt. You are getting the send-off of an old friend! Goodbye, and thank you once more.'

They shook hands.

Seeing the artist off gave the earl a sense of relief. The house was resuming its normal state after all the events of past months, and everyone was hoping for a quiet year. The last conversation with the artist gave Ninian occasion to think once more of Sir Neville, the train-building magnate, who had come and gone without making waves; without raising so much as an adverse comment from anyone, not even from his mother the marchioness, who usually was first to find fault with anyone's manner or behaviour or speech or deportment.

'We are reaching the age of equality, Damian.' He patted the dog's head, wondering where the other lurcher was. Delight in discovery that the dog's limp was only caused by an errant but unusually sharp burr was equal to the satisfaction he got from seeing Geraldine happy, caring for the dogs and spending a lot of time at the stables. 'Everyone is a gentleman now. Everyone has the opportunity to build wealth, easier than we ever thought it possible. If one does not read the newspapers, one would think it was a new world, where catastrophes are easily avoided and hard work *always* provides money. If only that were really the case.'

They all came up the outside stairs from the forecourt towards him. Lady Croukerne, arm in arm with Athena, and Geraldine, who had Cosmo on a lead.

Angus brought up the rear, walking slowly, hands clasped behind back. The man had a number of decisions to make, and it was plain they were giving him cause for unease.

'Perhaps we can have a good chat after dinner tonight, Cousin Angus.' The sunshine made the earl feel a touch of beneficence.

'Perhaps, perhaps.' He was not a man of many words. He walked on, following the others.

'The house is quieter now, Papa.' Geraldine stayed behind. She seemed happier in a riding habit of striped fabric, which gave her face a lighter tinge. Unlike Athena, who had a clearer complexion, Geraldine had looked dreary and ashen in mourning. Still, her eyes held a subtle disquiet her father noted, but was loathe to observe aloud. Was it her engagement? All young women, perhaps, had reason to fear a new liaison that presented intimacy and familiarity developed with someone outside the family. He had to urge Edwina to have a few conversations with young Geraldine. But what could a mother say, with propriety and tact, which would not entirely scare off a young bride? Ninian had no idea.

'Are you happy, my dear?'

'Not to see you still in that chair, no, Papa.'

'A man is coming up from London to bring me a new one. But I don't mean that, my dear.'

'Oh – it might make *you* happier. You have been decidedly uncomfortable now for too long. I have watched your moods change.'

'How does it feel to be engaged to be married? That is what I mean.'

His second daughter turned to Lord Croukerne and smiled. 'I shall get used to it. What I like most is being able to stay on at Denisthorn. I also like it that Athena does not mind that I accepted Angus.'

'She does not.'

'I love to be in a position where offering Mama a home, no matter how old she gets, is not out of the question. You know I have always hated the thought she will get pensioned off to Cheltenham House. That is possibly the best of all.' She gazed upward to where her father's new portrait hung. 'But it won't happen for a long time. You will live forever, Papa!'

'Ha ha.' He did not want to be in that much pain forever, but Lord Croukerne did not want to worry anyone with his physical discomfort. It was enough for him to take Dr Gable aside and ask for an increase in the dosage of whatever it was they put into his water at night.

Geraldine's eyes were turned away from him now, but he did wonder what exactly was in them, and why she looked perpetually under some sort of cloud. He would never understand women fully.

*

Prudhomme and Fairley sat across from each other at the long table in the servants' hall below stairs. Fairley sat by the enormous dresser, ranged with the crockery they ate on at the servants' table, all brown and white transferware that had stood on those dresser racks for decades.

Prudhomme sat nearer to the fireplace, whose mantelpiece was cluttered with a host of pipes and boxes of cigarettes, and tumblers of spills and matches. At the far end of the room, where the wall was distempered a dark shade of ashes of roses, two windows were hung with drapes of almost exactly the same hue; thick pinkish-grey insulating fabric without which the room would have been damp and cold, seeing the hall was below stairs and half-buried in the ground like a semi-basement.

'Would you be so kind as to open the curtains wider? The light in here is poor. Wouldn't it be lovely if we could sit up in her ladyship's bright sitting room with our sewing?'

'Ha ha! Fairley, your dreams and aspirations are miles above yourself.' Prudhomme did not mind rising to fix the curtains. Passing the glass cupboard and upright piano on the way to the windows, she picked up a scrap of fluff fallen from her darning to the floor. She had just paused after threading another needle, and Fairley was in the middle of the tricky business of letting out the waist of a pair of gentlemen's trousers.

'Wasn't Formby's playing good last night, though? I enjoyed watching him learn more.'

'He'll get better than Mrs Beste if she's not careful. Yes – he's picked it up surprisingly quickly.'

'He tends to stay back and practise, now, when we all take to the village.'

'And how do you know that, Fairley – what do you do when you stay behind, if you do?'

'Why! You told me what to do yourself. I wash my hair. I mend stockings, I tidy my things, and I save my money.'

'What about your reading and writing?'

'I've always been good at that. It was hard finding things to read at my mam's, but here, the shelf down near the fire is good, and besides, Mr Herring has a shelf of his own, and so does Mrs Beste.'

'That'll be the day, when Mr Herring lets one of the servants borrow his precious books. They must all be too highbrow for the likes of us.'

'I'll get there, for sure.' She looked sideways at Prudhomme, who had bitten off an end of thread with her front teeth. 'And I'll let you know when I do.'

Prudhomme laughed again. 'It's good to have optimists in the household.'

'No need to be arch. I like to be happy. Beats being miserable hands down.'

Prudhomme nodded, and started to tidy away her box. 'That's it for today. On Wednesday I'll start hemming Lady Geraldine's new petticoats and shifts.'

'She will have to start a trousseau soon. I've never worked on one. Is it a lot of hard work?'

'Did you not see that article in the *Ladies Home Journal*?'

'Ooh, yes – about the trousseau of the princess who got married in April? She married her cousin!'

'Isn't that what Lady Geraldine will be doing? Isn't Mr Angus Crownrigg a cousin of sorts?'

'Distant enough not to make them worry, apparently. I didn't understand how Queen Victoria's granddaughter is *German*.'

'Prince Albert! Prince Albert was German. But the princess's trousseau ... can you imagine? There would be more than two velvet gowns.'

'Perhaps two years' worth of shifts and nightwear, a year's evening and day dresses ... though nowadays fashions change so rapidly. I've never done so much new work.'

Prudhomme shrugged. 'It will be my first time too. The dressmakers will have to visit *again*. A lot of silk and lace and slippery work, is my guess.'

'Fiddly, fiddly.'

'Indeed. Don't you wish she'd look happier about it, though? I thought being engaged was a young woman's idea of a wonderful time in life.'

'Oh I don't know – they know much less about life and love and children and mothering than we do, these young ladies. Never seen a farm animal or a pet born, never understanding what it is to share ... never seeing the real sacrifices of mothering ... or the prospect of sharing a bed with a stranger – a man, at that – it might be a fearful thought.'

'But they don't have to, these fine people, see? They don't have to share. With enough rooms for a village of people, they don't have to share much space at all.' She lowered her voice to a whisper. 'My lady is only visited occasionally by his lordship. The big yellow suite is practically hers alone.'

'I know. I know. It's exactly what I meant, Prudhomme.' She gave her companion a meaningful look.

'I hardly think the young lady even knows what to think or what to expect.'

'It's not like us who grew up in small confines, is it? I mean ...' she smiled. 'In a small one-up one-down, with everyone cramped in together, it was no mystery about the movement and moaning and heavy breathing at night.'

Prudhomme lifted a finger to her lips. 'Hush now. With us it was muffled laughter and slap and tickle, my mam called it. Hush now, that's enough about that.'

'I think Lady Geraldine cannot bear to think of the future.'

'It's not like she was the kind to sigh and have romantic thoughts of who she might marry one day. Lady Athena is more that type. She has romantic thoughts, and writes enough letters I think must be romantic. But not her sister.'

'Think so?'

'Well – you're their maid. You might have a better picture of who thinks of what. Lady Athena is very slight and feminine. Lady Geraldine gives the distinct impression that all she wants to do is ride, ride, ride. She's more like her father. Come along now. Tidy your work away because one of the girls will be in to set our table in a minute.'

'I haven't even heard the upstairs gong. Ah – there it goes now.'

*

Angus Crownrigg stood and took another draw of cigar smoke, to which he was not yet fully accustomed. He looked at the glowing tip and thought it might not be too disloyal of him to decline to join his second cousin Ninian in a smoke on some evenings. He enjoyed the dinners, but the cigars were not entirely to his taste. They might think him staid and stodgy in this house, where it was as if time stood still, and there was little to amuse him. The thought made him smile.

Edinburgh was long ago and far away, and doing business by letter was not only inconvenient, but full of the hazards that accompanied written calculations and presumptions made by colleagues separated by hundreds of miles. That was something he had to remedy. There was one man he could promote to a more responsible position, and it would allow him time and occasion to commute – *commute* they called it – between Edinburgh and Cheltenham regularly. It was also not an impossible proposition to open a branch in Cheltenham.

He looked into the hearth flames and tried to form logical and precise thought. A branch, yes. A branch of his bank in another city.

But there was also the prospect of being caught in the country, without social diversion of the kind Edinburgh offered. He was used to dances and a good club, at least; the conviviality of living in the busy centre of a large city, and a literary circle that did more than just read plays and poems.

Cousin Ninian must have read his mind when he asked if Denisthorn was boring him. Not bored, no – he was not bored, and the prospect of impending marriage was a good thing. But he did wonder whether being buried at Denisthorn was not worse than being a widower in Scotland.

He had passed a number of weeks in which he had thought long and hard. Meeting the Croukerne sisters was awkward, and having occasion to speak with Lady Octavia and Miss Blockley had put him into a kind of mental fidget. It was part wanting to impress Lord Croukerne, part getting used to the extent and responsibility of his future legacy, and part the proximity of four refined young women, who were very different in bearing, education, and accomplishments than the ones he was friendly with in Scotland. It was a most discomforting time, that first fortnight. He was better now, and he had made some decisions, of which one was mandatory and inescapable.

He had reached the peak of what many considered prime marriageable age. He was almost twenty-seven, a widower, and prudently – and socially – needed to form a union. And now, it was a matter of making a union that did not upset his new position. Bringing a strange woman to Denisthorn, he knew, was not something easily done. For two paralysing days, he grappled with the realization it was either Athena or Geraldine, and sheer common sense – even though she seemed averse to even speaking to him – pointed to Geraldine.

His second or third .... or whatever cousin she was! ... happened to be a delightful young woman with a lot more verve and attraction than her older sister. It was a good move to engage and attract her. She was young, enthusiastic, and knew a great deal about how the place was run. A great deal more than Athena, at any rate. And she looked a lot more comely and less stick-like. No, it was a good move that he made.

'Have you got a date in mind, Cousin Angus? For the wedding, I mean.'

'June or September, I would say. But it's not for me to say. Lady Geraldine will no doubt consider the timing herself, and perhaps discuss the benefits of either month with her ladyship.'

Lord Croukerne took a long inhalation off his cigar. As he exhaled white smoke, which dissipated quickly and filled the room with the fragrance of exotic tobaccos, he waved the cigar in the air. 'Hm. While all that is going on, a family visit to my mother at Cheltenham House is in order. We shall descend on her ladyship *en masse*, and it will be a jolly ensemble, I am sure. Because my mother could not be here for too long at Christmas, it will be a re-enactment of the announcement I made at the table, I suppose.'

'The dowager marchioness was indisposed, I take it?' Angus remembered her indulgence in the sweet wines, and was not surprised when it was announced she would return to Cheltenham House late on Christmas Eve.

'She is well advanced in years. She used to pop back and forth in a brougham at the drop of a hat, creating quite a stir and attracting attention even as she drove through the village, such was the speed at which she insisted the coachman flew.'

Angus could well imagine the shiny dark green brougham that belonged to the marchioness hurtling through the narrow village road. 'Her carriage is kept at the tavern, isn't it?'

'Yes – my mother keeps one groom. There used to be a larger carriage and two horses, until a couple of years ago – she has since slowed down ... but still talks of planning another trip to the Continent.'

'That is something Geraldine and I have not yet discussed – our honeymoon.'

'Ah, there are still a lot of plans and arrangements to make. There is the matter of arranging a visit from your people in Scotland.'

'There are none, I'm afraid.'

'None! Surely you have an uncle ... or ... I see, of course, no brothers either. My goodness, we are going to have to get around that obstacle somehow or other, for the sake of my wife and my mother. And my wife's sister at

Gallantrae. They will all think it rather odd that there is no visit from your side.'

'I have thought about it. There is a distant uncle, related to the people on my mother's side. Mr Phineas Gow. He is a barrister.'

'Oh, capital! You must write to him at once.'

'I hope it was not inopportune, but I have already done so.'

'Excellent, Cousin Angus. I like that kind of anticipation and preparedness. Shall we join the ladies? I expect Godwin is waiting outside to push me along.'

'I should be honoured to take you, Cousin Ninian.' Angus came round behind the wheeled chair and pushed him towards the drawing room. It must have been the subtle squeak from the wheels that prompted Godwin outside to throw open the doors.

CHAPTER TWENTY-EIGHT

In which the Marchioness of Harpensted makes a personal
announcement
and
Lady Geraldine has second thoughts

Lady Croukerne regarded her mother-in-law as closely as she could without drawing attention to her concern about the older woman's health. 'Yes, I do understand.'

'I do not think you do, my dear Edwina. Now that their engagement is formal, Cousin Angus will take off, back to Edinburgh, as is quite fitting and expedient. He must attend to his affairs, must he not? And Geraldine can throw herself into wedding preparations.'

'We have not yet had a visit from his relatives, but yes, I do suppose Angus must go.'

'And he must present Ninian with his situation and circumstance. Being the director of a bank puts him in what one would call nowadays a *good* position. But for all we know, he might have nothing at all – the young man might gamble it all away, before it is *earned*.'

Lady Croukerne's face was the picture of despondency. 'The fact he works and *earns* is in itself something unusual. We are not used to employment of that sort, are we?'

'We must all work, Edwina. It is a *biblical* thing. Ninian works extraordinarily hard. We ladies do what we can for charities and such. We hardly sit *still* for the work that must be done. Here we are, with Christmas hardly over, that we do not start receiving requests for Easter attendances, to open this fair and commemorate that event, and preside over some meeting or memorial, sit on some committee or other. Spring and all the garden shows are upon us!'

'Yes – it is why we keep such detailed and exact appointment diaries. But we are not employed. And neither is Ninian.'

The marchioness pursed lips and tilted her head. 'The world is changing. There used to be a time when it was rare for money to be discussed or for it to change hands. We live in the *age of transaction*.'

'I thought they are calling it the industrial age.'

'With industry comes transaction, my dear. The currency of exchange is money, filthy and vulgar as it is – to be regretted, but inescapable.' She winced and placed a hand to her side.

'Oh Mother – are you in discomfort? Shall I call Mary? Should I ring for her?'

There was no answer for a second's interval.

'Perhaps I should ring for ...'

'No, no my dear. It is a mere twinge from faulty posture. I am no longer twenty or thirty, as we all plainly see.'

'Faulty posture, that must be it.'

'We were talking about Cousin Angus's departure.'

'But it has not occurred or been announced.'

'If he has any sense, decorum and propriety, the man will repair back to Edinburgh for a period, to attend to his affairs. He can correspond with Geraldine in the usual way, and send Ninian an account of his property and prospects.'

'Property and prospects.'

'Hm. It will not do at all for a young couple to be inside each other's pockets during an engagement. It's unseemly and tempting, and sets tongues wagging. Besides, you do not want to spend half a year in the wearying role of a chaperone, and neither does Athena, who had better look around her long and hard if she is not to be regarded as on the shelf, the spinster sister, now.'

'I do hope it will all go well and agreeably.'

'Ninian will bestow a nominal fortune on Geraldine, and Angus will enjoy the interest. I suppose they will marry at Denisthorn, and live ...?'

Lady Croukerne raised a hand to a worried forehead. 'It is so confusing. I hope it is somewhere close by. So confusing!'

'It is not at all. Remember Angus is no upstart. He is heir to Denisthorn. He might have been raised differently, but he has noble blood, and comports himself like a gentleman. That at least is a very good thing, in my view, and in the view of society. He is no *upstart*. And I do not think he will take Geraldine away after they marry, to live in Edinburgh, do you?'

'Oh no! I think they might stay at Denisthorn. You see, if ...'

'I have no intention of dying, to accommodate the family and vacate Cheltenham House.' The older woman pursed her lips again, but there was a twinkle in her eye.

'Angus must get the hang of running Denisthorn. Ninian has said it a hundred and one times. He must make sure it's in good hands. Besides, his present condition is not conducive to hard work on the estate.'

'You're right. With Ninian in a wheelchair, it is all the more advantageous to have a short engagement, my dear. Have you thought of that? And then the young couple can stay at Denisthorn and help Ninian as much as possible. It is really a good arrangement, when all is said and done.'

'A brief engagement! Will people not think there are ulterior reasons for not waiting at least six months?'

The older woman shifted position, winced and stood. 'Might we not sit at the table? I must change position to be more comfortable.'

'Of course.' Edwina held out a hand and helped her mother-in-law to a chair.

'Thank you, my dear. Now, I was not saying they should marry in unseemly haste. But it makes sense for them not to wait longer than necessary. Do you see my reasoning? Will you not tell Ninian?'

'I shall tell him every word we have spoken. He likes to know about our conversations.'

The old marchioness's hooded eyes hid a sparkle. 'I do hope you are discreet. Ladies discuss so many things men could not possibly grasp. What are you looking at?' She turned her head to see what Edwina had seen out of the bay window overlooking the garden.

'For a minute, I thought it was Frederic out there, running with a hoop and stick.'

'Frederic! Are you quite all right, Edwina my dear?'

'Oh, I see him often. I glimpse his shadow in the corner of an eye, turn to look, and he is gone.'

'Edwina, my dear.'

'He is.'

'He is really gone. Frederic is dead, my dear girl.'

Lady Croukerne looked away. 'Oh, please do not say that.'

'Whether I say it or not, death is death. The truth is the truth, and we must face it. Now ring for tea, or we shall famish, right where we sit.'

*

Mr Herring and Mrs Beste were ensconced in the butler's office, both with heads down, pencils in hand, and eyes fixed on their individual books. With a wedding on the horizon, there was much to discuss, plan, and prepare.

'I find it rather inconvenient and confusing not to be given even the indication of a date ... or a season!'

'Mrs Beste, I do suspect they do not know themselves. Easter is too early, and so, perhaps, might June be.'

'Of course June would be perfect. But Mr Crownrigg is still with us. I should have thought he would have returned to Edinburgh sooner than this.'

'Denisthorn Hall is a huge place, Mrs Beste. The young couple can keep out of each other's way quite conveniently.'

'But it's hardly seemly.'

'Her ladyship, I suspect, does think that an old-fashioned custom. But to appease his lordship – who thinks like we do – she did mention something about Lady Geraldine spending time at Gallantrae with her aunt.'

The housekeeper sighed with relief. 'What a perfect solution.'

'And Lady Athena is off to London again!'

The butler shook his head. 'I am not sure if that is a mere wish expressed by the young lady, or a real plan. Lady Athena finds herself in an invidious position, outshone by a younger sister who is not yet presented, without any indication of a suitor in the wings ...' Herring shook his head. 'I don't know about you, but I never expected this would happen.'

'Lady Geraldine might very well be presented at court as a young married woman, after the wedding.'

'It does happen.'

'Of course it does – that's not what I am worried about. I'm worried about the brave face Lady Athena is putting on. I do not believe she is as happy as she leads the household to believe.'

'I heard from Fairley that she still writes to Mr Alastair Updike.'

The butler put down his pencil, and screwed and unscrewed the cap of his fountain pen.

'Do you find that pen good?'

'It's excellent. That sounds like gossip, Mrs Beste, the detail about Mr Updike. And I should not tolerate the least skerrick of gossip. I have made myself clear on this a number of times.'

'Oh pray do not be so stern. She writes many letters,

and receives many too. And yes, when she gives them to the footmen, some are addressed to Mr Updike. It's a fact, not gossip.'

'Well, well. Now tell me, her visit to London. Might it not be motivated by an effort to socialize more?'

'Of course it is. The House of Lords will meet after the holiday, his lordship will be in London, so the Belgrave house will be open, and Lady Athena will be there too.'

'In the company of ...?'

'Perhaps Miss Blockley, from Minsterworth. And Miss Purl might be put upon to make the journey and keep them company. And it would not surprise me one bit if there is a party and Mr Updike is present. Why that look of surprise?'

'Miss Purl?'

'Miss Purl's usefulness as a governess is sadly over, and remember, she is of a genteel family, impoverished but genteel. Her ladyship was caught in the horns of a dilemma about what to do about Miss Purl's situation. I think she is the fifth daughter of the fourth son of a wealthy mill owner, or something like that.'

'The poor dear. Such a lovely character, and naturally not a servant, and not family, either. A strange in-between world, Miss Purl inhabits.'

'Only think ... if she goes on to acting as companion and chaperone to Lady Athena ...'

'... it would be a solution on a number of fronts.'

'You speak like a campaign strategist, Mr Herring.'

He drew his brows together over the renowned prominent nose, and placed a Napoleonic hand inside his jacket. 'You flatter me, Mrs Beste.'

*

Geraldine knew that Athena hated her sitting on the end of her bed, but she did throw herself down and she did sigh, which was also something her sister did not like either.

'You bring Papa's dog into my room, and you sit there like ...'

'Cosmo is on a leash, Athena, on account of his healing paw. He cannot be allowed to gambol about outdoors with Damian.'

'So he can gambol around in here.'

'Do you know, there was a time when we shared a room, with Nurse next door, and we would spend hours reading to each other and dressing each other's dolls.'

'And now all we do is quarrel ... and you are abandoning me, going to *London*, with *Miss Purl*. Lord Ullingsbroke has two spinster cousins, and you choose Miss Purl.'

'Oh Geraldine. I'm not ...'

'Indeed you are, and I don't know what to do.'

'There's nothing to do. You are engaged to be married to Cousin Angus. Mama says he will return to Scotland on the train soon, and you will set a date and everyone will start to prepare for the big day. Whether I'm here or at the house in London ... will it make a difference, Geraldine? Will it?'

'Mama keeps saying it would be expedient for you to find a husband, seeing I am ... I am ... Oh, Athena – I'm so tired of the situation.'

'Already? Husbands are not found so easily, or so expediently. It's hardly been two weeks. It's a new engagement. New!'

'Ten days. The problem is ...' The younger sister spoke with a strong voice. She stood, and the dog struggled from a squat onto all legs too. 'Sit, Cosmo.' He sat, and Geraldine burst into a loud bout of weeping.

'Geraldine!' In an unusual show of tenderness, Athena took her sister in her arms. 'Whatever's the matter?'

'The truth is I would much rather stand in the breezeway at the stables talking to Mark than anywhere else at Denisthorn in conversation with Cousin Angus.'

'Mark? One of the grooms? Whatever are you saying?'

Sobs wracked Geraldine and rendered her speech unintelligible.

'No, wait ... what?' Athena went to her top tallboy drawer and pulled out half a dozen beautifully laundered handkerchiefs, pressing them urgently into Geraldine's hands. 'Stop. Stop. You'll make yourself sick with weeping. Your eyes – your eyes will swell. Stop.'

'Mark, Mark.'

'Who is Mark?'

'Mary Mark, I mean the groom ... I mean stable boy ...' she wept and sobbed. 'I mean stable girl. Girl groom.' She buried her face in a fistful of crushed linen hankie.

'Geraldine, you're not making any sense.'

'I don't know him. I don't know *anything* about him.'

Athena made her sit on the foot of her bed. 'Do you mean Cousin Angus?'

'Yes. We have hardly spoken for ... I don't know. We haven't really said much to each other.'

'Surely you will have plenty of time for that.'

'What do we have in common?'

'You both ride well. That's one thing at least. Geraldine, why did you accept him?'

The girl rose, wiped her face roughly and stood in front of her sister's dressing table mirror. 'I need a basin of hot water and a flannel.'

Athena rang for Fairley. 'She'll be up in a minute. You look dreadful.'

'Thank you.'

'No – I'm sorry. Your eyes are red. You need a nap, perhaps, a powder, a cup of tea, and a rest. I don't understand why you accepted Angus if you have no feelings for him. I thought ...'

'You do too much thinking for anyone's good.'

It was Athena's turn to offer thanks. 'Please do take a chair. Don't sit on the end of my bed. I think I know something about you, Geraldine. You love Denisthorn. You want the Hall. This is your home, and your home will fall to Cousin Angus, so ...'

'Don't make me cry again.'

'You can write to him. Call it off.'

'He's *downstairs*, Athena. I won't write to him. I have not had a change of heart.'

The older sister folded her arms. '*Geraldine*. That's what it looks like to me.'

'You do know how difficult and insulting, and how humiliating it is to break off an engagement. We heard of one such breaking off in Cheltenham. There was a court case. No one breaks off an engagement. Why ... Angus has sent to Edinburgh for a ring! A diamond ring with a cairngorm in the centre, made especially for me!'

'Oh, how lovely! How ...' The older sister made a hopeless gesture with both hands.

'See? Do you see? I'm in this up to my neck, to put it in vulgar words. Grand-mama would *wring* my neck if she knew how I feel.'

There was silence and they listened to the wind that whistled past the corner, through the battlements on that side of Denisthorn Hall, against the shuttered windows on the unoccupied floor above, and among the trees below.

After a long silence, Athena stirred. 'Grand-mama would have done exactly what you did. In your place, she would have made the same decision ... the same choice.'

Geraldine's pink-rimmed eyes widened. 'Do you really think so?'

'Yes, I do. Perhaps a little visit for tea to Cheltenham House would make you feel better. Talk to her, heart to heart.'

'Talk to her? You mean listen to her.'

'I know she can be a bit of a dragon, but she speaks sense if you analyse it without emotion. And that's what you have done, Geraldine ...'

'What have I done?' It was more a rhetorical exclamation, a cry of despair, than a question.

Athena picked up two fallen handkerchiefs and placed them on the dressing table stool for Fairley to see to. She straightened a brush, uncapped a scent bottle and stoppered it again. 'You have addressed your future and that of Denisthorn without emotion, but with a lot of ... of sense and determination. And decisions like that are usually the ones that work. Or so I read. Papa is rather proud of you.'

'That was a long speech for you, Athena.'

'Oh pray do not take up Mama's attack about the way I speak. I said Papa is proud of you.'

'But he must think I am in a sentimental whirl of romantic love.'

'I wonder.'

Fairley came in, and was sent back again quickly to fetch a basin and flannel.

'There's a lot to do, and plan, and prepare for, Geraldine. I think you have a lot to look forward to. We all do.'

***

Here ends Book One in the Denisthorn Hall series. If you have enjoyed this novel, you can leave a brief review on its Amazon page.

To read more about the Croukerne family, Geraldine's wedding, the secret of the Keats room, Angus's past, Lord Croukerne's convalescence, and Athena's search for a suitor, do not miss Book Two.
Click 'follow' on the Amazon book page for updates on the author's publications. You will be notified of the next release.

Lightning Source UK Ltd.
Milton Keynes UK
UKHW041811071019
351157UK00006B/1794/P

9 780648 650287